BARNACLES AND BEDLAM

THE WAR SAGA OF A MOTLEY CREW

GH00357363

BY

PAUL B. BEHM

BARNACLES AND BEDLAM

THE WAR SAGA OF A MOTLEY CREW

PUBLISHED BY
SAGA PUBLISHING
P.O. BOX 3621
LAGUNA HILLS, CA 92654-3621

To my wife, Dorothy, and my daughter, Vicki

with love

ACKNOWLEDGEMENTS

I wish to express my gratitude to James F. Scheer, who helped greatly with suggestions and editing, to Walter Hardy who through the years encouraged me to complete this book, and especially to my wife, Dorothy, whose unwavering enthusiasm and editorial assistance made this book possible. I am also grateful for the detailed information supplied by fellow crew mates, William McKelly, the late Raymond Daugherty, and the late Wes Hewson.

I am indebted to my fellow crew mate Kenneth Anderson for most of the pictures of the expedition, to Pete Jacobelly, formerly chief engineer of the *S.S. Lane Victory* and a former director of the San Pedro Chapter of the U.S. Merchant Marine Veterans World War II for his technical assistance, and to the cooperative personnel at the U.S. Naval Historical Center and the National Archives in Washington, D.C. where I researched the records to determine what happened to that old lumber steamer, the *S.S. W.R. Chamberlain, Jr.*, after May of 1943, when she was turned over to the navy and renamed the *Tackle*.

PREFACE

The events surrounding the voyage of the *S.S. W.R. Chamberlain, Jr.* to Massawa, Eritrea, and the activities of the salvage crew at the naval base there should not be forgotten in recording the history of World War II. After retirement from his professional life as an attorney-C.P.A., the author found time to record his oft-recalled experiences as purser, some of them hilarious, some tragic, on that memorable adventure well over half a century ago.

With the aid of ship's papers, carbon copies of letters written to stateside friends and conversations with fellow crew members, using a few fictitious proper names, he has reconstructed and depicted, with some latitude, the events of this expedition.

The men who participated in this endeavor deserve applause. They sailed that old converted lumber steamer through German submarine infested waters in the early part of the war without benefit of naval escort. At Massawa they worked under extremely difficult conditions to open the Massawa harbor for use by the Allies during a critical period of the war.

BARNACLES AND BEDLAM
TABLE OF CONTENTS

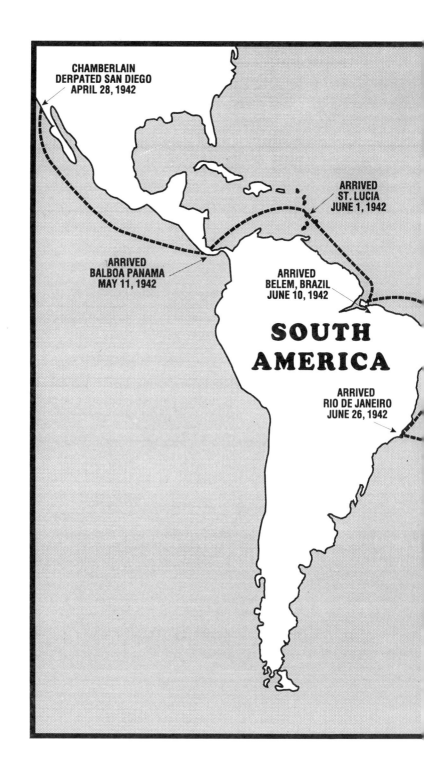

CHAMBERLAIN
DERPATED SAN DIEGO
APRIL 28, 1942

ARRIVED
ST. LUCIA
JUNE 1, 1942

ARRIVED
BALBOA PANAMA
MAY 11, 1942

ARRIVED
BELEM, BRAZIL
JUNE 10, 1942

SOUTH
AMERICA

ARRIVED
RIO DE JANEIRO
JUNE 26, 1942

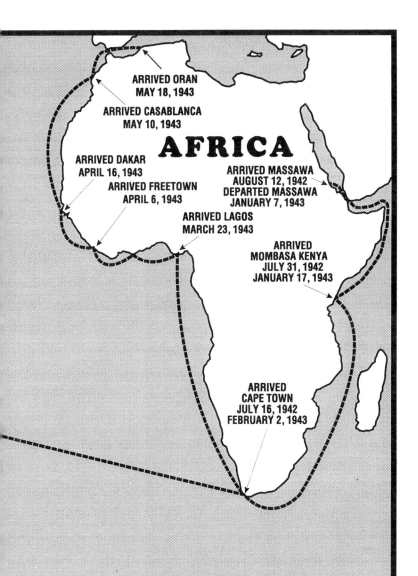

ARRIVED ORAN
MAY 18, 1943

ARRIVED CASABLANCA
MAY 10, 1943

AFRICA

ARRIVED DAKAR
APRIL 16, 1943

ARRIVED MASSAWA
AUGUST 12, 1942
DEPARTED MASSAWA
JANUARY 7, 1943

ARRIVED FREETOWN
APRIL 6, 1943

ARRIVED LAGOS
MARCH 23, 1943

ARRIVED
MOMBASA KENYA
JULY 31, 1942
JANUARY 17, 1943

ARRIVED
CAPE TOWN
JULY 16, 1942
FEBRUARY 2, 1943

Route of the Chamberlain

CHAPTER 1

AFRICA BOUND

THE WAR: Prior to April 28, 1942, the day the S.S.W.R. Chamberlain, Jr. sailed out of San Diego bound for Massawa, Eritrea, German submarines torpedoed and sank eighty-seven U. S. merchant vessels in the North and South Atlantic Ocean and in the Caribbean Sea, and Japanese submarines, cruisers and planes sank thirteen U.S. merchant vessels in the Pacific and Indian Oceans. A total of 1268 American lives were lost in these attacks.

From information appearing in:
   A Careless Word...
      ...A Needless Sinking
   By Captain Arthur R. Moore
   APPENENDIX I AND APPENDIX II

Above the clatter of winches and the clang of metal-capped booms as they settled in their cradles, the voice of the bols'n sounded, "Batten down the hatches."

The deck hands scurried about, tying down the deck cargo and covering the holds with tarpaulins.

The *S.S. W.R. Chamberlain, Jr.*, an ancient lumber vessel, vintage 1912, newly painted a battleship gray, was supposedly ready to sail from San Diego at the front end of World War II, just months after the Japanese bombed Pearl Harbor.

From its railing, I watched the final preparations for departure, exhilarated by the prospect of our voyage to the port of Massawa, Eritrea, in the Red Sea, to participate in the salvage of sunken ships and prepare it for use as an Allied naval repair base.

My enthusiasm evaporated as reality hit me.

Could this old tub, this senior citizen of the seas, held together with library paste and a mustard seed of faith, make it halfway around the world to East Africa, through waters bristling with the most modern killer submarines devised by the ingenious minds of the Germans?

As I surveyed the ship with the newly installed military armor—a machine gun on her fo'c'sle, a machine gun on either side of her flying bridge, and a three-inch cannon on her poop deck—I felt as reassured as if this weaponry were popguns and pea-shooters.

Yet I couldn't fault Bill Flanagan, who had been sent from Washington four months before by the U.S. Army Engineers to locate and oufit a mother salvage vessel, for drafting the *Chamberlain*. After the post-Pearl Harbor panic and the frenzied wartime search for ships, only the dregs were left; and I couldn't help thinking that the *Chamberlain* was an uncontested all-American dreg.

The fact that two prospective captains and three prospective chief engineers could not be persuaded to sign on after they had made a superficial inspection of the ship haunted me.

I was mystified as to why Thomas P. Hansen, who struck me

as being well-balanced mentally and not a crapshooter by nature, signed on as captain. Perhaps it was because he had been a salvage man for the better part of his thirty-five years at sea, and this mission entailed the raising of ships scuttled by the Italians in the harbor of Massawa only a year before.

There had been multiple malfunctions during our trial runs, but it was too late for me to back out. Another chief engineer had walked off the ship before the first scheduled trial run. On the second try, the engines failed to respond—a seemingly important impediment to our reaching Massawa.

On the third attempt, Captain Hansen managed to get the ship away from the dock, but a steering gear defect kept us going around in circles. I hoped this wasn't prophetic of our mission.

After correction of the steering malfunction, the *Chamberlain* had her fourth trial, a run from San Diego north to San Pedro and back. Our vessel exceeded all my expectations; it completed the round-trip. However, a towering column of black smoke interspersed with sparks spewing from its short smokestack was not likely to keep our ocean passage a secret from Nazi subs. Nor was the steady roar of its engines.

I tried to take comfort in knowing that the ship's officers were pros—except for me—and would somehow get us to our destination before an enemy torpedo got to us.

However, the crew was something else. Invariably when I thought of the crew, the word "motley" came to mind.

Among the seventy-nine members, consisting of salvage officers, deep sea divers, divers' tenders, welders, machinists, shipfitters, electricians, boiler makers, and carpenters, many of whom would have to double as the ship's crew on the long voyage, there were but few professional seamen.

My reverie ended in a collision with a view of reality on the deck below—tender farewells of at least twenty women in the embraces of our crew members.

I felt a twinge of envy. It would have been great to say goodbye to someone who would miss me until I got back.

Then bits of dialogue in male and female voices floated up to me:

". . . I'll write every day.". . ."Oh, God will I miss you.". . . "Take care of the kids." . . ."I won't be alive until I'm in your arms again," interrupted by a loud voice behind me:

"Okay, everybody. All visitors ashore!"

As the reluctant exodus began, I turned to Flanagan, a small, wiry Irishman with intense dark eyes. He never wasted words, and they bit like the thrust of an ice pick. "Where in hell's the captain?" Before I could get my mouth in gear, Flanagan struck again. "Doesn't the skipper know there's a war on? You sail at 13:30."

"I think I can reach him," I replied.

"Don't THINK! Do it NOW!"

I did it NOW, rousing him by phone at a nearby hotel where he and his wife, Lilly, were sharing their last intimate moments before his departure.

"Captain, the Coast Guard has been aboard and checked out the crew, and Flanagan insists we leave by one-thirty."

About one o'clock the skipper lumbered up the gangplank. It struck me that this medium-height man, in his navy blue jacket sporting four gold stripes, was as wide as a professional wrestler. He was the image of a typical Norwegian sea captain of the old school, with his ruddy skin, his oversized bulbous nose, and a long livid gash low across his forehead.

A wire carrying cage harboring a black alley cat swung from his right arm. Now on deck, he spied me scrutinizing number three hatch piled high with bulgy sacks of Irish potatoes, crates of lettuce with green leaves protruding, cartons of freshly dressed chicken, and a mountain of boxed canned food.

"Paul," he boomed. "Take this damn cat!"

What was I supposed to do with the cat?

Handing me the carrying cage and pointing to the stacks of provisions, he bellowed. "This stuff has to be stowed. Where in hell is the steward?"

"Flanagan fired the steward yesterday. He put me in charge of the mess hall."

"Damn! You're my purser! Also warehouseman in charge of the machine shop tools. You know anything about running the galley?"

"No, sir."

"My God!" groaned the captain. He looked up at the cloudy sky and roared, "There's a storm brewing. Get those mess hall supplies stowed before we hit the sea." He stalked off to the wheelhouse.

I climbed up the stairway to the boat deck, passed two lifeboats suspended on davits, and at my cabin door looked down at the black cat becoming restless in solitary, promising, "You'll get out in a second." I opened the cage and the feline jumped out, shook itself, sniffed, explored its new home, and found a resting place on my bunk. I jammed the papers on my desk into the drawers to keep them from sliding off when we hit the high seas.

Back on number three hatch, I stared at the Mount Everest of provisions, wondering how to move the stuff.

How the hell was I going to get any men to stow the supplies? Two weeks with the ship had taught me that we had some of the world's most talented goof-offs. This dilemma was interrupted by a heavy hand on my shoulder. It belonged to my friend, G.H. Carlyle, who had talked me into signing on for this expedition.

"Paul, I hear the skipper wants those supplies stowed. You're in charge of the mess hall crew. Get them to do it."

"Good idea, G.H.," I replied, and was grateful for his suggestion. He had signed on as salvage foreman, but for the *Chamberlain's* voyage the captain had designated him the ship's master-at-arms, permitting him to wear an officer's cap that inflated an ego which needed no bolstering.

He wielded considerable influence, thanks to nature's gift of a blocky body, his overwhelming self-confidence and his great ability to con people.

"On second thought, the mess men are tied up serving lunch," I added.

"Don't worry. Let's go find some willing muscles."

Knowing G.H.'s talent for promoting almost anything, I followed him hopefully to the stern of the vessel.

Some members of the crew leaning on the railing of the afterdeck were engrossed in observing proceedings on the dock below. Expeditor Flanagan, surrounded by three laughing women from his San Diego office, stood on a platform constructed on the dock. They tied a bottle of champagne to a rope suspended from a pole.

"This is hardly the *Chamberlain's* maiden voyage," jeered G.H. "He can't be serious, wasting a good bottle of champagne!"

But he was and he did!

Carlyle grabbed two nearby idlers by the arm.

"Guys, the captain wants you to stow mess hall supplies on number three hatch."

"Okay," they grumbled.

The next two didn't want to cooperate.

"What the hell," one bitched. "I was signed on as an electrician, not as a deckhand."

G.H. assumed an authoritative, yet confidential tone. "You know the ground rules. We're all part of the crew 'til we get there. We've got to pull together." He winked knowingly. "You'll be doing me a big favor."

I had to admire the Carlyle con.

Pied Piper Carlyle had a dozen men following us by the time we reached number three hatch. Then we were bumping into each other coming and going with boxes and crates, stowing the food stuff in the storeroom and refrigerator.

The *Chamberlain's* deep bass whistle blew. From midships, the mate bellowed an order to deck-hands, "Cast off the lines."

The deck trembled with engine vibrations as the ship lurched backward; then the *Chamberlain* reversed gears and moved forward, her stacks thrusting out black smoke. We swung around and headed out San Diego Bay toward Ballast Point and the open sea, passing gray ships undulating at anchor—aircraft carriers, cruisers, destroyers, submarines, and patrol boats.

I returned to number three hatch. The twelve helpers had dwindled to nine, and they were dawdling. My morale dropped.

" Come on fellas," I pleaded. "It'll take just a few more trips."

OTTO JAEGER, CHIEF MATE ENROUTE TO MASSAWA, CAPTAIN THOMAS HANSEN

The big mound of provisions made me a liar. As the ship gathered speed and rocked hesitatingly, moving the provisions became a game of balance.

A sailor called down to me from the flying bridge, "Hey, Purser, the skipper wants you!"

Heading for the stairs, I begged my helpers, "Carry on, fellas. We've gotta get this stuff stowed fast." Upon looking back, I saw some of them scattering. And then there were none.

I found the pilot on the flying bridge standing by the compass alongside the helmsman at the wheel, while the captain and Chief Mate Jaeger examined the 50 caliber anti-aircraft gun on the starboard wing.

As I approached the skipper, he turned to me and ordered, "Paul, take roll call to see that everybody's aboard. I hope we haven't left any men ashore. We'll be dropping off the pilot in twenty minutes so report back here before then."

I got a whiff of alcohol mixed with puffs of tobacco smoke from his pipe.

"But Captain, the provisions are not stowed yet," I protested.

"Paul, you heard what I said!"

"Yes, Captain, but there are still fifty bags of potatoes and thirty cases of tools in the machine shop to be stored, besides all the supplies on number three hatch."

The captain sputtered, "What in hell was Flanagan thinking of when he put you not only in charge of the machine shop tools, but also the mess hall, besides making you my purser!"

Then he turned to the chief mate, a stocky Norwegian whose sunburned, weather-beaten, and scarred face attested to many years before the mast.

"Jaeger, get your men to stow the food supplies on number three hatch and tie down the boxes in the machine shop."

Relieved of that problem, I picked up the crew list from my cabin and made the rounds. As the ship rocked, so did I. After climbing down several flights of iron steps into the engine room, I was nauseated by the overpowering smell of oil, the oppressive heat, and the loud thumping of the machinery. A hint of bitter digestive juices began to burn my throat. Oh, NO! I just couldn't get seasick in front of the crew.

Chief Engineer Culpepper, six feet of prattling dogmatic Irishman with flaming red hair and a temper compatible therewith, helped me check off the engine room crew, otherwise known as the "black gang". Outside, the fresh sea air settled my stomach for the moment.

After counting noses in the galley, I grabbed the arm of Consuelo, one of the messboys.

"I've got the captain's hungry cat in my cabin. How about taking it something to eat."

Ear-deafening grinding of lathes and the shrill buzz of saws emanated from the machine shop as I entered and checked off the few men there. I then made my way to the fo'c'sle.

Inside the blackout curtain seven seamen were gathered around an oiler waving a greasy rag and yelling, "Look what I found in the bilges!"

"So what, you dumb bastard. It's just a rag."

"Rag, hell! It's a woman's panties."

He spread the dirty, lacy underwear on deck.

"They probably belonged to that buxom blonde welder working in the hold in San Diego," suggested Tom Moyer, one of our diesel men. "What a pair of boobs she had."

I surveyed the fo'c'sle with its twenty-five tiers of two bunks each, checked off the names of those present and headed for the poop deck. Thank God the provisions on number three hatch were being stowed.

After checking the deck crew, I reported to the captain on the bridge, "All men are aboard."

Captain Hansen nodded approval, and I continued: "But I counted five black eyes, one broken nose, three taped fists, and a couple of scarred ears. And there's Axel. His face looked as though it had been run over by a Greyhound bus."

"Yes, I know about Axel, but he's tough and the best seaman aboard."

"Oh, by the way, Captain. One of the oilers found a woman's panties in the bilge."

"There are better places to find panties," the Skipper replied, a mirthful twinkle in his eyes, adding, "Right where they're supposed to be."

A sudden idea occurred to him. "You don't suppose they've got a gal stowed aboard for the trip?"

I laughed. Secretly, I wondered.

After we passed the lighthouse at Ballast Point, the pilot boat came alongside. The pilot, having navigated our ship from Sampson Street dock through San Diego Bay, climbed down the Jacob's ladder.

We were on our own, heading for Panama.

As the *Chamberlain* picked up the roll of the sea outside the harbor, the receding skyline of San Diego seemed to roll, too. Unsteadily, I stumbled into my cabin, the bitter juices again backing up in my throat. The contents of my stomach began to move upward. At least, the real seamen had not seen me, an officer, in this condition.

The full impact of mal de mer hit me. I grabbed a bucket, vomited and writhed; and, with my last ounce of strength, collapsed on my bunk, crowding the skipper's cat, which I had pitched into my cabin earlier.

Later, the sound of bugle calls blasted out of the air- conditioning vent. I bolted upright, and the frightened cat cuddled up, apparently for reassurance. Was this a call to arms?

"We'd better get on deck," I muttered to the black ball of fur, swinging my feet out of the bunk. Another wave of nausea caused me to vomit, the sour stuff ending up in the bucket.

To hell with the bugle alarm! Let the damn ship sink; let the world blast itself to pieces; let Gabriel blow his cheeks out. I was prepared to die without a struggle.

About ten minutes later the bugle calls stopped, and G.H. Carlyle burst in. A sharp moaning and screeching of Scottish bagpipes came though the air-conditioning vent. Bewildered and in misery, I turned toward G.H.

"What in hell's going on?"

He smirked. "That's just the doctor's damned idea of phonograph music—bugle calls and bagpipes. That guy is the only army man aboard, and he's not going to let us forget it."

Carlyle looked into my bucket.

"Paul, get hold of yourself. Seasickness is just in the mind."

I resented his platitudes but was too weak to argue.

The cat jumped to the floor near Carlyle's feet, staggered for an instant, then puked on one of his shiny new shoes.

"Damn!" he cussed.

I refreshed his memory, "It's just in its mind, G.H."

Carlyle grabbed a handkerchief from his hip pocket, and as he wiped the vomit from his shoe, the ship's engines stopped.

"Paul, I almost forgot to tell you. They're trying to fix the main condenser. I'd better see what's happening."

He threw the dirty handkerchief into the bucket on his way out.

When the engine vibrations halted, I thought I'd feel better. But there was no respite. A few minutes later, the ship, caught in the crest of a wave, rolled back and forth at a thirty-five to forty-five degree angle. I braced myself to keep from falling out of the bunk. My chair and the articles stowed in the drawers began sliding. I couldn't get up to tie anything down.

Then a screeching wail reverberated through the air- conditioning outlet, and the doctor's phonograph was silent.

The ship rolled and tossed for several hours while the engines were stilled. So did I. I didn't die—much as I wanted to.

CHAPTER 2

SIGNING-ON STORY

THE WAR: Although the U.S.Army had repelled continuous Japanese attacks by air, sea, and land on Bataan and Corregidor in the Philippines from January 5, 1942, General Johnathan M. Wainwright was forced to surrender his fifteen thousand men remaining on Corregidor on May 5th, 1942.

After two long hours the swaying of the *Chamberlain* halted. She leaped forward, her decks quivering under the rhythmic pounding of the engines. I lay sprawled in my bunk, thankful that at least the ship no longer rocked. For the first time since leaving San Diego I found time and energy to think.

The captain had assigned me this cabin, one of twelve occupied by ship and salvage crew officers, commenting, "As purser you'll need a lot of room to spread out."

Occupied by the ship's owner during the lumber steamer's better days, it was second in size to the captain's own cabin and well-furnished with a chair, vinyl-covered alcove seat, built-in desk and bunk, washbasin, and a bathroom with a shower and john. Drawers beneath the seat and bunk provided convenient storage space. My portable phonograph was secured on a newly built shelf adjacent to the bunk, and my records, among them,

Mendelssohn, Tchaikovsky, Victor Herbert, Brahms, and Grieg, were stowed in a rack below.

No fault could be found with my living quarters. A room on the Queen Mary would not have given me any more satisfaction. But the question of the wisdom of joining this expedition gnawed inside of me. And how in the hell did I get myself talked into signing up to serve simultaneously as steward and warehouseman (for neither position was I qualified), as well as purser.

In January of 1942 my draft board had ordered me to report to the army for induction by the middle of February, rudely interrupting my easy-going life in Hollywood as a magazine circulation representative of Dell Publishing Company.

The army held no enchantment for me so I applied for and was granted a clerk's rating in the navy, based on my typing ability. I was given a month's grace before being required to report for duty.

I terminated my apartment lease, stored my personal items with friends and wound down my job with Dell. In the midst of these preparations to depart for navy boot camp, I was surprised to get a phone call from my friend, Gunnar H. Carlyle, twenty-six years my senior. I had been out of touch with him for over two years.

G.H., as he was known, was an unusually affable person with a forceful manner, a firm handclasp accompanied by an instant smile. By virtue of his extraordinary lung power, a self-absorbed determination, and a posture that reflected his supreme ego and self-confidence, he quickly hypnotized those people easily influenced, and antagonized those who resented his officious manners. He was a little short on patience and not unduly sensitive to the feelings of others. On the other hand, no one could deny that he was faithful to his friends—and I considered him my friend.

On the phone he sounded puffy, blustery and cocky. "Paul, how about going on a trip to Africa?" he exploded, knowing my weakness for travel.

"G.H., I just put my bid in for the navy and I'll be sworn in by the end of February."

"Well, stop in to see me in San Diego at the San Diego Marine Construction offices", he urged. "I'll just bet I can get you out of the navy's clutches."

I had adjusted my thinking to a hitch in the navy; and, in view of my past experience with G.H., I was wary about his proposal that I join him on a nebulous trip to Africa.

I had met Carlyle about three years before in his office at the Crossroads of the World, a commercial development on Sunset Boulevard near Vine Street in Hollywood. I was on disability pay, convalescing from an injury to my knee as a result of a fall while clerking at a Los Angeles supermarket. It seemed a good time to seek out other work so I responded to Carlyle's advertisement promoting a Pan American Fellowship Society.

He spoke enticingly about possible lucrative rewards in activating a Pan American organization, although no salary was promised. The plan involved promoting Spanish language schools, trade with Latin American countries, and harnessing American technical knowledge for sale to Central and South American industrialists. Looking back on it, the idea didn't have a prayer, taking into consideration Carlyle's lack of expertise in this area. But his persuasive manner won me over.

He regaled me with stories of his early life as a cadet in the Danish navy and as a cabin boy on sailing ships out of Denmark. He also recounted his exploits as a deep sea diver, including his experience in salvaging U.S. destroyers—the *Delphy*, the *S.P. Lee*, the *Chauncey*, the *Fuller*, the *Woodbury*, the *Nicholas*, and the *Young*—all of which were beached in a fog off the California coast at Honda Point on September 1, 1923. At the time, I had no way of knowing his gift for embellishment and his need to have a few pipe dreams to wake up to every morning.

He balanced his paunchy, broad-shouldered body on the two hind legs of his chair. His large mouth broke out in a broad, ingratiating smile, exclaiming, "Now we've got to live while we're working this fellowship idea, Paul. Here's a plan to get a steady income for us in the meantime."

He opened up his desk drawer and handed me a miniature orange crate filled with kumquats, its label reading: "This is the box of oranges I promised to send you from California."

"All these tourists coming here want to send a souvenir home to impress their friends, and what's better than a little box that looks like a miniature orange crate? It'll cost us about four cents to put the box together and fill it with kumquats, and we can sell it for twelve cents to the souvenir shops. That'll be a two hundred per cent profit." As he spoke, his piercing eyes met mine. His passionate zeal was contagious, and my response was enthusiastic.

"What are we waiting for?"

"We'll need some money." He sat back in his chair, folded his arms and waited.

"I've got thirty-four bucks in the bank," I volunteered, mentally calculating that a 200 percent profit would bring in sixty-eight dollars.

"Okay, bring it around. That'll put us in business."

The Kumquat Project somehow never materialized, but it later came to light that my thirty-four dollars took care of his delinquent house rent!

His next promotion concept was even more exciting. It involved an exploration trip to Peru to investigate mining claims which a member of the prominent Leguia family of Peru, an acquaintance of G.H., insisted had considerable value. The Peruvian's father had been president of Peru a number of times, but after a few inquiries, we learned that our contact was out of favor with the country's then current leaders.

Still undaunted, G.H. and I next prepared a homemade brochure for presentation to the publicity department of a large movie theater chain, depicting printed autographed pictures of movie stars on stamps to be given away at theaters to promote attendance. As usual, G.H. oozed with confidence when he presented the plan to his contact at the Fox Westcoast Theater chain office, who, without hesitation, turned it thumbs down.

All of G.H.'s schemes expired along with my disability pay. It became necessary for me to again obtain mundane employment as a clerk in a supermarket.

Even after reviewing these past letdowns, I couldn't resist following up his offer for travel to Africa. I visited him at the office of the San Diego Marine Construction Company at the foot of Sampson Street on San Diego Bay.

He greeted me effusively. "Let me show you around." He led

the way to a ship tied up at the dock.

"That's the *Chamberlain*. They're making a mother salvage vessel out of her. She's going to Massawa on the Red Sea, south of the Suez Canal, to salvage a lot of ships scuttled by the Italians. The sunken ships are blocking the entrance to the Massawa harbor, and the English and our navy urgently needs that harbor for a repair base. This is a great opportunity for you. How about signing on?"

"Who would I be working for?"

"Johnson, Drake & Piper. It's a big construction outfit from back east that has the contract with the U.S. Army Engineers. They're hiring all the personnel, buying the equipment and materials and getting the *Chamberlain* in shape. Flanagan is in charge here. In Massawa, Ellsberg, a commander in the navy, will run salvage operations."

"How do you fit in, G.H.?" I asked.

"I'm Flanagan's assistant, helping him get the men he needs. I expect to sign on as a salvage foreman."

Carlyle pointed to the workmen scurrying from the dock to the ship carrying lumber, tools, and supplies. "You can see they're doing a lot of work on her."

I couldn't help but be impressed. "But what can I do?" I asked. "I don't know the first thing about salvage."

"Don't worry. I'll see to it that there'll be a place for you."

As usual, he had all the confidence in the world regarding his ability to promote, but considering his prior record of failures and my lack of knowledge about the Red Sea area, I was wary and decided to seek information about Massawa and its environs at the local library before taking the plunge.

When the Italians took over Eritrea during the 1880's, the port of Massawa was the center of Middle East intrigue, dope smuggling, slave trading and Arabian violence and crime. In 1922, Mussolini, after assuming dictatorial powers, had succeeded not only in making the trains run on time but also rescued the Italian economy from chaos. By the 1930's, Mussolini decided to acquire an African empire for Italy.

Massawa became a naval base for the Italian fleet, complete with floating drydocks, machine and carpentry shops, and served as a supply base for the Italian army in preparation for an invasion of Ethiopia. A highway and railroad were constructed, connecting Massawa to Asmara in the highlands. In 1936 Mussolini's planes and bombs succeeded in conquering Haile Selassie's spear-wielding army.

In June of 1940, after Europe was overrun by the German armies and Hitler appeared to be winning the war, Mussolini, anxious to share in the spoils, declared war on France and England. In the following four months, Italy's armies, from their positions in Ethiopia and Eritrea, attacked and occupied the Sudan and took over British Somaliland.

By April of 1941 the British army assembled a large force, including Free French, British recruits, South Africans, East Indians, Sudanese and Scots, and invaded Ethiopia from bases in Kenya. Having freed Ethiopia from the Italians, the English army pushed on to Asmara and Massawa in Eritrea.

To deprive the British of the use of the Red Sea port, the Italian admiral in charge of the Massawa base ordered the scuttling of all ships, drydocks, cranes, and anything else afloat there. The Italians maneuvered twelve freighters across the entrance to the naval and commercial harbors, placed bombs and mines in their holds, and sank those vessels to prevent the Allies from using the harbors. They also placed bombs in twenty-eight other vessels, both freighters and passenger ships, and sent them to the bottom of the Red Sea.

Five destroyers, the bulk of the Italian Red Sea fleet, steamed out of the Massawa harbor just before the British entered, but the British navy pursued them, sank several of the ships, and the others were scuttled by their Italian crews.

As of the first of February, 1942, most of continental Europe was under the direct or indirect control of Nazi Germany; and, in the German drive to conquer Russia, Hitler's forces were beseiging Leningrad and threatening Moscow. In the Pacific, the Japanese had occupied Hong Kong, Wake Island, Bangkok and Sarawak, and had invaded Burma, Borneo, New Guinea and the Philippine Islands, and their armed forces were at the gates of Singapore.

In North Africa, the German objective was to capture the British naval base at Alexandria and the Suez Canal, which would give the Axis powers access to the oil kingdoms of the Middle East. General Erwin Rommel had been dispatched to Libya in early 1941 to command the *Afrika Korps*, and by February of 1942 he had succeeded in capturing the port of Bengazi, which had been taken by the British from the Italians two years before. The British Eighth Army, under General Sir Claude Auchinleck, retreated to a defensive position south of Gazala, near the port of Tobruk, which had also been captured from the Italians in January of '41.

The war situation looked bleak, indeed.

Now on the brink of making a decision, I found myself in a quandary. If I were inducted into the navy with a rating, perhaps I would wind up in a safe, but dull, stateside position while the world was being torn apart.

Carlyle's offer was far more intriguing. Adventure had always appealed to me, and I had never visited the Middle East. I didn't relish the idea of melting away in the extremely hot climate of Massawa, but there I would be free from the strict discipline of the armed service and still make a contribution to the war effort. That was the deciding factor.

Back at the San Diego Marine Construction Company office, I searched out Carlyle at his desk.

"Say, G.H., see if you can get me on the *Chamberlain*."

Grabbing me by the arm, G.H. introduced me to W.E. Flanagan, a likeable Irishman, who, nevertheless, was quick-tempered, explosive, impatient, and hyperactive.

"Paul would be a big help to you here in the office, Bill. But he'll need a draft board deferment."

"Do you type?" queried Flanagan.

"Sure do."

"When can you start?"

"Well, let me see . . ." I was concerned about giving my employer enough notice.

"How about right away? Take that desk over there." He pointed to a large desk piled high with file folders.

That evening I called my boss, the West Coast circulation representative of Dell Publishing Company, and advised him that I had joined Flanagan's staff.

Flanagan requested a deferment from my draft board, and it

was automatically granted because of the triple priority status of this expedition.

Within a week Flanagan, at the suggestion of G.H., signed me on the ship as warehouseman to be in charge of its $500,000 cargo of small and large tools and salvage gear and equipment. Never mind that I didn't know a caliper from a left-handed monkey wrench.

In preparation for the voyage, a local hospital nurse delighted in jabbing my arms and buttocks, mainly the latter, with needles to innoculate and immunize me against yellow fever, typhoid, tetanus, cholera, diptheria, and typhus.

She joked, "We'll have you back on your seat again in no time."

It had taken more than three months to reconstruct and refit the *Chamberlain*, a long-neglected lumber steamer. The U.S. Army Engineers managed to acquire her at a time when the army, navy, and merchant marine service were commandeering just about any ship that succeeded in staying afloat. I suspected that the ship had been scrutinized by each service and summmarily rejected as a disaster.

Be that as it may, her size was ideal for a salvage supply and repair vessel, with gross tonnage of 2264, overall length of 310 feet, breadth of 44 feet, and depth of 19 feet. In the conversion from a run-down coastal lumber boat into a salvage supply vessel—no less run-down as we were to learn—the ship had undergone radical changes. Like other lumber vessels, her bridge and officers' quarters were on the aft part of the ship, with most of the intervening space between the bow and afterdeck utilized for carrying lumber during her heyday.

Since the first of the year, the fo'c'sle had been built up from the deck to provide a mammoth dormitory for most of the salvage men, who were also to serve as part of the ship's crew en route to her destination. A machine shop and a carpentry shop had been constructed midships to house lathes, grinders, saws, and other equipment.

She was a most unusual looking ship with her deck cargo of large crates and two motor launches and the alterations to her structure, strange enough to confuse friend or foe. Even a connoisseur of ships would have been at a loss to identify the purpose for such perversion of the ship's lines, or the nature of her mission. Certainly she was one of a kind.

In anticipation of Massawa's high temperatures, an air conditioning system was installed. It consisted of two five-ton frigidaire units that funneled cool air into all living quarters and the mess halls.

Powerful diesel generators had been set in position to provide electric current and power for the cooling system, the refrigeration plant, and the machine shop. Blackout curtains had been hung in all quarters, and switches were added to turn off lights automatically when a door opened.

When the ship was scheduled to make its trial run, Captain Hansen requested that a purser be assigned to help him with administrative details. Again with Carlyle's enthusiastic endorsement, Flanagan designated me for the job. As warehouseman, it was my job to inventory the tools and equipment brought aboard and to maintain a record of their use. In view of my experience as a supermarket manager in Hollywood, I felt better qualified to serve in the more prestigious position of purser.

In the excitement of the proposed voyage, I gave no thought to the difficulties that would arise in working two jobs.

When I related the endless sequence of problems encountered during the ship's trial runs to my Los Angeles buddies, they begged me not to sail with the *Chamberlain*. I had hoped to talk some of them into joining me on this expedition. After several weeks with Flanagan, I was confident he would hire anyone recommended by me.

"Paul, I don't think the odds of surviving are good," warned Irving Wallace, later to become a best-selling novelist. I had known him since 1934 when he joined me on an adventure trip into the jungles of Central America.

"Pablo, I'd rather take a chance in the army," concluded James F. Scheer, a budding author and a friend of long standing.

Just a few days before departing, five of my friends gave me a last supper in Los Angeles at the Pirate's Den, a restaurant featuring a fortune teller. I desperately wanted to believe in her palm reading when she enthused over my long life line, which supposedly assured me of my safe return.

The day before sailing, the steward hired by Flanagan to buy the ship's provisions and to supervise the Filipino mess hall crew was caught taking bribes from the ship's chandler and promptly fired.

Flanagan, determined that the *Chamberlain's* departure was not going to be delayed a single day and desperate to find a replacement, took Carlyle's suggestion that I should also serve as steward.

I protested taking on the work involved in three positions, but Carlyle insisted, "It'll all work out, Paul. You'll have a lot of time free from your purser's duties while at sea."

"But I know nothing about running the galley," I protested.

"What makes you think the mess hall crew and cook and baker do?" He laughed heartily at his remark.

I felt some obligation to Carlyle for getting me on the ship in the first place and decided not to bitch further.

Flanagan had acquired two sea-going tugs for the salvage project. The *Intent*, captained by Edison Brown, a west coast salvage master, and manned by experienced salvage personnel who had previously worked for him, sailed from Port Arthur, Texas, for Massawa, Eritrea, on February 26th, a couple of months before us. The *Resolute*, captained by Oiva Byglin, an unskilled salvage man, was scheduled to sail with a crew of salvage men at a later date.

Other salvage men had already flown to Massawa and were actively engaged in reconstructing the Massawa Naval Base.

Finding salvage workers for the Massawa project challenged Flanagan's ingenuity. The navy had already hired most available experienced salvage men and deep-sea divers for the purpose of clearing Pearl Harbor of the wreckage of warships bombed in the disastrous Japanese attack on December 7th, 1941, and to construct naval bases on our East and West Coasts and in the harbors of a number of foreign countries.

Until the ship sailed, my job was to assist Flanagan by typing up reports, applications, and correspondence. By advertising, contacting salvage companies and divers, including those employed by the motion picture industry, he managed to assemble a salvage crew for the *Chamberlain*. Most of the artisans such as the welders, boilermakers, carpenters, and machinists, were well qualified in their own specialties, but many of the divers and tenders were inexperienced in salvage work.

Before our trial run to San Pedro, Flanagan assigned the men to positions aboard the vessel, compatible with their experience. Iron workers, welders, and boilermakers were designated to serve in the engine room as oilers, firemen, and wipers; carpenters, divers, divers tenders and salvage men were assigned deck duties; and electricians were selected to work in the machine shop to keep the ship's diesels operating.

The captain, chief engineer, and the steward and his staff were to be compensated by a weekly salary, whereas the remaining members of the expedition were to be paid at an hourly rate, with a miniumum pay based upon a forty-eight hour week, and time and a half for overtime. I was expected to work in my three capacities for just one salary.

While en route to Eritrea, the men were scheduled to be on duty seven days a week. Overtime for the extra day was never discussed. Seamen were never compensated for overtime at sea even though they worked from Monday through Sunday.

It was inevitable that problems would ensue.

CHAPTER 3

BEGINNING OF A FEUD

THE WAR: The U-Boat tanker built for the German Navy in early 1942 carried torpedoes, supplies, and 600 tons of fuel, making it possible to refuel and resupply its submarines at sea. During the month of May, 1942, its fleet of 32 U-boats, thus serviced, sank 111 ships in the Caribbean and eastern seaboard.

G.H. turned on my bright cabin light as he came in and shook me awake.

"Paul, it's already 6 o'clock. The skipper's asking for you."

What could the captain want with me at this early hour? Had I goofed?

"And he's asking about that cat of his," G.H. added.

The ship grunted and groaned in irritating rhythm, undulating like a camel in motion. But a night's sleep had renewed my courage, settled my stomach and restored my dignity.

The cat awoke, meowed wailfully, and sought out the leftover food provided by the messman.

I dressed hurriedly, swooped up the feline and tramped out on the windswept deck under a sky adorned with white billowing clouds, sullied only by a trail of black smoke from the ship's stack. Exhilarated by the cool morning air, I was ready for any challenge.

At the skipper's door, with the purring cat curled up in my arms, I whistled "Roll Out the Barrel" and knocked firmly.

"Come in!" he commanded.

Seated in an armchair at his desk, clad in his grayish long johns and puffing away at his pipe, he boomed, "Sit down."

I sat, inhaling the foul-smelling smoke and studying his weather-beaten face for a clue to his mood. The lines on his forehead, emphasized by the large scar, did not encourage familiarity.

"Your cat, sir," I offered, holding it by the scruff of the neck.

The captain cuddled the cat in his arms, then deposited it on the settee.

Glaring at me with half-closed eyes, he growled, "I heard you whistling. You've gotta learn never to do that at sea. It brings on bad weather."

He pointed to the cat. "Take care of him. Belongs to my wife. She calls him Ernie. Lilly thought I needed company."

When he mentioned his wife, I detected a slight smile on his lips. He puffed thoughtfully at his pipe.

"Now Purser, first, I want to give you a word of warning. We'll be handling a lot of sensitive material. Keep it confidential."

"Yes, sir," I mumbled.

The skipper leaned over, waving his smoking pipe in my direction. "Now about the steward's department. I know you're not trained for that job, but we're stuck with you. If you have any problems, bring 'em to me. Keep the crew happy. Nothing will upset 'em more than lousy food."

The ship lurched unexpectedly. My stomach settled back on the rebound, but Ernie wasn't so lucky. He heaved and heaved, making a real mess on the settee. It was obvious that Ernie was a landlubber.

The skipper rose from his chair, his face livid. "Get that cat out of here and send a messboy to clean this up."

I put Ernie in a box in the machine shop, but he jumped out and followed me to the galley.

The odor of burning food infiltrated my nostrils, and no cook was in sight. A large pot of soup boiled over on the stove. I turned off the heat, and, upon opening the oven door, a flood of smoke and the smell of cremated chicken filled the air. Loud voices in the mess hall alerted me to a hot poker game in progress among the galley crew.

Trying to disregard the offensive smell and the recurring impulse to throw up, I passed the large refrigerator and work-tables and entered the mess hall, pleading, "Fellas, those chickens—they're burning!"

The kitchen crew, sitting on benches around one of the long tables, raked in their chips and got up. I complained, "Must we have chicken again today?"

Bennie Godines, the roly-poly chief cook, stumbled toward the galley, rationalizing, "Cooler, she full. Gotta eat chicken before we get to other meat."

It now occurred to me that the entrance to the freezer was in the cooler, which was piled high with crates of dressed chicken, directly in front of the door to the freezer; and the freezer, too, was packed to the ceiling.

I followed Bennie and tapped him on the shoulder. "Let's

talk," I said, leading the way back to the mess hall where we sat on one of the benches. A record player in the corner of the messroom blared forth jazzy dance music.

"Can't your boys move the chicken crates and take out other meats from the freezer? We can't have chicken every meal," I shouted above the loud music, still hesitating to use the clout of my unwanted position as steward.

"My boys busy," the cook insisted. "Gotta prepare chow. No time to dig into freezer."

"But lots of time to play poker," I remonstrated. "The captain doesn't want any complaints from the crew about the food. Let's give the men a variety. Say Ben, send one of your men to the captain's quarters. The cat made quite a mess on his settee."

In spite of my instructions, chicken continued to be featured daily.

Ernie was right on my heels. He apparently recognized Consuelo, who had brought him chicken bits the night before. When the cat brushed luxuriously against the messman's ankle and purred, Consuelo picked him up and petted him lovingly.

"Say, Consuelo, what about keeping this cat fed?" I asked.

From then on, Ernie transferred his allegiance to Consuelo, who fed and cared for him and took him into his bunk in the fo'c'sle at night. Although relieved that the cat was now in such good hands, I couldn't help feeling a touch of regret that he switched his loyalty so easily.

I climbed up to the boat deck and found Carlyle supervising a couple of seamen tossing overboard empty cartons that were piled up in front of the sick bay.

"Hey, G.H.," I yelled. "Save me a box."

Carlyle grabbed one of the remaining cartons out of the clutches of a deckhand. As the last of the sawdust and wrappings went over the side, our ship's doctor, Lieutenant M.E. Chasen, U.S. Army, came out of the sick bay.

"You, there," he drawled. "What the devil are you doing with my packing boxes?"

The doctor, a reserved, six-foot, 190-pound southerner, his cheeks pink and puffed, had a love of authority—his own. He had been selected to accompany us because of his experience in treating tropical diseases. While stationed in Liberia, he specialized in learning about the bloodsucking tsetse flies which thrive on the African continent and attack animals and humans, transmitting the flagellate protozoan parasites that cause human sleeping sickness.

Hands on hips, Carlyle turned to the doctor. "You talking to <u>me</u>?"

"Yes, I'm talking to <u>you</u>. Don't you know there's a war on? Those boxes were stamped with our ship's name and destination. You trying to help the Nazis?" The doctor's voice rose an octave above his normal speech.

Tact was a lost art with G.H. whose patience was easily tested. He forged his way with daring and a touch of arrogance, and his temper flared with little provocation. The feud had started.

"I don't let any SOB army punk tell me what to do." Carlyle's cutting words carried across the ship's deck.

Doctor Chasen's face turned crimson. Accustomed to strict army discipline and no flack from civilians, he threatened, "I'll get you for that. Wait 'til we get to Panama!" With that he stalked off.

"You wouldn't get an 'A' in diplomacy," I admonished G.H.

"He's crossed me a couple of times, and I don't take that shit from anybody."

To change the subject, I asked, "Isn't the gun crew due to try out that three-incher this morning?"

Carlyle nodded.

I persisted, "Do you think she'll ever go off? Someone said she's been parked in a public square since 1915. Besides, how could our crew learn much about guns in three days of briefing back in Diego?"

Instead of answering, Carlyle said, "I've got something for you."

He grabbed my arm, led me to his cabin, and reached into a box on his bunk. "Since the skipper made me master-at-arms, he gave me half a dozen thirty-eight's to pass around. You get the first."

"The fellas would sure laugh me off the deck if I wore a gun," I protested.

He handed me a six shooter and a box of ammunition. "It'll come in handy if you have to tote any ship's money around."

When I tried to insert a bullet into the ammunition chamber, it wouldn't fit.

"Say, G.H., these bullets aren't right for this gun."

Carlyle examined them.

"My God! it's screwed up just like everything else on this tub. Flanagan gave us thirty-eight police special ammunition and regular thirty-eights for guns!"

There was a sudden blast and the ship shuddered, throwing both of us against the bunk.

"Maybe that three-incher blew up!" I yelled, dashing out to the afterdeck.

The three-incher on the deck above was still there, but the boys firing her were picking themselves up from the deck.

Carlyle gasped in disbelief, "I didn't think she'd go off."

The doctor stood in the doorway of the sick bay surveying its interior, his left arm akimbo, his right arm pressed against his forehead. A glance inside disclosed a broken medicine bottle on the deck, and a strong odor of a druggist laboratory emanated from the sick bay.

After one salvo, the gun would not reset itself. When the men dismounted the barrel, it became apparent that six inches of the inside of the barrel had been painted. After removing the paint, the gun crew successfully fired four more salvos.

CHAPTER 4

COMPLAINTS! COMPLAINTS

Let's Face It
We are undoubtedly the screwiest crew ever assembled on one ship. This is one of the few things we agree on. We have enough licensed skippers to chop up the boat into equal parts and make a race for it. We have bakers and boilermakers, carpenters, and cooks, divers, riggers, ex-pugs, welders, ex-rumrunners, and most every trade you can think of. We beef most of the time, argue the rest of the time, and seldom agree on anything.

From the *Hawse Pipe Herald*, unofficial journal
of the *S.S. W.R. Chamberlain, Jr.*

Five days days out of San Diego, at officer's mess, First Mate Jaeger asked Cletus Stirewalt, our radio man, what was happening in the outside world.

"I've got war news and it isn't good," he blurted out. "The Japs are closing in on Corregidor. Our army there can't hold out much longer. German subs are sinking more than one of our ships every day, some of them in the Caribbean!"

Gloom hung over the officers. Chief Engineer Albert

Culpepper commented, "Looks like a long, dirty war." He turned to the skipper. "I'd like a word with you, Captain."

"Me, too, Tom," interposed Jaeger.

"You both meet me in my cabin after mess," Hansen responded. "And Paul, you join us. I've got some work for you."

After yet another meal of chicken, we proceeded to the captain's quarters. Jaeger entered, a husky old-time seaman who had served as captain on many a freighter. I admired his dignified bearing and unpretentious disposition as he removed his cap and sat upright in his chair, mouthing his inevitable pipe, a faraway look in his eyes.

We were joined by Culpepper, nicknamed "peckerneck" by the fo'c'sle gang because of his red neck. A tall, thin bundle of nervous energy, he sat on the settee, playing with his cap and looking furtively around the cabin, as fidgety as a race horse at the starting gate. I sat down next to him.

"Well, Mate," began the skipper, taking off his jacket, his left forearm revealing a tattoed dragon. Eyeing Jaeger, he asked, "What's on your mind?"

"Cap, I've got troubles. Those men Flanagan hired in San Diego to do salvage work in the Red Sea may be good men in their trade, but as sailors they're not worth the powder to blow 'em to hell. I have to teach 'em to do everything on deck. You'd think this was a school ship."

"I know, Mate," the skipper concurred. "The crew seems to think this is a holiday cruise."

"That ain't all." The mate was usually not very talkative. Now he didn't spare words. "They just won't stick to a job. They tell me that they're hired as carpenters, divers, or ship fitters, not as sailors. I get a dozen fellas painting on deck. Leave 'em for five minutes and they're gone. Can't put 'em in irons. They didn't sign any ship's articles. They just agreed to sail the ship to Massawa."

**CAPTAIN THOMAS HANSEN AND
CHIEF ENGINEER ALBERT CULPEPPER**

The skipper, the mate, and the chief were all accustomed to sailing with an experienced and well disciplined crew, but only a few men aboard the *Chamberlain* had previously served in the merchant marine service. While working in the San Diego office, I snooped through the personnel records of the men and was impressed by the quality of manpower that Flanagan had managed to acquire. There were some misfits, but many of the welders, mechanics, boilermakers, carpenters and electricians had been highly paid on shore jobs. Most were not psychologically suited for the routine jobs on board ship.

The skipper paced the floor, took a few puffs from his pipe, then pointed it at the chief. "Before we get to your complaint, let me have my say. I'm beginning to learn why a couple of other skippers walked off this ship. But come hell or high water, I'm taking her to Africa. I've got my troubles and I want you each to shoulder your own. You're responsible for the morale of your men and don't forget it." He pulled down his Prince Albert tobacco can from the shelf above his desk and refilled his pipe.

Culpepper's irascibility surfaced as his words tumbled out in a loud voice that resounded in the cabin. "It isn't only the men, skipper, it's this son of a bitchen ship that's got me turning handsprings. She should've been sold to the Germans and they'd probably lose the war trying to run it. Even after working on the condensers yesterday afternoon, about two-thirds of the tubes in the main condenser still leak. The main condenser should've been re-tubed in Diego. Water still gets into that forepeak tank. Our main throttle valve also leaks like hell. I wouldn't trust this tub to respond promptly to change of direction if we ever have to go in convoy."

"Yeah," Jaeger contributed. "The lifeboat davits won't swing out, water gets into the chain locker, cables block the machine guns so they have little scope, our steering gear won't work properly, fire extinquishers are empty and I could go on for an hour about what's wrong with this junk heap."

The chief cut in with his usual vehemence. "And those men Flanagan assigned to me. They're useless. You can drown 'em all. My engineers and I'll run the engine room ourselves. Not only are they dumb about the engine room, but they don't want to learn. Three of them are now in sick bay pretending to be seasick. When I told doc all they needed to cure 'em was a day in the engine room, he says, 'They're not fit for duty!' "

The captain vowed, "Anyone who has been in sick bay because of seasickness won't get shore leave. Pass that word along. No, Purser. Write a notice and post it in the mess hall."

Just then Scottish bagpipe music screeched out of the air-conditioning outlet drowning out our conversation. The rolling ship had not ruined the doctor's phonograph.

"That damned music," groaned the skipper. "If that doctor wasn't an army man, I'd lock him up." He reached up to the air-conditioning unit and closed the outlet, but the weird sounds still filtered in. For a few moments he puffed at his pipe. Then he continued, "Now, you've got to get the men together, talk to 'em and get 'em to cooperate. Send 'em to me if you have to."

"That's not all," Culpepper persisted. "The lousy grub isn't fit for pigs."

The master's hand trembled as he took his pipe out of his mouth. He and the chief were not tuned in on the same frequency. "Not good enough for pigs, is it? I'm eating the food, and I'm not complaining. Now don't make any more trouble, Chief. I've heard enough out of you."

Culpepper's expression turned sullen, but he knew he'd better shut up. He got up and a gloomy Jaeger followed him out on deck. I was right at their heels, but the skipper stopped me.

"Purser, we haven't talked yet."

While the door was open, Jim Cook, a short, well-built, handsome specimen of a man, flamboyant and assertive, stepped in. His resonant voice boomed, "May I have a word with you, Captain?"

He had been hired as a diver, based upon his diving experience on the West Coast. Previous to that, he had operated his own boat, equipped with twin Packard engines, in the Upper Bay of the Hudson River, taking passengers around the harbor of New York. He had the confidence of the men in the fo'c'sle. Contrary to the musical tastes of the fo'c'sle gang, he loved operas and piano concertos and insisted upon playing his records at odd hours.

"Well, what do you want?" The captain's voice was crisp.

"I've been elected delegate for the crew and they've asked me to take up some complaints."

The captain waved him to a chair and sat upright at his desk. After many years before the mast, Hansen's eyes were invariably half-closed as a protection against the bright sunlight. Now he squinted. The veins in his forehead bulged. But all he said was, "Well?"

"We must have overtime pay for Sundays," Cook began.

"What?" The Old Man roared, his eyes wide open.

Not to be intimidated, the delegate said in a firm voice, "Our contracts read that we are to put in a forty-eight hour week and that we get time and a half for overtime."

"How much are you getting a week?" queried the captain.

"A hundred dollars."

Sailors' pay was closer to forty dollars weekly.

"You want overtime pay for working Sundays?" asked the skipper incredulously. "I've never heard of a sailor collecting extra pay for Sunday work at sea. It just isn't done."

The delegate wasn't going to be bullied. "O.K., so we won't work Sundays."

"Then we'll stop her in mid-ocean on Sundays," the skipper muttered sarcastically. "Now what else are you beefing about in the fo'c'sle?"

Cook's voice no longer carried much conviction. He blurted out, "It's the food, sir. The bread tastes sour, the soup is over-spiced, and the everyday chicken is burnt and tough."

Obviously, my stewardship of the mess hall and the galley created all kinds of problems. The Captain scratched his sixth match within the past half hour, took a few puffs on his pipe, squinted at the delegate and pointed to the door.

"Get out!" he ordered.

Cook hesitated. The captain gripped the arms of his chair and started to stand up. Cook swung around and left in haste.

The Old Man banged the ashes from his pipe as he settled down again, and muttered, "What the hell do they expect? Some of the men came aboard with fifty-three pieces—a deck of cards and a spare sock. Now they want to live like kings."

I ventured a chuckle, but the skipper continued in a serious vein. "Now about the steward's department. Talk to the cook and do something about the menu before we have a mutiny."

"Sure thing, Captain," I agreed, wondering what I could do to make my influence felt in the galley.

"Also, I want you to prepare several notices for posting on the mess hall bulletin board. You already know about giving no shore leave to those who spent time in sick bay with seasickness. Also prepare a notice warning the men not to throw anything overboard until one hour after sundown and also to remove all labels and identification marks on items thrown overboard. And make a notice ordering the men to turn over to Carlyle all radios, cameras, guns, and ammunition. I'll sign 'em after you type 'em up."

It later developed that in spite of the posted notices the crew kept cameras, radios, and guns. Fortunately the retained cameras did record the progress of the expedition.

Next morning I found a typewritten sheet shoved under my cabin door, titled, *Hawse Pipe Herald*. One of the seamen had gone to the trouble of typing an unofficial newspaper with his hilarious comments and gossip about the ship's officers and men.

From then on, the paper appeared at unpredictable times. I relished the cleverness of the editor and always looked forward to the next issue. I was never able to learn his identity. Since many of the comments were barbs directed at specific members of the crew, the author must have thought it best to sign the news letter with the pseudonym, "Hawse Pipe Harry". Looking up the word, hawse, I learned why he had chosen that name. It referred to that part of a vessel having openings for the passage of cables. To the editor, it meant a channel for transmitting gossip.

About mid-morning Dr. Chasen emerged from sick bay with nurse John Vargas at his heels. Two members of the crew had been stricken with a mild case of food poisoning, and the doctor had announced at breakfast his intention to inspect the ship to determine the source of the infection.

NURSE ART ALLUISI AND NURSE JOHN VARGAS IN SICK BAY

In view of the complaints about the food, the captain conceded, "If you can keep the rest of our crew healthy, go to it."

The doctor opened the door of the cooler.

"My God!" he exclaimed. "What a mess!"

It was impossible to get into the freezer with so many crates of food stacked against its door.

Chasen exclaimed, "I can't believe it! What's all this chicken and butter doing in the cooler? You know it'll spoil quickly. Hey, John, make a note of this, and you, Paul, see to it you have the whole cooler and freezer repacked." The nurse nodded his head, and, although offended by the doctor's officiousness, I did likewise.

Chasen slammed the cooler door shut and I followed him into the galley where the Filipino crew was preparing another batch of chicken. I stood in the doorway watching the baker knead the bread dough while the doctor poked around the kitchen inspecting the pots and pans. The baker, looking flushed, wiped the perspiration from his forehead and brushed his nose on his sleeve. Then he sneezed into the bread dough.

"You there," Chasen barked. "I want you in the sick bay at once."

The baker looked puzzled. "Me gotta bake bread."

"Dump that dough!" the doctor ordered. Then he turned to me, scolding, "Do you permit such unhealthy practices?"

"I never noticed it before," I muttered.

The doctor stalked out with the baker in tow.

Chief Cook Bennie grabbed me by the arm. "What's idea you bring doctor in? Doctor take my baker. No run galley without baker. Me quit."

"I had nothing to do with that. He's only trying to do his job. Besides, you can't quit. You're under contract. If you don't stick, the captain can put you ashore when we get to Panama and then you'll go in the army," I threatened.

The cook shrugged his shoulders. "I only cook. I no bake bread."

Searching for a replacement for the baker, I scouted the fo'c'sle where four of the boys were playing poker and several others lounged in their bunks.

"Does anyone here know anything about baking?" I asked. "The doctor hospitalized the baker, and until he's out of sick bay, we need someone to bake bread and pastries."

"Well, I did a hitch in the navy doin' bakin'," volunteered Watson from his bunk. Signed on as a welder, he served as a fireman in the engine room but apparently preferred the baker's job that would give him more free time.

I hesitated in view of his dirty hands and face and his filthy bed clothes, but since no one else volunteered, I motioned to him. "Okay, you report to Bennie in the galley right away and I'll make arrangements with the chief for your transfer."

Watson called out as I headed for the door, "By the way, Steward, Peters says he worked in a hotel once and could run the galley better'n you."

Here was my chance!

"Where is Peters?" I asked.

Employed as an electrician, Peters was working on one of the diesel motors in the machine shop. He was an intelligent twenty five-year-old, who kept to himself. His build was wiry, his height medium, his face nondescript, but his manner was engaging.

"Say, Les," I shouted at him above the whining of the lathes. "I hear you've had hotel experience and have been bragging about being able to run the galley and mess hall better than I."

"Well, to tell the truth, you heard right." he boasted.

"I'll talk to the skipper and try to arrange for you to take over the steward's job. You're welcome to it as far as I'm concerned."

Following up on my job as warehouseman, I surveyed piles of cartons in the machine shop containing tools, equipment, and salvage gear for which I was responsible. The cartons had been stacked between the machinery to prevent them from being smashed as the *Chamberlain* rolled from side to side while parked in mid-ocean undergoing repairs to its condensers.

Upon paging through the pile of invoices, I did not recognize any item, and I knew the responsibility and the tedious work of a warehouseman was also not for me.

In the engine room, I accosted Culpepper.

"Say Chief, our baker is in sick bay. Watson said he could take over until the baker is well again. He was a baker in the navy. Is that okay with you?"

"Maybe he's a better baker than a fireman," the chief said resignedly.

Encouraged by the prospect of relinquishing the steward's position, I pressed him further. "I think you should assign someone from your department to take charge of the tools and salvage gear pilled up in the machine shop." I felt certain he preferred to have the tools under his control without having to requisition them from me.

"Purser, that's a good idea," the chief responded with enthusiasm. "Let's talk to the Old Man about it."

In the skipper's cabin, I confessed: "Captain, I know nothing about the tools and salvage gear in the machine shop. The chief is willing to assign one of his men to take over my job as warehouseman."

"That's okay with me Paul. Now as to your job as steward. I'm getting more complaints about the food."

"Captain, we may have an answer. I've talked to Les Peters, and he said he had hotel experience with food and was willing to take over."

"Well, send Peters to me." The skipper's face lit up. "Your work as purser will take a lot of your time, and each of the other jobs requires someone's full attention."

I dashed down to the machine shop to locate Peters, relieved that I had extricated myself from my two headache positions.

CHAPTER 5

PANAMA INTERLUDE

Fo'c'sle Subdivides

The fo'c'sle, because it is a growing little community, finally took to naming its streets. Hereafter, the port side will be known as Beverly Hills, the starboard side will be known as Wilshire Boulevard, while just forward of the toilets will be known as Skid Row, or the other side of the tracks. When questioned, the boys from Skid Row snarled and said, "Yeah, so what, we're doity and we like it. Besides, we never could sleep good when beds is made."

From the *Hawse Pipe Herald,* unofficial journal of the *S.S. W.R. Chamberlain, Jr.*

Meandering from my cabin to the engine room to consult with Culpepper about his repair list, I paused at the railing to watch porpoises leap out of the water in graceful curves alongside the vibrating ship and then dive back under to repeat the rhythmic gymnastics.

The ship's funnel puffed away enthusiastically, its black cloud of smoke spiralling into the atmosphere, inviting any and all marauding enemy craft to use our ship for target practice.

The chief sat at his desk in the hot engine room, his slender perspiring physique bare to the waist; but the members of the black gang—the firemen, oilers, and water tenders—leisurely stalked about, indifferent to the debilitating heat and the strong smell of oil.

Remembering his complaints, I shouted above the rhythmical pounding of the pistons, "You'll probably need a lot of repairs, Chief, when we hit Panama."

As usual, he didn't lack for words. He leaned back and propped his feet on his desk. "We'd be better off just getting another ship. This one needs almost all the engines and equipment rebuilt or replaced, and even then I wouldn't trust this tub." He handed me a scribbled sheet of paper.

I had problems deciphering the long itemization for typing. It included the re-tubing of the main condenser, repairing the main throttle valve, overhauling the steering gear, and fixing the leak in the forepeak tank.

First assistant engineer James Gibson, greeted me from his desk in the engine room. He was a baldheaded, well-built man of forty-three. His quick smile was counterbalanced by two haughty, steely blue eyes that commanded respect, and I kept my distance. He had a terrible temper but usually regained his composure quickly. However, he never forgave anyone who crossed him.

Pointing to one of the oilers, Gibson shouted, "Hey, Armstrong, get your ass down below and clean out the bilges, and be quick about it."

Now Horace Armstrong was a former prize fighter, a heavy-set specimen of a man. Although formidable-looking, he was very popular with the crew. According to the scuttlebutt, he and the first assistant had tangled in a number of acrimonious verbal exchanges. Armstrong had been rewarded by being assigned to the dirtiest jobs in the engine room.

The veins in Armstrong's neck bulged out. In an aside to one of the oilers, he confided in a voice loud enough to carry throughout the engine room, "Just wait until we get to Massawa. That bastard'll be sorry he tangled with me."

Back on deck, I approached Jaeger, the chief mate, who reluctantly consented to take off a few minutes from working with his crew to give me a rundown on deck repairs needed in Panama. He repeated the complaints he had previously itemized in the meeting with the skipper.

I scratched my head. "Looks like we'll be in the repair yard in Panama for awhile."

"Ja, if we make it to there," was his sarcastic reply as he turned back to supervise the deck crew.

After two weeks at sea, a pilot came aboard at Balboa in Panama and directed our vessel to the oil dock. Dr. Chasen had ordered the radio operator to signal ashore for an ambulance, now waiting at the dock, to take messman Felix Bonife and diver's tender Edwin Maitland to the hospital. Bonife had persistent headaches, and Maitland, a former prizefighter assigned to the post of helmsman, had complained of dizzy spells. We always knew when he was at the helm because the ship then weaved from port to starboard. We needed bodies for the *Chamberlain*, and apparently health was not an important factor in signing on.

Axel, our bos'n, having boarded our ship severely beaten up, should also have been hospitalized in Panama. One of the few experienced seamen aboard, he was a grim-faced, well built, gruff sailor—a loner, and a heavy drinker. He could move the heaviest objects with ease. I wondered how he could have suffered such a beating in view of his great strength. I believed him when he said that six men had jumped him. "You should 'a seen what I did to dem six," he gloated.

The first two days after our departure from San Diego, he worked more energetically than any of the other seamen, in spite of his agonizingly bruised face and his inability to eat solid foods. On a liquid diet for the third day, he reported to the doctor and spent the next five days in sick bay, coughing up blood. Chasen decided that Axel's condition needed only rest. Later, it worried me to see Axel working on deck, still obviously suffering from that beating.

Anxious to set foot on *terra firma*, many of the crew donned white shirts and business suits and lined up at the railing, ready to leap on the gangplank for a dash to the nearest bar.

Ernie crouched nearby, eyeing the dock and meowing. "Gee, Ernie, what's the matter, are you hungry? Aren't you boys feeding him down in the galley?" I asked.

Wes Hewson, one of the electricians, piped up, "Hungry? Hell! He's sex starved like the rest of us. We're going to pick up a mate for him ashore so at least he doesn't have to go on the prowl at every port. We should be so lucky." The gang snickered.

"Say, Purse," asked Okie, one of the ship's best poker players. "How much money do we get here, and when do we get it?"

"Yeah, and what about the shore passes?" piped up Hewson.

I shrugged. "I don't know. The ship's agent hasn't boarded yet."

The authorities ordered the *Chamberlain* to anchor in the shipyard within sight of the quay and wait for a berth in the repair yards. In shifting from the dock to mooring, the forward steam line powering the anchor windlass cracked and had to be replaced before our ship could move under its own power.

Army and navy officials boarded us that afternoon, and shortly after, a Standard Oil Company shore boat pulled up alongside.

Culpepper handed me a scribbled note. "Paul, add this to my repair list."

Upon deciphering, I amended his repair list to include the replacement of the steam line leading to the anchor windlass and rushed it to the skipper's cabin, where military officials were inspecting our ship's papers.

Hansen emphasized the fact that we were on a priority mission and that the *Chamberlain* needed urgent repairs.

"We've got a six weeks' backlog of work in the shipyard, and it's all top priority," countered one officer, starting for the door. That was the cue for all the officials to depart, leaving the skipper, the Standard Oil Company agent, and me wondering how many days or weeks we'd be stuck in Panama.

The agent had several thousand dollars available for a draw, but the captain decided, "We'll just give them ten dollars apiece. More than that and they'll get into trouble."

The agent hesitated, then in a serious tone confided, "Did you know, Captain, German subs sank nine U.S. ships in the Caribbean last month?"

The thought of traveling through the Caribbean was terrifying, especially in view of our slow speed and our smoking and sparking smokestack.

"Our radio man reported some sinkings, but I had no idea there were that many," the skipper responded.

After the agent left, I broached the subject of our itinerary, hoping for a safe and interesting sightseeing trip around South America. "Are we sailing around the Cape, Captain?" I asked.

"I don't know, Paul. Let me worry about that. You take care of your department." We heard the loud voices of the men outside the captain's door. "Give the men their draw before they mob us. Remember, just ten dollars apiece."

The contract with Johnson, Drake & Piper provided for a weekly cash payment of ten dollars to each crew member, the balance of the weekly wage to be deposited to the credit of the respective crew members at the Bank of Manhattan in New York City.

The boys crowded around me as I left the captain's quarters, clutching the passes and money. "Okay, fellas, I've got the draw. Line up at my cabin."

John, the carpenter, was the first. When I handed him a ten-dollar bill and his pass, he protested, "My God, ten dollars! You can't even get a good lay for that here."

"Weren't you winning at poker?" I asked.

"Winning, hell! That Okie cleaned us all out last night."

Grumbling about their "measly draw," the men made for the gangway where shore boats were lined up to take them to the dock. The skipper had forgotten about his notice forbidding shore leave to any crew member who had sought refuge in the sick bay for seasickness, and I didn't remind him.

Shore passes in hand, the men ignored their officers' orders to take turns maintaining a fifty percent security watch. Even some of the officers deserted the ship.

William Alsabrook, nicknamed Okie, was one of the last to get his pass and ten dollars. He was a slender, easy-going, intelligent fellow who hailed from Muskogee, Oklahoma, where he had a reputation as a professional gambler.

"What do you need the dough for?" I asked. "Didn't you take the boys to the cleaners in poker?"

"I can always use a little more." He winked at me. "Aren't you coming ashore?"

"Naw!" I mumbled dejectedly. "I've got work to do."

But that evening I, too, dashed ashore. The taxi driver deposited me at the Cantina Americano in the heart of the Panama City's night club district. I looked forward to a relaxing evening.

The Cantina was reminiscent of a saloon during the frontier days, its tables and chairs scattered without symmetry and a long bar dominating the scene.

Merchant and navy seamen sat around a half dozen oblong tables, while others stood three deep at the bar. The rumble of their voices was suddenly drowned out by the loud beat of the rhumba blaring forth from the phonograph stashed on a corner shelf.

I recognized Carl Freeman, Thomas Cahill, Clarence Gregory and Horace Armstrong, oilers and water tenders from our black gang, occupying one of the tables.

"The Purser," sneered Gregory, our six-foot-four salvage boilermaker, grabbing my arm with his gorilla paws as I approached. "Let me buy you a drink out of that piddling ten bucks you gave me."

"Say, instead of you buying me a drink, I'll buy you one." I wrenched myself free from his grip and sat down next to him.

"I knew you were okay," he bellowed, punching my arm with a sledge-hammer blow. "I got news for you, Purse, I'm quitting. I'm going no farther with this fuckin' bucket."

All but Armstrong joined the refrain, "Me, too!"

Ours would be a short trip if the crew deserted.

"You know you've got the draft board to worry about if you get off here." It was the only argument I could think of.

"You fellas are quitters," Armstrong burst out. "Even that bastard, Gibson, isn't going to get me off this tub by making me clean the bilges."

A big, amiable seaman from another ship, who had imbibed bountifully at the bar, approached and placed his hands on the table to support his weaving body.

"I'm celebratin'," he slurred. "Our ship come through the Caribbean and we're still alive. Yup, I counted six oil slicks. But those subs didn't get us." Then he weaved his way back to the bar, leaving us to contemplate the hazards that lay ahead of us.

Gregory, now even more worried, complained, "Well that wasn't exactly a pep talk, was it Purse? What chance have we got makin' it?"

"Don't worry, a submarine would never waste a torpedo on our tub," I countered, tongue in cheek.

"Maybe you're right at that, Purse," Freeman agreed. "The chief and the first assistant treat us like dirt, the second assistant is drunk all the time, but who wants a hitch in the army, anyway? At least, we're free agents."

"I'm wasting my time here," interjected Cahill. I"m going to a spot where I can find some dames." He left abruptly.

After another couple of beers, the rest of us returned to the ship. I wondered how many of us would be aboard at departure time.

The skipper haunted the offices of the army and navy command in his attempt to get some action on the ship's repair jobs, but the *Chamberlain* remained anchored day after day in the Balboa shipyard. The crew didn't object as long as there were frequent shoreboats for their daily tours to the local bistros and bordellos. Although here their cash draw was only ten dollars, they had been paid their full wages prior to sailing from San Diego.

The skipper paced the deck and complained, "Six days in Panama and they haven't started our repair work. We're supposed to have triple-A priority. Paul, write a telegram. I'll take it ashore and have it sent to the U.S Army Engineers in Washington. They may get these brass-hats in Panama off their butts."

"What do you want me to say?"

"Tell 'em our ship needs critical repairs and that the Zone officials are giving us the runaround; that we've been here a whole week and can't get any action. And write a letter to Johnson, Drake & Piper in New York explaining why we're delayed here. Our office should know why we're spending all this time in Panama."

We were interrupted by Jaeger. "Captain, those sixteen

cases of beer are aboard. Where do you want 'em?"

"Bring 'em in here," the Old Man ordered. "D'ya think I'd trust anyone else with 'em?"

"Okay, if that's where you want 'em."

Upon returning a half hour later with the drafted telegram and letter, I found him and the mate counting cases of beer.

"Fourteen cases," he grumbled. "What the hell is this?"

"Well, I checked out sixteen cases down at the gang plank." The mate sounded indignant over being in the middle of this controversy.

"So the crew is stealing beer from me already," the skipper groaned. "You can pass the word around, Mate, there won't be any more shore leave until those two cases of beer are brought in here."

The mate sighed. "I'll see what I can do."

He enlisted the second and third officers to search the ship. One case was discovered in the diesel room, but no amount of searching or threatening could produce the other. There were rumblings among the men.

"Aw, shit," Okie complained, reflecting the feelings of the other men. "Why should I lose my shore leave? I didn't steal that fuckin' case of beer."

Art Vatne, the second mate, accosted me in the passageway. "Say, Purse, would you type a couple of letters for me?"

"Sure," I agreed.

The youngest of our mates, his slim, erect figure was a marked contrast to the muscular and hefty body of Jaeger. He spent much time with his sextant, even when not on watch, charting the ship's course. Having little imagination, when he went ashore he invariably headed for the nearest bar, his goal to become intoxicated.

**SECOND MATE, ART VATNE,
WITH HIS SEXTON**

He invited me into his cabin and handed me a couple of hand written letters for typing.

"Are you thirsty?" he asked.

"Sure am," I replied, my mouth watering in anticipation.

Pulling out a drawer from under his bunk, he reached in for a couple of bottles of beer. He opened them and handed one to me, bragging, "Just like a rabbit out of a hat, eh?"

Even though it was warm, beer never tasted so good, and I leaned back on the settee to savor it. Then I noted the Panamanian label.

"Say," I gulped twice as the realization hit me and the beer almost went down the wrong pipe. "Where did you get this?"

A snide look came over Vatne's face. "Oh, I picked up a few bottles ashore."

"Hmm, same brand as the skipper's," I remarked pointedly.

"Okay, so I took it from the Old Man. And why the hell should he have sixteen cases of beer? To hear him sqawk, you'd think he lost his only case of Scotch."

A pang of conscience came over me, and I nervously stashed the empty bottle in Vatne's wash bucket and left.

The captain decided to forget his threat to restrict shore leave and never again mentioned the missing case of beer.

Upon the skipper's return from a trip ashore the next day, he informed me that the local censors had refused to permit the dispatch of our telegram to the U.S. Army Engineers. No doubt the navy personnel at the repair base feared censure from Washington officialdom.

After another day's wait, the captain and I went ashore once more and attempted to send the telegram, but again the censors refused.

Hansen, the representative from the Standard Oil Company, and I taxied to the army command post where we cornered a colonel and demanded, in no uncertain terms, that the *Chamberlain* be repaired at once. Action was promised.

The next morning a tug towed our disabled ship to the

repair dock.

At 10 A.M. on Sunday, as usual, I opened the slop chest, otherwise known as the ship's store, to the members of the crew for the sale of cigarettes, gloves, shoes, and other supplies. I took an inventory of the merchandise, prepared an order for replacements, and took off for the skipper's quarters to get his signature. A curly-headed young army captain entered at the same time.

"I'm from army intelligence," he volunteered as he sat down on the chair facing the captain. "May I speak to you alone? This is a matter of some delicacy."

"This is my purser, Mr. Behm," the skipper interjected. "You can trust him."

I was pleased that the skipper included me in what seemed like a confidential meeting of some import.

The officer hesitated and after a disapproving glance in my direction asserted, "We've had a report that you may have a saboteur aboard. We have information that a certain Gunnar Carlyle threw empty crates overboard bearing the address of your destination; that he started a lot of rumors on your ship; and that a number of your fire extinquishers were emptied."

It appeared that the doctor had carried out his threat.

"I can assure you, Captain, Carlyle is a loyal American—and not a saboteur," insisted Hansen. "Dr. Chasen, our ship's doctor, must have passed the word on to you. There's bad blood between the two, and the doctor is just trying to get Carlyle into trouble. I'll vouch for him."

The army captain was not satisfied with the skipper's assurances. "May I have your permission to interrogate the members of the crew, Captain?" he asked.

"Go right ahead," answered Hansen.

Later in the day I asked the Old Man whether the army intelligence officer was continuing his inquiry on Carlyle.

"He said he was satified there was nothing to those charges."

CHAPTER 6

THE WATCH ON THE CARIBBEAN

Fo'c'sle Society Note
Citizens of Beverly Hills side of the fo'c'sle are up in
arms at the invasion by Pete Watson, our new baker, of
their exclusive district. A citizens' committee headed by
Jim Cook has hastily been organized, but to no avail.
When asked for a statement, Watson lay back in his
dirty sheets and snarled, "Them bums has got a lot of
noive just cause I don't bleed blue. Anyhow, I pay me
rent and dats vot counts."
   The Citizens Purity League of Beverly Hills are non-
plussed and plan early action. Jim Cook says, "We'll
snub him, that's what we'll do."
   From the *Hawse Pipe Herald,* unofficial journal
   of the *S.S. W.R. Chamberlain, Jr.*

After eight days in the repair yards of Balboa, it was our des-
tiny to transit the Panama Isthmus via the Canal and brave the
submarine-infested waters of the Caribbean, alone.

   In spite of the threats by members of the black gang to quit
ship, I reported to the skipper on the bridge: "All of our crew are
accounted for except for the two men hospitalized at Balboa.
Oh by the way, we picked up a mate for Ernie, and doc brought
two screeching parrakeets aboard. Now we can expect a duet

or two with the bagpipes."

A pilot boarded us in Balboa to take our vessel through the Panama Canal. Since the highest point across the Isthmus through which the fifty-mile canal meandered was eighty-five feet above sea level, locks were designed to raise and lower ships traveling between the Pacific and Atlantic Oceans. Our engines were shut down at the entrance to the first set of locks. Canal workers on both sides of the lock attached towing cables from locomotives, called mules, to our bow and stern. Our ship was pulled into the first chamber, and the steel gates closed behind us. Water flowed into the chamber through openings in the bottom of the lock. In fifteen minutes, the rising water lifted us to the level above, which then opened its immense doors, and mules pulled the ship into that compartment. When the gates to the rear of the vessel closed, the process of lifting us to the next chamber was repeated.

While viewing the tropical paradise, memories of my prior journey through the Panama Canal in 1935 surfaced. I was then a deck passenger, in my early twenties, on a Grace Liner out of La Libertad, El Salvador, en route to Havana on my way back home to Cedarburg, Wisconsin, after searching out La Fuente de Sangre (The Fountain of Blood) during six months of adventure in the jungles of Central America with Irving Wallace and Walter Hardy.

Wallace had learned about this phenomenon of nature in his writing research. After plodding through the Honduran jungles during the dry season, we solved the mystery of the Fountain of Blood upon discovering a cave with pools of reddish water. Our guide informed us that during the rainy season a stream of blood-colored water flowed out of the cave, staining the river below for miles. As we entered the cavern, many bats fluttered about in confusion. Later, a laboratory analysis of the fluid we obtained from the cave revealed the presence of manganese, iron, and bat waste matter, kept in colloidal suspension. We had hoped for a much more dramatic explanation.

But now, my *Chamberlain* adventure had scarcely begun.

Leaving the Miraflores Locks, we entered Miraflores Lake, fifty-four feet above sea level. The Pedro Miguel Locks lifted our ship to eighty-five feet above sea level, and then we sailed under our own power through the narrow Gaillard Cut and into Gatun Lake. At the Gatun Locks, our ship descended eighty-five feet to the Caribbean Sea, and by nightfall we anchored in Limon Bay, which served the cities of Cristobal and Colon.

My job as purser kept me busy while in port, but at sea my time was my own—that is, until the skipper appointed Carlyle and me blackout wardens. This duty required us to make periodic checkups from dusk to dawn, enforcing the "No Smoking" on deck rule, keeping the doors of the cabins set on blackout switches, and trying to ensure that no light showed on the vessel.

Alternating with Carlyle, I stood watch the first night from 8 P.M. to 1 A.M. and the next night from 1 A.M. to 6 A.M.

Limon Bay, where I began my evening vigil, was under an absolute blackout, three enemy submarines having previously surfaced and shelled the cities.

About midnight while gazing at silhouettes of the Colon buildings framed against a starry sky, I heard footsteps, then a rasping voice, "Hey, Paul, why are you prowling the deck this time of night?"

Recognizing that it was the chief engineer, I turned around and replied, "The Old Man put me on blackout watch, Chief."

"Blackout watch? Jumping Jesus, what they really need is some son of a bitch who can keep our smokestacks from shooting sparks at night and belching smoke in the day time."

"I thought they fixed that at Balboa."

"Balboa, hell! All those bums did was look at our forepeak tank and say it was okay. Then they fiddled around a little with our condenser."

"Didn't they repair that?"

"Hell no. Our main condenser is leaking as bad as ever."

"Say, Chief, what is a condenser anyway?"

The chief stood beside me, silently staring at the shadowy shapes of ships bobbing in the dark water of the Colon harbor. I wondered whether he had heard my question. It wasn't like him to be quiet very long.

Finally, in his grating voice, he began, "Well, the condenser is a device that reduces the steam coming from the boilers back to water. When the water becomes steam, it expands and pushes the pistons, and that's what turns the propellors.

"Throughout the condenser there are lots of pipes carrying salt water that's pumped in from the sea. The steam from the boilers surrounds the pipes, and the salt water cools the steam and turns it back into water. The water collects at the bottom of the condenser and is pumped back to make steam again. You understand?"

The chief paused. It sounded like he was reading from a

textbook.

He continued. "Now then, after awhile salt water corrodes the pipes in the condenser and pinholes show up. Steam circulating around the pipes shrinks sixteen times in volume when it condenses to water, and the suction from the shrinking steam will pull the salt water out of the pipes and mix it with the pure water. When the water coming from the condenser again reaches the boilers, the salt separates from the steam and clogs the pipes in the boiler, and that's what causes the damned corrosion."

Culpepper paused for breath. "That's when we have real problems. We've got to stop the engines in midocean and plug the holes in the condenser pipes with sawdust when our gauge shows too much salt in the condenser. That's only a temporary remedy until we can plug the holes ashore, or replace the pipes."

I pressed the chief further. "And why does our smokestack blow out that black smoke?"

"That's because there isn't complete combustion in the boiler, and with the *Chamberlain* we just can't correct that because we have a short smoke stack. This ship was built for peacetime use and it didn't matter then how much smoke came out of the stack."

"What about the sparks shooting out of our funnel?"

"Well, carbon gets into the stack and burns, causing the sparks. We have to blow the tubes often to get rid of the carbon. Again, because it's an old ship there isn't enough combustion. If they had given us new condenser pipes in Panama like I asked, and if we had a taller stack, it would help a lot. Besides water leaks into our forepeak oil tank, and that causes sparks when the oil burns in the boilers."

"What about the main throttle valve?" I asked.

"Where the screwy hell do you think I've been all day? Right at that main throttle valve while we were going through the Canal past the locks. She was leaking so bad that if we had to stop quick-like, and with all the Canal traffic, we might've had an accident. That would've been the end of this son of a bitchen ship, and the end of me. Oh, they took it ashore all right in Balboa. Now she's leakin' bad as ever."

It began to look as though we had spent the last two weeks in Panama for the sole purpose of giving the crew a Roman holiday—a boon to the pubs, pimps, and brothels and a little more American lend-lease down the international sewer.

"There must be a hex on this ship."

"Yeah," Culpepper agreed. "I wanted to get off this blasted tub myself in Panama, like my three engineers tried to. They spent five days being kicked around from one office to the other but were told they'd lose their licenses, be fined, and get bounced into the army."

"Is it really that hard to get off?"

"Looks like they've got us boxed in."

I spied the flare of a lighted match on midships and scurried over, yelling, "Hey you! Douse that light!"

Coming closer, I recognized the intermittent glowing of a pipe being puffed. I gulped. What went with the pipe was an old sweatshirt, the lowers of a pair of gray drawers, a pair of run-down slippers and the captain.

He laughed good-naturedly.

"Sorry, I didn't know it was you, Captain."

"Don't apologize. Just keep on your toes. You've got to keep this ship blacked out on your watch, 'cause tomorrow we'll be out in sub territory."

When he walked, his pigeon-toed feet came down like those of a punch-drunk fighter, and his body swayed back and forth in rhythm, even though the ship was not moving. I kept pace with him, waiting for him to elaborate. He stopped behind a bulkhead to relight his pipe, and then, before discarding the match, he snapped it. One could locate the captain by following broken, burnt-out match sticks on deck.

He felt like talking. "The navy wanted to send us around the Cape; said it was too dangerous to risk this crew of salvage men and cargo. But I argued with them. The war might be over before we got there, and we've lost too much time already. No, we have to take that chance going through the Caribbean." Whenever Hansen spoke about the mission's urgency, his voice assumed a quieter and deeper tone.

Neither of us spoke as we paced the deck in the dark night. Finally he broke the silence. "Say, Paul, I forgot to tell you. The laundry we sent ashore in Panama City followed us by train across the Canal. It's on number three hatch. Get the steward to take care of it."

I interrupted Les Peters in his usual poker game in the fo'c'sle. We dragged a couple of the laundry bags into the machine shop for inspection. Peters pulled out a filthy wet pillow case and a sheet from one of them.

"My God! they must have dragged this though the Panama Canal," I exclaimed.

"Looks more like they dragged it through those swamps we passed," he retorted.

The next morning as we sailed into the Caribbean, I strolled out on deck to be greeted by dirty sheets, towels, and pillow cases fluttering in the light breeze. We were truly a laundry tub. The sea was calm, almost like glass, and strangely quiet. I took a few deep breaths of the pure air.

Then I spied the mess—glistening pools of oil on the surface of the water, life preservers, pieces of life boats and other debris. God! The enemy was for real!

A shout came from the starboard watch station, "Ahoy, bridge, we're passing through an oil slick."

And from the bridge came Jaeger's booming voice, "Wake up, you slow bastard. We've been passing through it for the past thirty seconds."

At four bells (10AM) our engines stopped. I dashed out of my cabin and met Carlyle on deck.

"What's up?"

"They're fixing the steering engine. There's always something wrong with this miserable ship," he lamented.

In the officer's mess, the skipper complained to the chief, "We passed through two oil slicks this morning. Can't you get more speed out of this ship? She's only doing seven knots."

"Well," Culpepper answered sarcastically, "if you'd gotten those damned condensers fixed in Panama, I could. But the bastard won't do any more. We'll soon be running out of sawdust the way we're feeding her."

The captain drank his coffee in silence.

Culpepper, who never missed an opportunity to gripe about

something, persisted. "As long as we're dead pigeons, why the hell don't you get that steward to give us steaks and eggs instead of this chicken stew?"

"Chief," snapped the skipper, clutching his pipe as he got up, his face livid. "I don't want another word out of you about the food. When I come down here to eat, I want peace and quiet, not squawks. I've got enough worries on my mind."

At mess, Culpepper invariably brought up controversial topics for discussion, from the legitimacy of bastards to the question whether women should be allowed in the fighting army. His opinions were usually contrary to those held by the other officers, and when anyone expressed a viewpoint different from his, he became belligerent, thus usually ending any intelligent discussion of the subject.

Actually, the chief no longer had reason to complain about the food. After taking over, Les Peters had improved the quality of the meals considerably. He shuffled the provisions in the freezer and cooler so that the eggs, butter, bacon and other meats were stored in the freezing unit. Many cartons of spoiled food had been tossed over the side.

"They feed better on this tub than on most other boats," volunteered Carlyle.

"What the hell kind of ship you ever been on?" the chief hectored G.H.

"Maybe not on as many ships as you, but I stayed longer," G.H. responded, building up to an explosion. Some of the officers guffawed.

Culpepper took the bait. "You're a smart bastard. Think you know your way around."

Carlyle's blood pressure shot up. His face was a flaming red.

"Why don't you take him down a peg?" interposed Dr. Chasen.

"I can handle my own affairs without you putting in your fart's worth." The chief waved his hand in the doctor's direction. "You're causing enough troubles around here as it is with your report to the army intelligence."

I hardly expected Culpepper to defend Carlyle, but when it came to an army man attacking a fellow sailor, the men stuck together.

Chasen got up from the table and walked out.

On several occasions, the chief had taunted G.H. Just the day before, also in the messhall in the presence of the other officers, he had turned to G.H. and said, "I heard that the boys in the fo'c'sle intend to take away your pistol."

At times G.H. wore a pistol as the badge of his office as master-at-arms.

"There isn't a man big enough aboard this tub to do it!" had been his reply.

G.H. got up and stomped over to the chief. "I've had enough of your gibes. Come out on deck, you bastard."

The chief hesitated a few seconds, and then followed Carlyle. Culpepper was six feet tall, but slim, while G.H., although of medium height, was built like a wrestler. On several occasions he had bragged about his stint as a jujitsu contestant.

The messhall emptied as the officers pursued the two rivals. On deck, G.H. grabbed the chief's shirt collar with his two heavy hands, choking him. Culpepper's cockiness vanished. He didn't even try to defend himself.

"I don't want any more guff out of you," Carlyle's voice echoed over the deck.

Third Mate Olsson and I grabbed Carlyle's arms. He let go his hold on the chief's collar, and the chief, humiliated, stalked off toward the skipper's cabin to bitch.

Thereafter, the chief and Carlyle took pains to ignore each other.

CHAPTER 7

MAN THE LIFEBOATS

News Flash
Okie Alsabrook says, "I don't reckon I'll have any
trouble gittin' settled in Massawa, cause some of my
kinfolk took Californy without firin' a shot."
Missing Persons Column
Dear Harry, 'the Hobo,' Herz. Please come back to
the fo'c'sle. All the fellows miss you.

From the *Hawse Pipe Herald*, unofficial journal
of the *S.S. W.R. Chamberlain, Jr.*

Ernie's agonizing shrieks echoed from number three hatch
as he recoiled from an attack by the big orange-colored cat that
boarded in Panama.

Someone shouted, "Fight on midships!"

In no time, the men made a semi-circle around the cat arena.
Then there was just one big ball of orange and black, claws and
teeth sunk in for the kill.

"Ernie!" I yelled helplessly. "Ernie!"

Carlyle dashed into the machine shop for a bucket of water.
The boys cheered, "Kill him, Ernie!"

I heard the chief's voice, "Ernie, you black bastard, get him
by the throat!"

G.H. sloshed water over the yowling cats and they slunk away in opposite directions. I grabbed Ernie, a sorry mess of blood and water, a tuft of orange fur clinging to his mouth.

"Fine cat you picked up in Panama, Wes," Carlyle jeered. "Should think with all your experience you could tell the difference between a male and a female."

I tried to comfort Ernie, patting his quivering body. "I'd better get you to sick bay."

"Sick bay? I've got some stuff in my cabin. Bring him along," offered Carlyle. "I wouldn't trust this cat to that horse doctor. Considering those chattering parrakeets he picked up in Panama, he'd want to protect his own interests."

G.H. opened a bottle of peroxide and nursed Ernie's wounds. It appeared that his pride was injured more than his body. He jumped off the alcove seat and sneaked into the open closet.

"Say, G.H. I didn't know you had rifles aboard." I pointed to half a dozen of them stacked up in the corner where the cat had taken refuge.

"Oh, I traded those six pistols and the bastard ammunition at the Panamanian police department for these rifles and a barrel of bullets," he explained, dismissing the incident. I had to admire his ability to promote. There were several more questions on the tip of my tongue when G.H. grabbed my arm."Hear that?"

Sparks voice came over the air-conditioning duct."That's the report, Skipper. One ship torpedoed thirty knots due east. Another calling for help about fifty knots north."

The trade routes of the Caribbean were well-known to the

German high command, and their submarines were disrupting the flow of oil from Curacao and Aruba, as well as the transport of tin from Caracas, bauxite from Maracaibo, and nitrate from Chile via the Panama Canal, all necessary commodities in our prosecution of the war. During the first seven months of 1942, the U.S. Navy just did not have vessels available to patrol the Caribbean, or for escort duty.

As the bugle calls drowned out the remainder of our radio operator's report, G.H. grumbled, "There goes the doctor's damned phonograph again."

Later in the day, Jaeger joined the Captain and me on the bridge to report, "Captain, there's a ship on the horizon off our starboard bow."

Hansen took a long look through his binoculars. "We've got watches all over the ship. Haven't any of the men reported this?"

"Nope," replied the mate.

"Can you make out what kind of a ship she is? I can see her masts. Can't be a sub." Before long, the ship disappeared over the horizon.

Fifteen minutes later, Okie, who had been assigned lookout duty in the crow's nest, reported to the skipper on the bridge.

"Captain, was there something over there?" He pointed to the right of the mast.

"You mean off the starboard bow?" asked Hansen.

"Yeah!"

"Well," the captain growled. "Why didn't you report it when you first saw it?"

"Oh, I thought I saw something and wasn't sure, and then it

was gone. Since I was coming off duty in a little while, I decided to tell you about it then."

"My God! All you had to do was lift up the telephone in the crow's nest and report it. What do you think you're on duty for?" He called the third mate over.

"Mate, climb up to the crow's nest and see if the man on duty is really watching."

"Okay, Skipper," Olsson replied.

Ten minutes later he came back from his search with five much abused detective magazines. "This is why they ain't watching the skyline, Captain."

Hansen jutted out his jaw. I knew he was making a mental note to put out another notice.

Crew members equipped with binoculars were posted on four hour watches on the fo'c'sle deck, the poop deck, and on both the port and starboard sides of the vessel. They had been ordered to scan the horizon and alert the officers on the bridge if any vessel appeared. Invariably, these men shot the bull with fellow crew members and seldom bothered to look seaward. In spite of the numerous oil slicks and debris that we passed through, they often slept on duty, oblivious to all dangers.

On my lonely blackout watch, until my eyes got accustomed to shapes and steps, I felt my way in the dark, bumping into guide wires, kicking boat chucks, and knocking my head against doors and walls. But the worst part of the job was staying awake.

Every half hour, the tolling of the ship's bell reverberated through the night. Eight bells designated the hours of four, eight and twelve. The half hour following marked the hours of four-thirty, eight-thirty and twelve-thirty. Each additional stroke of the bell marked the succeeding half hour.

I had become acclimated to life at sea and could now balance myself, even in the roughest weather, maintaining my equilibrium by simply leaning forward and backward and from side to side as the ship rolled.

This night was particularly black. I leaned over the railing on the lower deck and watched the dark shadow of water rushing by. I relished the sensation of moving, even though the ship's vibrations were sometimes aggravatingly monotonous. Travel, for travel's sake, was the life I loved. After graduating from high school, I had hitched rides by auto and on freight trains. One especially satisfying experience found me sitting on the narrow step platform of a railroad tank car, my arm twisted around the metal bar surrounding it to keep from falling off as it passed grazing cattle, wooded hills, and raging mountain streams.

I congratulated myself on having been stripped of all accountability as a steward and warehouseman, giving me ample time to just enjoy being on the move.

Sparks still shot from the smokestack. It seemed useless to carry on my duties as blackout warden when the ship, itself, so flagrantly violated blackout regulations. But it did give me an opportunity to dawdle on deck.

At last the sun's first light filtered in on the horizon. I made my way to the fo'c'sle, jerked open the door, thereby triggering the light switch to "off," brushed aside the blackout curtain and walked into the darkened interior.

A voice bellowed, "Hey, close that damned door."

Another voice threatened. "Keep your hands off that dough."

The door slammed shut and the lights flashed on. My eyes, now accustomed to the fo'c'sle lights, revealed four of the crew sitting around the table clutching poker hands. Miscellaneous snores resounded from the fifty bunks nearby.

"Sorry fellas about stopping your game," I apologized, opening the refrigerator door. "Just wanted a cold pineapple juice. Say, don't you guys ever sleep?"

"Not while there's money floating around," answered Wes Hewson, throwing in a dollar bill to open the pot in his usual carefree manner.

Then it came! A blast from the ship's whistle rent the air— three, four, five, six times. The boys temporarily froze in their places. The bell alarm sounded the warning to man the lifeboats, and bedlam broke loose.

The poker players took time to pocket their money and then made a dash for their bunks to claim life preservers and valuables.

From the bunks came a sleepy voice, "Shut off that damned telephone."

Another, "Where's my wife's picture?"

Still another, "Hey, Tom, pay me those thirty clams I won in yesterday's poker game."

Jim Cook dashed for the door. Wild screeching ensued as the lights went off.

When the lights clicked on again, I, too, made a beeline for the door. Upon passing the head, I saw Jim Corbett, one of our electricians, in shock, glued to a toilet. Bill McKelly helped me carry him out on deck where he fell in a heap.

Pandemonium ensued. Flashlights beamed here and there in

spite of the first blush of the morning sun.

"Put out those lights!" I yelled.

Someone else shouted, "Throw the damned light overboard!"

One of the carpenters, completely nude, gave his flashlight a mighty heave, and the beam made a brilliant arc before it splashed into the water.

No one tried to jump in, but several of our sailors fell on deck in their rush to reach a life boat.

Dashing to my lifeboat station on the midship deck, I found G.H. already cranking out the boat with the help of a couple of boys from the deck gang.

The voice of the skipper boomed from the bridge.

"Okay men just swing out the lifeboats and swing them back again."

Then the signal came. Three short bells! The boat drill was over!

The skipper had forewarned me about the boat drill. "The men don't know there's a war on. We've got to bring 'em down to earth. I'd like to have a boat drill in the middle of the night, but we might lose a few men that way. Just keep your eyes open on blackout watch to be sure no one jumps overboard when the alarm sounds at sunup."

The terrorized mess hall crew, still immobilized in their bunks, never made it to the boat stations.

Harry Herz, nicknamed, "Hobo Harry", was the first one to man his assigned post by the lifeboat. The boys had given him that pet name because he seldom slept in his bunk, traveling around the ship night and day, catching a few catnaps now and then. He was in constant fear of a submarine attack. His clothes always dishevelled, bags sagging under his bloodshot eyes, we found in him an interesting diversion.

For a few days after the boat drill some of the boys kept their life preservers handy and remained fully clothed, even as they slept. Many stashed a getaway bag, filled with their valuables, in a convenient location; but after the initial scare, most reverted to their former carefree habits.

CHAPTER 8

G.H. CARLYLE

Notice to Helmsmen
All helmsmen will report to the bridge as soon as
possible to be fitted for bullet proof vests. Our super-
gumshoe, G.H. Carlyle, is on the prowl.

From the *Hawse Pipe Herald,* unofficial journal
of the *S.S. W.R. Chamberlain, Jr.*

Carlyle had time on his hands. Employed as a salvage foreman for work upon arrival at Massawa, he was a virtual passenger en route, although all the other men aboard were assigned
active duties. As master-at-arms, he was required to keep order
on the ship and had not yet been called on to act in that capacity. As blackout warden, he spent little time patrolling on his
duty nights.

To keep in the good graces of the captain, he invaded the
galley on a regular basis to prepare tasty Danish pastries which
he carried to the skipper's cabin. He had not forgotten the culinary art he had mastered as a ship's cook in his younger days.

Although disapproving of some of his tactics, I acquired a
real fondness for G.H. He symbolized the adventurous spirit that
had inspired me on many occasions. Besides, he had gone out
of his way to get me on this expedition, always fostering my

best interests—except when he had promoted me for three jobs aboard ship.

On the third day out of the Colon harbor, at the end of my blackout watch, just as the first rays of the morning sun crept over the horizon tinting the eastern sky in a glorious display of various shades of red, I spied the skipper knocking on Carlyle's cabin door. My curiosity aroused, after waiting a few minutes I, too, made my way to his quarters, knocked, and upon being invited in found Hansen lounging on the alcove seat in his long johns, sipping from a glass, the contents of which must have come from the whiskey bottle on the book shelf above G.H.'s bunk.

"Sit down, Paul. Want a drink?" asked G.H.

It was too early in the day. I refused, and made myself comfortable on the alcove seat.

"Carlyle was telling me how he got started in salvage work," volunteered Hansen.

"Yeah. After working on a few ships as a cook and seaman, I decided to work ashore in New York City as a grocery clerk but was fired after one month. To forget my troubles, I headed for Coney Island.

"There were a lot of people crowded around a sailing ship sitting high and dry on the beach watching a man on the ship's deck dressed in a deep-sea diver's outfit. I pushed my way aboard, paid my twenty-five cents and looked on as the diver climbed down into a large water-filled glass tank. He worked on some pipes and other gear for over half an hour. I went back five times that afternoon to see him perform again and then searched out the owner for a job. To my surprise, he hired me as a diver's tender and in five weeks gave me the diver's job. After two years there, the Scandinavian-American steamship line took me on as a maintenance diver."

By this time the skipper was getting restless and even refused a second glass of whiskey.

"I'd better see what the boys on the bridge are up to," he mumbled as he got up, then brushed aside the blackout curtain and shuffled out.

As Carlyle stowed the bottle of whiskey in the drawer below the settee, I spied three more bottles stored there.

I looked at him inquisitively. "I didn't know you imbibed." He always opted for a cup of coffee or a nonalcoholic drink whenever we went out on the town together.

G.H. threw up his arms. "Oh, I just keep the whiskey for the Old Man. He comes in here every morning for his daily slug."

I knew that he and his wife, Peggy, were believers in the Christian Science philosophy and religion. On a number of occasions I found him reading from Mary Baker Eddy's *Science and Health with Key to the Scriptures* kept on the ledge above his bunk. I recognized the correlation between his abstinence and his religious beliefs, and I understood why he refused to take any medicine for his high blood pressure.

On one occasion when I found him reading Mary Baker Eddy's book, he explained, "Peggy insisted I bring it along, and she made me promise to read from it every day."

Anxious to hear more about his salvage experiences, I asked, "Have you ever been involved in a treasure hunt?"

"Yeah, Paul," G.H. laughed. "My contract with the Scandinavian-American Line provided for a weekly wage, plus one-half of everything that I recovered from the river bottom. All that ever went down to the bottom of the Hudson River was coal and copper; until one day, while trunks were being unloaded from the hold of a passenger ship, a sling broke, and four of them slid into the river and sank to the bottom. That night a woman knocked on my door and, out of the blue, offered me a thousand dollars to recover her trunk, which she said contained some valuable diamonds."

"How did she get your address?"

"From the watchman at the dock. Anyway," he continued, "early the next morning I rushed down to the dock figuring it would be my big day. Instead, an agent from Lloyd's with whom the cargo was insured, as well as two U.S. Secret Service agents, met me. They advised me that one of the trunks might contain smuggled diamonds. I got into my diving gear, and, after stumbling around in the murky river bottom, I managed to tie a sling around each trunk, and the ship's booms lifted them, one by one, onto the dock.

"A hundred thousand dollars worth of diamonds were hidden in the trunk owned by that woman. She was taken into custody, and instead of the thousand dollars she had promised me, I got twenty-four thousand dollars as a reward after filing a finder's claim with the customs office. Then, I accepted an offer for a diver's job with Lloyd's, which took me to Galveston, Texas."

CHAPTER 9

ST. LUCIA HAVEN

Flash Impression of St. Lucia: Central Avenue with an English accent.

Random Thoughts While Dreaming: I think I'll get a bag of flour, a case of canned milk, a couple of bars of Palmolive soap and settle down in St. Lucia.

From the *Hawse Pipe Herald*, unofficial journal of the *S.S. W.R. Chamberlain, Jr.*

The *Chamberlain* smoked its way over the Caribbean through oily, debris-infested waters, reminding us of the proximity of enemy submarines.

The Navy authorities in Panama had directed the captain to proceed to Trinidad for refueling and further sailing orders and a new identification signal for our use in the waters of the South Atlantic when challenged by U.S. or allied war vessels.

"We'd be sitting ducks if we sailed to Trinidad," mused the skipper at mess. "Those waters are crawling with enemy subs. Isn't that right, Sparks?"

"Yup," agreed Stirewalt.

"We'll steer clear of that place," Hansen decided.

The chief asked, "Where will we refuel then?"

"Don't know yet," responded the captain.

Five days out of Colon, the condenser problem again created a crisis in the engine room. Culpepper demanded that we seek haven at the nearest port for emergency repairs. After consulting the map, Hansen ordered the helmsman to steer for the port of Castries on the island of St. Lucia despite the fact that it was within sight of Martinique, then a possession of Vichy France, where German submarines found a safe harbor and a base for its operations.

The tropical island of St. Lucia had been an English crown colony since 1814, but before that date possession between France and England had changed no less than fourteen times since its discovery by Columbus in 1502. The landlocked harbor of Castries was one of the best in the West Indies. As part of its agreement to transfer destroyers to the war-plagued British, the U.S. had acquired a ninety-nine year lease on St. Lucia land and constructed an air and naval base there.

Forty-nine year old Sparks, naked to the waist and in shorts, looked up from his desk as I entered the open door of the radio shack. Having turned off the air-conditioning vents, he basked in the warm Caribbean sea air. The blue varicose veins in his legs bulged out, attesting to many years balancing in front of a ship's radio set while the vessel rolled from starboard to port.

Because of the hazard in these waters, Sparks slept little, attentive most waking hours to radio reports of war news and warnings of approaching danger. In spite of his long vigils, his eyes were clear, sparkling with understanding and lucidity of thought. It was a lonely watch and he welcomed company.

"Just learned we're going to St. Lucia," I said. "Any interesting news?"

"Yeah! A U.S. destroyer was torpedoed and sunk near there a few days ago, and now I got a report that a sub was sighted not too far from us. That's the fifth report of a sub in our area in the last few days. So say your prayers," he warned.

"Anything new about the African front, Sparks?"

"Rommel is raising hell there. Let's hope the British can hold out or we might find Massawa overrun by the Germans."

After the port authorities opened the submarine net that blocked the entrance to the harbor of Castries, a local pilot boarded the *Chamberlain* and escorted us to a location within sight of the docks, where we dropped anchor. A shoreboat came alongside at about 2:30PM, and Hansen boarded, dressed in full uniform in spite of the humid heat, to report to the local Standard Oil Company agent.

The silhouette of tropical vegetation delineated the edge of the sandy beaches. Many of the men, some dressed up waiting to go ashore, gazed longingly at the island paradise; but they had to content themselves with watching native boys recover coins tossed by them into the crystal clear water. They also busied themselves exchanging cans of food for bottles of rum with the boatmen coming alongside the gangway.

Two freighters and two U.S. destroyers bobbed at anchor nearby. From the flying bridge, Lewis C. Whittaker, our gun crew captain, an ex-navy man, attracted the attention of a signalman aboard one of the destroyers with our signal lights.

We crowded around him as he interpreted the flashing lights from the destroyer. "She's the *Blakely*. Her bow was blown off by a torpedo. If she had been hit twenty feet astern, there would have been no *Blakely*, and no survivors. She was struck at four bells in the morning near Martinique. The *Blakey's* instruments had picked up electrical impulses that the destroyer's officers thought were from shore engines, but must have come from the sub. She limped into the harbor of Castries, where, luckily, a tug from Myron, Chapman and Scott was engaged in salvaging two freighters torpedoed by a German submarine in the harbor three months before. After that attack they installed a submarine net across its entrance."

So the destroyer Sparks had reported as sunk survived after all. The personnel on the tug were constructing a wooden bow on her so that she could sail to New Orleans for repairs.

Although the island was a British protectorate, it was now practically deserted by the British authorities. Even the Governor's house was vacant.

The signalman on the destroyer warned us that Castries was overrun by U.S. sailors and airmen on leave, all competing for the attention of the local dark beauties.

The captain opened my door at five bells the next morning, demanding, "Paul, wake up. We're going ashore."

Not bothering about breakfast, I joined the skipper at the gangplank, both of us in shirt sleeves. He signaled one of the bum boats alongside to take us to the dock.

At the Hotel Caribbeana, a middle-aged, ebony-skinned, buxom native woman with fine facial features, greeted us. "I'm Margo," she said.

We were the only patrons.

Walls adorned with pictures of English horsemen in red coats and riding breeches on the hunt reflected the British influence. The decorations were very much out of character in this Caribbean Island cafe. The furniture consisted of five small tables, each surrounded by four chairs, and a phonograph resting on a table near the entrance. There were no bottles of alcohol to be seen.

Margo served us gin and tonic from her supply in the adjoining room.

After taking several gulps from his drink, the captain turned to me. "You know, Paul, I wired our New York office to let them know we were stopping here for repairs. They wired back promptly. Look at this."

He handed me a telegram: "Cable immediately. How many survivors?"

Our New York office personnel must have read the recent statistics on the number of ships sunk in the Caribbean during the past two weeks and jumped to the conclusion that we had been attacked and thus needed repairs. Actually, it was more likely that upon spotting our ship a German submarine commander would have decided that she would sink on her own, so why waste a torpedo on her.

"Won't they be surprised to learn that we're all still among the living, Captain."

He pulled a tobacco pouch from his shirt pocket, stomped his pipe full, lit it, then took another sip of his drink. "I wired them that we were not hit but came in here for work on our condensers."

Then ship's business was put aside while the skipper filled me in on his experience as salvage master with Myron, Chapman and Scott on Pacific Coast jobs. As he drank, he overcame his reticence about discussing his early years and reminisced about his first trip, as a cabin boy at the age of nine, on an eight masted schooner out of Germany, hauling grain to America.

"The skipper of that ship was the most disagreeable man I ever sailed with. Nothing pleased him. He kept me running all day long."

Margo planted her ample body on the chair next to the captain. "Don't see many merchant sailors in here these days, maybe 'cause the Germans are sinking most ships headed this way."

Putting her hand on the skipper's arm, she asked, "Did your ship bring in any food supplies? A supply ship got sunk near here a couple of days ago, so our stores have no flour, meat, or canned goods to sell."

"No, ours isn't a merchant ship," responded the captain. "I guess the war's changed your life a lot."

"It used to be carefree. Now with the military base, we're always upset. For my business it's good, but not for my people." She spoke with a clipped English accent, acquired during years of occupation by the British.

"You speak English well," I observed, admiring her diction.

"I taught here for many years."

"There are a lot of local boys lounging around town. Isn't there any work for them?" the skipper asked.

"There's plenty of work out in the sugar fields, but most boys now have a little education and don't want to do that kind of labor."

She jumped up and asked, "What about some calypso music?"

She put a record on the phonograph, and the cabaret reverberated to a calypso ballad, set to rhythm similar to that of the Brazilian samba. The beat of the music was exciting. Margo explained that the songs were initiated by the early slaves during the time they were allowed to relax. They improvised words and music, usually mimicking known individuals. When the tempo rose, everyone shouted in approval, *"carrizo"*, which in Spanish means reed or cane. Eventually, somehow, *carrizo* became calypso.

Margo left to serve another patron.

We finished our drinks and after Hansen emptied his pipe in the ashtray, he turned to me. "Now, Paul, before you make out the shore passes for the crew, check with the mate and the chief for the names of those who spent time in sick bay claiming to be seasick. Don't give them any passes."

We returned to the dock about noon and watched our ship being moved from anchor in the middle of the bay to a location alongside a British freighter at the pier. We had to climb aboard the freighter en route to the *Chamberlain*.

"Give the men their passes and their draw, but remember, only to those who deserve them," the captain ordered. This proved to be the magic cure. After St. Lucia, seasick sailors avoided the sick bay.

I distributed local currency equivalent to ten American dollars to each crew member and shore passes to the deserving ones, who lost no time scrambling over the British freighter on their way to the nearest bistro.

On a walk around the city I found the cobblestone streets surprisingly clean, but the wood-constructed buildings were in dire need of paint and repairs.

Tempting piles of mangoes, coconuts, papaya, breadfruit, and squash were displayed in the open air market. I couldn't resist buying a papaya and with the help of my pen knife, relishing the succulent fruit.

The purveyors and native customers in the marketplace were predominantly descendants of slaves brought over from Africa. The women wore colorful gingham dresses, striped, plaid and polka-dotted, and knotted scarves around their heads. Occasionally, a woman grasping a broom passed us, going through the motions of sweeping the street even though there was no visible litter.

I stopped at the Hotel Caribbeana and was greeted by Hansen and Jaeger, both in very good humor.

"Come join us, Paul," invited the captain. I ordered the inevitable gin and tonic and we sang *New York Town, Sally*, and a few other ditties. Then to my surprise, our mate belted out a series of Norwegian songs, to the entertainment of all the patrons. This was a different side of Jaeger than I knew. I had him pegged to be ultra-reserved and stern.

Walking back to the ship, I encountered our chief carpenter and the third engineer. They couldn't restrain their enthusiasm.

"Say Purse, you should've been along! Three native gals latched on to us on Vigie Beach. We stripped off our clothes and they swam with us in the nude. To top it off, they suggested playing leap frog on the sand. They had no inhibitions. Funny, they asked no favors. And what a beach! Sand for a quarter of a mile out to sea. We're going back tonight."

We never lacked for drama. Wes Hewson, a dapper, moustached thirty-four year old, was a restless soul. His indulgent well-to do parents had satisfied his every wish from childhood on, and now he continued to pursue his every urge. He had a keen mind and curiosity for anything electrical and mechanical. Had he pursued a formal engineering career, he no doubt would have achieved great success. In spite of imbibing excessively in alcohol, he had maintained his position as the best electrician on the staff of Columbia Pictures in Hollywood and was frequently loaned out to other studios as a troubleshooter. He had put in a hitch in the navy as a diver, but signed on as an electrician on this salvage expedition.

In San Diego, William Flanagan had delegated G.H. Carlyle the task of helping him search for divers and other salvage personnel. G.H. had telephoned the lifeguard headquarters in Redondo Beach and was referred to Houghton (Hoot) Ralph. Hoot, in turn, contacted Ray (Huck) Daugherty and Wes Hewson. The three were old buddies.

Hoot and Huck were both experienced skin divers and had served for years as lifeguards in Redondo Beach. They had also worked for Hollywood motion picture studios preparing underwater scenes in *Northwest Passage, Hurricane* and sea stories for Jon Hall. They caught crabs, leopard sharks, and octopuses, and placed them in tanks where they were photographed by cameramen and superimposed on film. Huck owned a fishing boat and with Hoot as a partner, they contracted out their services wherever diving projects were in demand.

Hoot was in his late thirties and had a tall, powerful physique. He became the stabilizing influence in the fo'c'sle. Never too busy to settle disputes among the men, his advice was frequently sought, and whenever violence erupted, his huge bulk intervened.

Daugherty had acquired the name "Huckleberry Finn," or "Huck," for short, after he had been seen on numerous occasions in Redondo Beach, barefoot, wearing dungarees and a straw hat, and carrying a fishing pole on his shoulder. He had a mild disposition and was often sought out by his crew mates to accompany them on shore excursions. Although he was only of medium height, just the sight of his stocky, muscular body served as protection and prevented many a brawl.

No one could ask for a better older brother or friend than either Hoot or Huck. They were both forthright, without guile, and adventuresome but not foolhardy.

Wes left our ship while it was moored to the British freighter. After our vessel had been shifted to an anchorage in the bay he returned from a heavy drinking session in Castries and walked up the gangplank of the freighter to which the *Chamberlain* had previously been moored. After crossing its deck, he confidently climbed over the railing and plopped into the water. Fortunately, even though drunk, he was an excellent swimmer. Some of the seamen aboard the freighter threw him a line and pulled him back on deck.

One of the fellows at the railing of the freighter yelled, "Hey, you lost your passport. There it is," pointing down toward the water.

They pushed him back overboard, and Wes grabbed his floating passport. In the meantime, a rowboat came alongside. He argued with the oarsman for a reasonable rate to take him back to our ship and finally made a deal; but upon reaching the

Chamberlain, Wes didn't have the money to pay his fare. Aboard, he approached Pearson, our second assistant engineer, to borrow a dollar. Pearson pushed him away in disgust. He had his own private stock of alcohol and was, himself, stumbling around drunk, the yolk of soft boiled eggs running down his chin.

"Sir, you're drooling." Taking a wet hankerchief from his pocket, Hewson, ever in charge of a situation, dabbed at the engineer's chin. He managed to borrow a couple of packs of cigarettes from his pal Huck to pay the boatman.

That evening one of the mess boys knocked at my cabin door and barged in, shouting excitedly, "They're lootin' number one hold, Purser, and loadin' our flour and canned goods into bum boats."

I rushed on deck, knocked on Carlyle's door, and the two of us made our way to the gangplank. We were too late to stop our men from shoving off in a bum boat loaded with sacks of flour and cases of canned goods.

When I informed the skipper of the theft, he paced the floor, frowning. "It's a serious offense to break into a sealed hatch." After a few seconds of deep thought, he continued. "You know, Paul, the natives here in St. Lucia are in real need. I want you to type a report that the men had my permission to take some provisions ashore, and that instead of taking our galley supplies, they mistakenly broke into number one hatch.

"Further, also type a note for the permanent record that I ordered a hundred-pound bag of flour to be sent ashore to our Standard Oil agent as a gesture of thanks for helping dispatch the *Chamberlain*. You might also mention there isn't an ounce of flour on the Island for the local people because of the sub blockade."

I was touched by the captain's benevolence.

About midnight, while prowling around deck, I heard a commotion at the gangway. I peered over the side of the ship and recognized Hoot and Huck arguing with a boatman. Someone was stretched out on the bottom of the boat. The argument settled, Hoot picked up the limp body, threw it over his shoulder, and climbed up the gangway.

Meeting him topside, I asked, "What's the trouble?"

Hoot mumbled, "Oh, Moyer passed out and we had to carry him back."

Moyer, one of our diesel men, a slender thirty-two year old, weighed over 140 pounds, but Hoot shouldered him with ease.

The next morning I asked Tom Moyer, "What were you celebrating last night?"

"Well, I was offered a job on a dredging project ashore that would pay better. This *Chamberlain* gang is screwy, and I'd sure be glad to get off this bucket. Then I was warned by the chief that I'd land in the army if I left the ship. So I was drowning my troubles."

In St. Lucia, the crew not only freely imbibed Mount Gay Barbados rum at a dollar a bottle, but they banked a supply for the voyage. The bum boat skippers exchanged many a bottle for flour, cans of vegetables, and coffee from the ship's supplies.

In Panama, the diesel crew, Jim Thornton, Tom Moyer, Bill McKelly, and Carlton Fromhold had ordered a liberal supply of pure alcohol in five-gallon containers, supposedly to be used for washing commutators, but actually providing their liquor supply for the voyage. With plenty of grape and pineapple juice aboard, tropical cocktails were freely available to the diesel personnel. But they jealously guarded the alcohol and kept it hidden from the rest of the crew.

Not only was the Caribbean infested with German submarines, but the U.S. naval authorities in Panama had warned us that the German Navy had indiscrimately planted magnetic mines in these waters. It was somewhat comforting to recall that prior to our departure from San Diego, the U.S. Navy had installed a degaussing cable on the hull of the *Chamberlain* to nullify the ship's magnetic field.

The Germans developed the magnetic mine in the early part of the war and had distributed them widely along shipping lanes. When submerged, or semi-submerged, they were detonated by the magnetic field of a vessel passing over or near them. In 1939, one of the German mines had washed ashore on an English beach. With the help of this specimen, the British had developed the degaussing cable.

In the ten days of our Caribbean voyage, we sailed through seventeen oil slicks and masses of ship's debris, proof that enemy submarines had been very busy.

CHAPTER 10

KING NEPTUNE OFFICIATES

Spokesman Resigns
Jimmy Cook formally announces his retirement as
spokesman for the fo'c'sle. You made a nice try, Jim,
but don't worry, you'll soon have the Black Gang
spokesman crying on your shoulder. What the fo'c'sle
really needs is a Choral Director to lead the greatest
collection of Blues Singers ever assembled in one
group.

From the *Hawse Pipe Herald*, unofficial journal
of the *S.S. W.R. Chamberlain, Jr.*

The third morning after our arrival in Castries, Culpepper
reported that the condensers had been souped up, and, as far as
the engine room was concerned, we could shove off anytime.
Shortly after midday the deckhands hauled in the anchor, the
pilot came aboard, and we were on our way, sailing past the submarine net and into the open sea.

As usual upon departure, I took roll call and reported to the
skipper that all men were accounted for.

"But Ernie and the cat we picked up in Panama are both
missing. They must have jumped ship. I hope that's not a bad
sign."

"Well, I'm not superstitious about that, but as far as Ernie is concerned, Lilly will never forgive me," lamented the captain, somewhat downcast.

Noting the calmness of the sea, the skipper's mood changed, and he mumbled with a devilish grin, "The boys must have paid all their bills in St. Lucia. You know there's an old superstition: the ship will run into heavy weather if sailors leave port without paying their bills."

We sailed parallel to the island, its bald-faced twin peaks of Gros Piton and Petit Piton standing out majestically from the green vegetation. We had the benefit of an Air Force plane escorting us that afternoon, scanning the sea ahead as we changed our course southward. Late in the day, the Air Force plane dipped its wings in farewell, and our ship was again a loner.

There were no porpoises in sight. I could only surmise that the subs had scared them into hiding.

Since the captain had decided not to call in at Trinidad, our next scheduled stop pursuant to instructions from the Panamanian U.S. naval base was Recife in Brazil. However, since oil had not been available at St. Lucia and we did not have enough fuel to take us to Recife, he decided to put into port at Belem, located just below the equator, past the mouth of the Amazon River. With all the reports of sunken tankers, it was a gamble that oil would be available in Belem.

It was my watch as blackout warden. Periodically, the smoke stack lit up the sky with sparks. The engine room's problems had not yet been solved.

I invaded the refrigerator in the fo'c'sle for a can of pineapple juice. The men, after their rum-inspired sojourn in St. Lucia, were sprawled in their bunks, asleep and snoring, instead of engaged in their usual all night poker session. It was a lonely vigil.

Back on deck, I watched the eastern heavens light up, and soon the sun rose slowly over the horizon, resting on the undulating waves in a red ball of fire. I relished every second that the sun's rays splashed colors on the eastern sky.

This sunrise brought back memories from eleven years before, when at age 20 I served a short term as seaman on the *S.S. Leviathan*, then the largest passenger liner afloat.

Having travelled to New York from Wisconsin with a companion in 1931, hell-bent on getting a job on a freighter that would take us to Europe, we searched the docks for a likely ship and found none. After a week of tramping the streets, my companion lost his courage and decided to return home. But I had told all my friends that I was going to Europe, and my pride didn't permit failure. Since my cash was depleted, I could only hope to accomplish my goal by becoming a stowaway.

Selecting the *S.S. Leviathan* from the *New York Times'* list of ships which were scheduled to sail in a couple of days, I visited the dock where she was moored. The entrance to the dock was guarded by a watchman. But I spied a heavy rope tied to a mooring post on the street, leading to the bow of the ship.

"That's it," I decided. "I'll climb it."

It seemed an almost impossible way to gain access to the *S.S. Leviathan*. I shivered when I considered the implications, looking down at the dirty river water ten to fifteen feet below, then up at the deck of the ship about forty feet above the water level. Still I was determined to board her.

At midnight prior to its sailing, a fog covered the city so dense that the skyscrapers were scarcely visible. The street lights were like dim candles dotting the way at intervals. The waterfront was deserted. After looking around to be certain I was not observed, I moved stealthily to the mooring rope. Entwining my legs around the rope to keep from sliding down, I ascended inches at a time and then rested a few minutes to catch my breath and renew my strength.

Halfway up the rope, the lace of one of my shoes came untied. It gradually loosened, and further up, dropped off, hitting the water with a splash. I dared not look down.

At last, only a few feet remained. I was weary. The muscles in my aching arms and legs wanted to give up the battle. My lungs begged for more air. The condensing fog made my clothes damp and uncomfortable; but that was not comparable to the agony of clutching the rope. A final burst of energy and my arms were within grasp of the ship. One last heave and I pulled myself up on the rope, through the scupper, toward the bitt around which the rope was fastened, and stretched out on deck, panting.

I located a hiding place under the seat of a lifeboat and waited there through the torturous morning hours while the ship's winches, loading cargo, clattered and groaned, each moment fearing to be discovered and sent ashore. At midday the ship's whistle signaled departure and a tug's horn answered. After exchanging signals for four hours, the tug gave a last hoot, and the *Leviathan* was on its way, alone.

With one shoe missing, I realized that it would be impossible to mingle with the passengers en route and sneak ashore upon arrival in England without discovery. I crawled out of my hiding place, limped with my stockinged foot to the railing, and waved triumphantly at the Statue of Liberty and the New York skyline receding in the distance.

"You're a stowaway, eh?"

I swung around to be confronted by a uniformed officer who escorted me to the captain's office.

The unsympathetic captain sentenced me to work two shifts, sixteen hours at a stretch, from four in the afternoon to eight the next morning. I didn't really mind. The two work sessions gave me the privilege of participating in six meals a day with the crew; and the work was preferable to remaining locked up in solitary in the ship's brig, where I had to spend my off hours. The cell had frequently been occupied by stowaways in the past, as was evidenced by comments, signatures, and dates scrawled on its walls.

Wearing a pair of work shoes donated by the master-at-arms, I scraped paint, washed decks, and moved deck furniture.

Each morning at dawn I goofed off, climbing up the mast to watch the morning sun creep over the horizon, spraying its various hues of red and yellow over the filmy, cloudy sky. Those sunrises remain forever in my memory bank.

When the *Leviathan* arrived in Southampton, England, a bobby from the local constabulary escorted me ashore to Bargate Prison, where I shared a cell with an Englishman, an ex-sailor, accused of receiving stolen property. He enthralled me with tales of his sea voyages and adventures in faraway places.

My two days in Bargate were too short, but I did hunger for better food than the sole diet of fresh bread and tea, morning, noon and night—and teatime, too.

Two bobbies escorted me back to the *S.S. Leviathan* for the return trip to New York and two work shifts and six good meals a day.

Aboard the *Chamberlain*, the sun was now well above the horizon. The colors in the eastern heavens faded, and so did my reverie.

One evening, attracted to the music of my Mendelssohn recording, Dr. Chasen and Wilford Wood joined me in my quarters. I welcomed the chance to become better acquainted with Wood, who had been personally recruited by Commander Ellsberg because of his long career as a deep sea diver. But like the doctor, he was reserved and impossible to fathom.

Surprised that Chasen was interested in listening to music other than his bagpipes and bugle calls, I offered to loan him some of my classical records, hoping to reduce the number of ear-splitting Scottish and military serenades issuing from his cabin.

He turned me down. "I can always come in and listen to yours."

Earlier that day I had noticed that one of the parrakeets in the cage hanging outside of the sick bay was going bald.

"Say, Doc, one of your parrakeets is losing its feathers. I was billed as a canary doctor in Canada in 1936 and treated many birds for everything from bald heads to dirty feet while selling bird food." I couldn't help bragging about my stint as a doctor.

"A canary doctor?" Chasen chuckled.

I persisted. "Why don't you drop a rusty nail in that bird's water. Iron should cure a bald head. And please, hang your birds on the other side of the sick bay. Their shrieks hurt my ears."

Taken aback, he said, "I'll think about it, Paul." But he never followed through on either of my suggestions.

On the sixth day out of St. Lucia, we approached the mouth of the Amazon River, where the dark blue waters of the Atlantic merged with the murky river waters thrusting 200 miles out from its estuary.

By midafternoon we crossed the equator, and that triggered a lot of activity on deck.

The ceremony, occasioned by the crossing of the equator, originated in ancient times with the appeasement of the sea God Poseidon, sometimes referred to as Neptune. It became a regular occurrence during the 17th century on French ships, where it was customary for the second mate to impersonate Neptune and induct all who had not previously crossed the equator by striking them with a wooden sword and dowsing them with a bucket of sea water.

Standing on the flying bridge, I watched the crew members erect a water tank on the main deck just below the bridge, fill it with salt water, fasten a chair on a swivel on the hatch just above the water tank, and install another chair below the hatch.

The members of the crew who had previously crossed the equator elected Gregory, our tall, robust boiler maker, to personify King Neptune. He wore a hemp crown overflowing to a full hemp beard that extended down to his stomach, and a laced hemp skirt was draped around his middle. The two members of

CLARENCE GREGORY AS KING NEPTUNE
AND HIS TWO ASSISTANTS

G. H. CARLYLE AFTER BEING DUNKED
GALVIN AND HOOT STANDING BY

THE CREW'S ANTICS
CROSSING THE EQUATOR

GLEN GALVIN AND
HOUGHTON (HOOT) RALPH

DICK SLATTERY, WILFORD WOOD,
TOM MOYER AND AXEL FREDRIKSON

WES HEWSON, LES PETERS
AND TOM MOYER

his court wore bandannas around their heads. One covered his left eye with a patch, jammed a cutlass in his belt, and supported his right knee on a peg. Some crew members, claiming to have been previously initiated, dressed up as pirates and assisted the court in carrying out the judgments imposed.

One by one the men were blindfolded and hauled before King Neptune. Each was then seated in the chair below the hatch and something was sprayed into the initiate's mouth. He was then escorted to the chair on the hatch, his face smeared with a brush which had been dipped into a can, and the chair was tipped backwards, dumping him into the water tank.

While enjoying the performance, I was surprised by a tap on my shoulder. Turning around, I was confronted by two of the crew dressed as pirates and wearing metal stars signifying badges of authority. One of them grabbed my arm.

"You're next, Purser."

I had felt secure on the flying bridge away from it all. Now escape was impossible. The two pushed and pulled me, resisting, down to the main deck to appear before King Neptune's court.

"The charges against you are serious," accused King Neptune. "You are charged with not giving the men a pay day when they were promised and not selling cigarettes on Tuesdays." I just shrugged my shoulders.

"Give him the works," he bellowed.

They blindfolded me and pushed me into a chair.

"Open your mouth," a voice commanded. I finally did and nearly choked on a mouthful of vinegar. Someone led me up a series of steps and pushed me into another chair.

Another voice asked, "Shave, shampoo or haircut?"

"Shampoo," I mumbled.

Something wet and sticky was smeared on my hair and all over my face.

Again a voice demanded, "Open up."

This time my mouth was inundated with catsup, and I felt it being massaged into my face and hair. My body was then catapulted backwards into the tank of water. Someone held me under, and after emerging, to my dismay, I was ducked again.

After my blindfold was removed, I managed to climb out of the tank, coughing and spitting out catsup and water. Someone whammed me with a paddle to the entertainment of the crew. To my great relief, that ended my induction.

CHAPTER 11

BELEM FEVER

News Flash

Tom (Ten Times)Moyer has been offered ten thou-
sand dollars and a half interest in Madam Za Za's if
he will only return to Belem and repeat his feat in the
lobby of the Grande Hotel. Moyer replied, "I must've
been inspired. I guess its them vitamins." We think it
was shellac applied externally.

Crazy Americanos

If a group of South American men came to our
country and acted the way we did in Belem, we would
get all steamed up about it and want to organize a
lynching party. They're not laughing with us. They're
laughing at us.

From the *Hawse Pipe Herald,* unofficial journal
of the *S.S. W.R. Chamberlain, Jr.*

A full moon blessed the night with rays shimmering on the
dirty waters of the mouth of the Amazon. Awaiting daylight and
the arrival of a pilot to guide us to the port of Belem, we
crossed the equator two more times, sailing up and down the
Brazilian coast, past the Amazon River estuary and wide island
of Marajo, to the mouth of the Para River.

In the early morning hours the captain spotted a pilot boat. After boarding our vessel, the pilot ordered the helmsman to proceed upstream, leaving the tropical trade winds and the salt spray scent of the Atlantic behind. We were welcomed by the sweet, captivating fragrance of wet earth, of leaves, of tropical plants. Bright green trees and bushes lined the shores. It was a ninety-mile journey pressing against the onrushing waters of the Para River, an arm of the Amazon.

By late afternoon we dropped anchor within sight of the docks of Belem. As the pilot reached the gangway from the bridge, Jim Cook accosted him.

"Any piranha in the river?"

The pilot nodded and waved his arms excitedly, emphasizing there were many.

The piranha, a member of the characidae family, is also called a caribe or tiger fish. Its usual length is fifteen inches, although sometimes it is as long as two feet. They swim in large schools and usually feed on other fish. With their strong jaws, they also attack humans and animals, tearing them apart in minutes.

Cook decided to test the waters and threw a large piece of raw meat tied to a rope into the fast-moving Para River. At first the bait was undisturbed; then a school of piranhas descended on the meat and in a matter of seconds savaged it.

I felt the oppressive heat, our hygrometer registering ninety percent humidity. Just one degree south of the equator, Belem, also known as Para, had an average yearly rainfall of eighty-six inches.

Another pilot boarded us in the rain early the next morning

and directed our helmsman to move our ship closer to the docks of Belem, but still at anchor some distance from shore. Before long one small motorboat filled with officials approached our ship from downstream, but the current kept sweeping the boat away from our vessel. The man at the tiller gunned her engine repeatedly.

Meanwhile a large launch, flying the Standard Oil Company flag and carrying a sole passenger, the company agent, tied up to our gangway. The motor boat with the Brazilian officials then managed to tie up to the launch.

Soon our ship swarmed with seven Brazilian bureaucrats who in their various capacities, demanded to see the captain. Among them were representatives from their customs, immigration, police, and navy. I led them to the captain's quarters, along with the Standard Oil agent who had also boarded.

"Your papers, Captain," one of the officials ordered.

After examining them, he threatened, "I'm fining you one hundred thousand milreis for illegal entry into this port."

The skipper demanded. "Hold on. I want to talk to the Standard Oil Company agent."

The agent pushed his way through the party of bureaucrats, grasped the skipper's hand and introduced himself as "John." He was a chubby, light-skinned Brazilian in his middle thirties, with a ready smile.

After studying the ship's papers and conferring with the captain, he informed the Brazilian authorities that our vessel was a naval auxiliary ship; that we were not carrying any cargo for Belem; and that we came into port in an emergency, seeking fuel.

Satisfied with the explanation, the officials left en masse, but not before extorting cigarettes that the captain had available for just such an occasion.

John gave us the bad news. "There's no oil in Belem. Hasn't been for at least two weeks. A couple of oil tankers headed this way were sunk."

Hansen asked, "Well, how soon do you expect another shipment?"

John shrugged his shoulders. "Any day now, if the next tanker makes it here. A couple of destroyers are waiting to be refueled. Several freighters are ready to sail but are stuck here because of the submarine menace."

He took two cigars out of his pocket and offered them to us. We politely refused. He lit his own and continued, "I'm ready to take you ashore, Captain."

Hansen turned to me. "Paul, you'll join us."

I grabbed his briefcase and my officer's cap, the only item of attire distinquishing me as purser, and followed them down the gangway into the launch.

John took a few puffs from his cigar, then settled back on the launch cushions.

"Captain, on my way to your cabin, your boys asked if they'll get any money to spend in Belem. I told them they could have all you'd authorize."

Again the captain's firm answer was, "Ten dollars apiece in local currency will be enough."

"That'll be just 200 milreis in Brazilian money." The agent's voice expressed disappointment. No doubt his fees were computed on the volume of our ship's expenditures.

Ashore, as we were riding in John's chauffeured company car, the agent pointed to the warehouses along the wharves and explained, "Before 1910 Brazil was the rubber capital of the world and those buildings were crammed with raw rubber for export. Belem was really prosperous then. Now they're storehouses for Brazilian nuts and piassaba."

I learned that piassaba is a coarse fiber obtained from palm trees and used in cordage or brushes.

We passed open booths at the marketplace displaying melons coconuts, bananas, peaches, a wide array of vegetables, dried fish, and pottery of beautiful designs and colors. Three distinct lanes channeled the heavy traffic in the streets—one for horses, one for old-fashioned streetcars, and another for bicycles and automobiles.

At the Caloric Co., the agency for Standard Oil, John produced a bulletin from his New York headquarters requesting that the agency give special attention to our captain, ship, and crew, and that we be provided with any stores, supplies, or help needed to facilitate our journey.

At our next stop the American consul advised, "Since yours is a naval auxiliary vessel, Captain, you should contact the naval attaché for fuel and ship's orders."

Then at the office of the naval attaché, Hansen presented our ship's papers, which included the demand that our ship be promptly expedited.

Upon examining them, the navy Lieutenant dismissed the skipper with, "Your ship is next in line to be fueled after the destroyers have been serviced."

The chauffeur then drove us to the Grande Hotel, the jewel

of Belem, where local elite and foreigners met for drinks and dining. Civilian patrons in business suits mingled with those in army and navy uniforms. We passed rows of marble-topped tables on the sidewalk, occupied by people in deep conversation over drinks. We then made our way to a table in a formal dining room, where we were soothed by the music of a trio— a pianist, a guitarist, and a violinist—from the balcony above us.

The captain commented, "John, I didn't expect to see so many foreign military and naval officers in Belem."

"Since the war began, it's a stop-over for planes flying between Africa and the United States," John explained.

We enjoyed a six-course meal, including a tasty steak, sardines, potato salad, and papaya, all for the price of twelve milreis or sixty American cents apiece.

At the Caloric office, we collected fifteen thousand milreis for the men, and the chauffeur drove the captain and me to the docks to board the Standard Oil launch back to our ship, still swaying at anchor in the Tocantin River.

"We'll move the ship alongside the dock first thing tomorrow and the crew gets shore leave then," shouted the skipper to the mate, loud enough for the benefit of the men crowded along the ship's railing. They almost mobbed me for the cash advance on my way to my cabin, where I handed out two hundred milreis apiece.

An American destroyer was anchored nearby, and motor launches took members of its crew ashore throughout the day. Ignoring the captain's orders, Wes, Huck, and Hoot stood at the railing, waving at the launch pilots to hitch a ride to shore.

Having imbibed heavily from his private stock, Wes stumbled down the gangway. His foot slipped on the lower step and he fell into the river. Huck grabbed a life preserver from one of the life boats and tossed it out. Wes didn't catch it. He floundered in the water and was carried down-stream.

Hoot kicked off his shoes and dove in from the main deck. It was an instinctive response for him. With powerful strokes, he overtook Wes, gripped his shirt collar, and swam upstream against the current, back to the ship.

There were loud cheers from the men as they watched Hoot help Wes aboard. It was fortunate that the fast-moving Para River had been slowed by the incoming tide from the Atlantic, which pushed the water level nine feet above its low tide level. It was fortunate, too, that the piranah had taken a holiday.

The next morning the pilot came aboard and guided the *Chamberlain* to dock at Pier ll. The sandbanks in the river constantly shifted, and only an experienced pilot could guide a ship safely in these waters. Woe to any enemy submarine or surface vessel commander who dared to pay a surprise visit to Belem.

The men trooped ashore like an army that had been marooned in the desert for six months. Some sought female companionship, invading the red-light district and monopolizing it for three days of shore leave. Others went on sight-seeing trips into Belem. Glen Galvin, employed as a diver's tender, was a former backfield man on the University of Southern California football team and a participant in several Rose Bowl games. He headed for the local cathedral to give thanks to God for our safe passage thus far. In fact, he never failed to kneel by his bunk in evening prayer.

Private homes had been converted into nightclubs harboring Brazilian damsels. The front living room became a small dance hall, where the lively beat of the drums poured forth from a jukebox or phonograph. Beer and rum flowed freely in an adjoining room furnished with chairs and tables. Our men monopolized the girls' time to the annoyance of the locals, who sulked over their drinks.

A few of the men immediately acquired steady girl friends for our stay in port, appropriating their entire time. After they returned to the ship, I learned that many had spent no more than forty to sixty milreis apiece. Some of the girls paid for their food, drinks, and in a few instances, even for their taxi fares and admission to the local movie house.

The story got around that one of our oilers who had latched onto a playmate ashore took the liberty of strolling down the hallway in the nude from his girl friend's room while she was off on an errand. When his paramour returned and found him chatting with another girl in a state of undress, she pounced on the rival, pulled her hair and punched her. Both screamed as they pummeled each other, cheered on by spectators emerging from other rooms in the house.

Then the police arrived, and, after ordering the two nudes to get dressed, took the girls and our crew mate to the local court. The judge listened to the stories of the rivals, winked at the sailor, then fined the girls each twenty milreis for disturbing the peace.

That evening, Tom Moyer, Huck Daugherty, and Dick Slattery, a crew mate, had a confrontation with police officers and spent the night in the local jail.

The next morning I invited Huck to join me for a drink in

my cabin and asked, "Just what happened to you guys last night?"

Huck sat back in the chair, his bulky frame squeezed against its arms. His face broke into a big grin as he reflected. Then he explained, "Well, we were leaving one of the joints and Moyer, in passing a bargirl, pinched her butt. She followed us out, screaming bloody murder in Portuguese. A guy in a business suit, standing at the bottom of the outside stairs, grabbed Moyer's arm. Moyer shook loose, and the fellow reached into his pocket, hauled out a policeman's badge and shook it in Moyer's face. Moyer grabbed it and passed it behind him to Slattery, and he tossed it to me. So I dropped the damn thing into a bucket of water nearby. Say, that cop was teed off. He pulled out a little gun, a 25 millimeter, and yelled for help. We laughed, but our fun ended when three cops in plain clothes circled us, called the wagon, and hauled us off to the jailhouse." Huck took a sip from his drink and shook with laughter.

Anxious to hear the rest of the story, I pressed him. "What happened there?"

"Well, the jailer paraded back and forth in front of our cell, waving his pistol. Slattery took off his shoes and threw them, one at a time, at the overhead light. On the fourth try he broke the bulb. The jailer came to the cell door and shook his gun at us, shouting in Portuguese."

Huck took a long gulp. "Next morning the police chief fined us each five milreis, made us pay for the light bulb and let us go. We could have been locked up for the duration.

"On the way back to the ship, we saw a lot of people gathered around a statue of a military man standing next to his horse, and guess who was sitting on the horse? Yeah, there was Wes, drunk as hell! When he saw us, he waved wildly and fell off. We picked him up and convinced him to join us."

On one of my visits to our agent's office I asked John, "Are the local police officers always easy on sailors? Some of our men stole a policeman's badge and gave him a hard time. If this had happened in the States the men would have been locked up for awhile, but they just spent a night in jail and were fined five milreis apiece."

"I heard all about that affair," he said. "The word has got around that you are from a navy auxiliary vessel, and the police didn't want to hurt the war effort. Otherwise, those men would'nt have gotten away so lightly."

Four days after we dropped anchor at Belem, an oil tanker arrived. Once again our agent informed us that the destroyers would be fueled first. The captain asked the naval attaché for a letter explaining the reason for our delay in getting priority fueling for the *Chamberlain*. The attaché pointed out that the navy had ordered the destroyers to hunt down a nest of submarines reported off the Brazilian coast, and that, for our own safety, the destroyers should have the first option on the oil and precede us into the South Atlantic.

Our ship was refueled later that day, and the following morning I accompanied the captain to the office of the naval attaché to obtain sailing instructions. The captain had not been informed that he had to bring along the code books, so we returned to the ship to get them. They had been stuffed in a canvas bag, ready to be thrown overboard in the event of an attack on the high seas; however, one was missing. I was on my way to the radio shack in search of the misplaced book when one of the crew grabbed me by the arm.

"Hey, Purse," he said. "What about getting me a carton of cigarettes out of the slop chest?"

"I'm in a rush," I exclaimed, trying to break away. "I'm looking for something for the skipper and he's in a huff."

"It'll only take a minute," was his response.

I decided to humor him and opened the door to the slop chest. Before I could get away, five of the men blocked the entrance, all wanting cigarettes. I knew that if I served them all, the captain would blow his stack, so I slammed the door, mumbling, "Gotta do an errand for the skipper."

My explanation did not satisfy Tom Moyer. Having spent the previous night in the Belem jail, he was disgruntled.

"Getting a big head around here!" he barked. "Can't you give us a civil answer?"

His right fist connected with my jaw. I retaliated with a feeble right to his chest and was thankful when the gang restrained him.

I quickly smoothed my hair, retrieved my cap, and hurried to the captain's quarters. He had located the missing book on the bridge.

The doctor's two parrakeets continued to chatter incessantly from their cage outside the sick bay. In Belem, four more passengers joined our menagerie—three monkeys and an Amazonian wildcat.

The wildcat, spotted like a leopard and no larger than an alley cat, was a hopeful contender for the honor of disposing of the parrakeets. It was a gift from John, our Belem agent. Caught in the jungle as a kitten, it had been tamed, became a family pet, and was very protective of John's children. However, it had also acquired a reputation as a hunter in his neighborhood. Every week or so it disappeared for a short time. Following its return, a neighbor would present a bill of indemnity for a chicken, or a turkey, or a goose. When the captain heard John's story, he agreed to take the cat off his hands.

Carlyle enthused, "Just maybe the parrakeets have had their day."

Carlyle appropriately named the monkey he had aquired ashore "Flanagan" in memory of the man who had expedited our vessel in San Diego. From then on any complainers aboard the ship—about the food, the contract, no overtime pay on Sundays, the miserly ten-dollar pay advance at each port of call, the condition of the ship—were told, "See Flanagan." Whereupon Flanagan just shook his head, rolled his eyes, and looked on with an all knowing expression.

Ever since boarding, Flanagan invited trouble. Frequently he sneaked into my cabin while I dozed and scampered off with some of my desk supplies. At other times I caught him with my sun glasses, poker chips, pictures, papers, and even a mirror.

After chewing up two of Jaeger's pipes and scattering papers over his cabin, the skipper decreed that Flanagan must be kept on a tether.

As we sailed south of Belem, the weather became colder, and Carlyle, feeling sorry for Flanagan, sewed a coat for him.

Then there was Ugly, a monkey with long spiderlike arms, a pot belly, and a long prehensile tail. He had the disposition of a saint. Nothing offended him. When someone scolded Ugly, he scampered off to the nearest seaman and begged for sympathy. He was a homely specimen and constantly scratched himself. He loved to cuddle in the arms of anyone who picked him up, but it soon became obvious that his weak bladder could make quite a mess.

Consuelo never got over losing Ernie at St. Lucia, and he now became very fond of Ugly. When he took the trouble to clean Ugly's fur and brush him, Ugly's eyes lit up as he caressed Consuelo's arms.

The third monkey, a wild marmaset that looked like a rat, remained in hiding most of the time.

When I reported to the captain that four of the crew were missing, he responded, "We'll sail without 'em." But just as the pilot stepped aboard, Cahill, Wilson, Foreman and Hughes appeared on the dock and dashed on deck over the rising gangplank.

While the pilot guided the *Chamberlain* past the sandbars down the Para River en route to the Atlantic, the captain asked me to write a letter to John. He had left his spare glasses somewhere in Belem and wanted our agent to try to locate them, perhaps by contacting the taxicab company, or the night club, or, to my surprise, a certain brothel. If found, he was to mail them to Massawa. He and John had gone out on the town, so John could retrace their steps. Apparently, he had followed his wife's advice: if he desired female companionship, he should pay for it instead of getting emotionally involved. I scrambled to get the letter ready for the pilot before he left the ship.

The military authorities in Panama had requested that the *Chamberlain* refuel at Recife, on the bulge of Brazil, and then sail on the long journey across the South Atlantic to Cape Town in South Africa. But the skipper, upon calculating the distance from Recife to Cape Town and taking into consideration the ocean current, the prevailing winds, the fuel consumption rate, and our fuel capacity, determined that we would run out of fuel oil long before our arrival there.

Our leaking forepeak fuel tank was causing serious problems, so the Captain decided to proceed to Rio de Janeiro to refuel and for repairs. He had performed an amazing job at each port of call to expedite the ship on its way despite all the obstacles imposed by the shore authorities. The sea route from Rio de Janeiro to Cape Town was much shorter than from Recife; the prevailing winds were favorable; and there would be adequate fuel for the *Chamberlain's* long journey, its maiden voyage into a vast ocean—a far cry from its coastal lumber hauling days.

When Hansen received his sailing orders, the naval attaché asked him whether he wanted a naval escort out of Belem.

He responded, "We've come alone this far. We'll make it the rest of the way, too."

I hoped he was right!

CHAPTER 12

WE'RE BOARDED

THE WAR: After seven Brazilian ships had been torpedoed off the coast of Brazil, its air force joined the U.S. Air Force in patrolling its coast in search of U-boats. Over the weekend of June 6th, 1942, the Brazilian pilots were credited with sinking one German submarine, and the U.S. pilots with two.

The *Chamberlain* bucked the headwinds, heaving and tossing, as we left the sanctuary of the Para River on June 14th, 1942. Fortunately, my own *mal de mer* did not surface. The captain chided at mess, "Someone didn't pay his bills in Belem."

The wildcat easily adjusted to the vibrations and rolling of the ship and surveyed its new domain. I became quite fond of the feline, and it nestled on my lap, keeping me company on lonely blackout watches.

Once in awhile its hunting instincts prevailed and it jumped off to stalk one of the monkeys. They always eluded capture. One night while leaping around the machinery as the ship rolled from side to side, it landed on a protruding boat chuck and broke a leg. I did not want to take it to the doctor, so G.H. and I placed the cat in a box cushioned with a blanket and carried it into my cabin. It had lost all its aggressiveness, and its whimpering kept me awake all night. It must have suffered internal injuries, because the next morning it breathed its last. I lamented the loss of its companionship.

Ugly wandered into the mess hall on a number of occasions and sampled sugar, meat, butter, and other food stuffs. To get him out of the habit, Toledo, the officer's mess boy, filled sugar bowls with salt and planted heavily-peppered meat in accessible places.

Not easily discouraged, Ugly continued to frequent the mess hall. Toledo caught the monkey digging into a sugar jar, carried him topside and threw him overboard. Consuelo, heartbroken, couldn't forgive Toledo for such a dastardly act and complained to Hoot, who punished him with a black eye.

Six days out of Belem, Okie, our lookout from his perch in the crow's nest, reported ships far out to starboard. The news traveled throughout the ship, and within minutes, most of the men not on duty were lined up along the railing. I joined them, anxiously searching the horizon for the threat. I spotted two warships steaming into view. They bore down on us at full speed.

There had been no report of enemy surface war ships in the South Atlantic, but if these were, in fact, German vessels, our fate was sealed.

A destroyer lay to about 700 yards off our starboard bow, its big guns trained on our ship, and signaled us to stand by. Our engines stopped and we tossed in the turbulent seas.

My heart missed a couple of beats as I anxiously gazed at the bobbing warships. Several men dashed for life preservers. Someone yelled, "Are those German ships?"

Wes Hewson, a former navy man, had his binoculars trained on the naval vessels. "Relax," he shouted. "That's a U.S. destroyer and cruiser."

The Skipper yelled down from the flying bridge to the men on deck, "Where's Whittaker?"

Our chief gunner dashed from the railing to join Hansen on the bridge. The cruiser executed a wide circle around the *Chamberlain*, its guns sighting us continuously.

The skipper turned to the mate on watch and ordered, "Hoist the American flag and our I. D. letters."

The destroyer, meanwhile, flashed its signal lights in Morse code.

"What are they saying?" shouted the skipper.

"They're asking for our secret code signals, Captain," responded Whittaker.

Hansen disappeared into the log room and returned with the signal given to him in Panama. The gunner flashed the secret code letters.

The destroyer came back with, "Incorrect letters. Stand by, we're boarding you."

The destroyer lowered a boat into the turbulent waters. The occupants were hidden from view by the water spray as their boat bounded from one wave to the next. When they drew near, we distinquished sixteen men crouching in their seats, several with machine guns clutched to their chests.

From the bridge, the captain shouted, "Throw down the Jacob's ladder so they can board."

As the boat scraped against the ship's iron plates, the officer in charge of the boarding party shouted, "Men, get up that ladder and take your places. If you see anything threatening, shoot. Now get aboard."

The men boarding were obviously U.S. sailors in view of their uniforms and the New York accent of the officer-in-charge; nevertheless, their behavior was menacing.

The first sailor arrived on deck and stationed himself above the Jacob's ladder, his machine gun trained on us. Two more sailors armed with machine guns climbed up the ladder, followed by a young navy lieutenant who surveyed the deck and, with an air of importance, demanded, "Take me to your captain!"

Wes Hewson, moved closer to the navy guard at the Jacob's ladder. The navy man, pointing his machine gun at Wes, barked, "Keep your distance."

"This way, Lieutenant," I volunteered, leading the way to Hansen's quarters. The officer, flanked by two of his armed men, followed close behind.

Meanwhile, six more sailors, pistols strapped around their waists, climbed aboard. Two of them took positions on the bridge, two in the engine room, and two in the fo'c'sle. These were followed by others who demanded to examine our cargo. They searched our ship thoroughly, while the guard stationed above the Jacob's ladder kept the sailors in the launch informed of developments. Some of our men tried to converse with the invading sailors, but they refused to reply, remaining soberly wary.

I was apprehensive. The evidence of sunken ships that we passed through in the Caribbean had been vivid reminders of the wartime dangers of our journey; but the threatening big guns of the cruiser and destroyer, together with the machine guns and pistols of the invading seamen holding us at bay, even though they were our own countrymen, were more than a little intimidating.

Dr. Chasen, who had hurriedly put on his army dress uniform decorated with all of his citations, approached the navy lieutenant while I was escorting him.

"I'm Lieutenant Chasen, U.S. Army," he pompously introduced himself to the naval officer. "Can I be of any service?"

The navy lieutenant brushed him aside without answering. Chasen was crestfallen.

The captain waved us in through the open door of his cabin. I had to admire his nonchalance as he deliberately lit his pipe. Two armed sailors took positions at his door.

The Lieutenant's voice was crisp and commanding, "May I see your ship's papers, Captain?" After studying them, he asked, "Where are the special code signals from Trinidad?"

"We didn't stop at Trinidad, Lieutenant," explained the captain.

The lieutenant frowned. "You realize, Captain, by not putting in at Trinidad, you put your ship in great jeopardy. There you would have received secret orders and signals that would have identified your ship as American, and you would have avoided this confrontation. But your papers are in order, and you may proceed."

Hansen, not to be cowed, said, "Well, Lieutenant, in any event I would prefer this encounter with our navy to those subs in the waters around Trinidad. Wouldn't you?"

The lieutenant didn't respond.

"Can you give us the right signal in case our navy stops us again?" queried Hansen.

"I am not in a position to give you that information, Captain."

"Did you take us for a German ship?" Hansen wanted to know.

"We were very suspicious. Our instruments warned us of your diesels. When we came closer and saw your fo'c'sle and mid-ships built up, and that you were equipped with eight lifeboats and four life rafts, machine guns and a cannon, and your decks were awash with men, we concluded your ship was no ordinary cargo vessel. By the way, what are those diesels for?"

"We have a large refrigeration plant aboard, together with an air-conditioning system, and we carry provisions for shore personnel in Eritrea. It gets to be 140 degrees there. We also have a carpentry and machine shop aboard that need a lot of electricity. Ours is a mother salvage vessel, and we carry divers and diving equipment for use in clearing the Massawa harbor of sunken ships." The captain sat back in his chair and relit his pipe.

"When we spied you, we thought you were a supply ship for the German submarines and fully expected to see the sides of your ship open up and reveal big guns ready to fire on us," the navy lieutenant explained. "We captured one last week."

"Maybe that's why the U-boats left us alone," the skipper said with a chuckle.

"Well, it's obvious there is more power aboard this ship than a cargo vessel would normally need. And then when you signaled the wrong identification and couldn't answer our code, we were sure we had cornered an enemy vessel. Yes, maybe you fooled the U-boat commanders, too."

With that, the navy lieutenant abruptly left, ordering the sailors standing guard to round up the boarding party and return to the destroyer.

CHAPTER 13

RIO DE JANEIRO

CHAMBERLAIN BLUES
Tell me not in mournful numbers
That this tub is low on oil,
For her engines there's no slumber
And the water is loath to boil.

In the tubes goes the sawdust,
Pine and fir and all the rest.
Plugging up the leaks we try
But our oatmeal is best by test.

Rio's far and time is fleeting,
And our hull tough, stout and brave;
Still the termites keep on eating,
and the bulkheads bend and weave.

And so we stagger down to Rio,
Waddling along your friendly shore,
With our boilers "Mucho Frio"
Quoth the Captain, "Nevermore".

Open wide your drydock Rio,
Why she floats I'll never guess.
If we make it down to Rio,
This floating mess deserves a rest.

From the *Hawse Pipe Herald*, unofficial journal of the *S.S. W.R. Chamberlain, Jr.*

As the sun rose on the 26th of June, we sailed along the Brazilian coast, escorted by schools of dolphins leaping high out of the water in their enthusiasm. Our stack was still puffing away like an habitual Cuban cigar smoker, leaving a trail of black smoke churning in the breeze.

The spectacle of Rio appeared at last! Mountains and forested hills, encirled by filmy clouds, dominated the background. Protruding granite buttes dotted the landscape.

Clearly visible as the clouds drifted by were Christ's outstretched arms on the statue welcoming us from its perch atop a tall peak.

Pilot-guided, we passed the beautiful white sands of Copacabana beach enroute to our moorings. Even at this early morning hour it was dotted with Cariocas in swimming and walking attire.

We passed through the narrow entrance to Guanabara Bay, and off our port bow an imposing bare granite cone-shaped peak came into view. It was Rio's landmark—Sugarloaf.

As soon as the ship's engines ceased throbbing, a dozen bum boats, each powered by two oarsmen, swarmed around us. Shouting wildly, the boatsmen waved bottles of the local sugarcane brandy, cachaca, demanding foodstuffs in exchange.

Our boys improvised an elevator system, lowering large cans of diced carrots, beets, and other foodstuffs on ropes, and the oarsmen then tied the bottles of cachaca onto the ropes for the return.

Cachaca was foul-smelling and unpalatable until mixed with grapefruit or pineapple juice. Even then, after just one drink, I took the pledge. Those of the crew less discriminating and less concerned about their stomachs and livers, imbibed freely. Quite a number of cans of foodstuffs were exchanged before the captain posted several armed men around the ship to keep the bum boats at bay; but it was an uncooperative vigil, and the bottles of Brazilian liquor came aboard by the dozen.

A launch pulled up alongside, and a half dozen Brazilian officials climbed aboard and invaded the captain's quarters, all demanding attention. After examining our ship's papers and requesting the reason for our stop at Rio, they each extorted a carton of Lucky Strikes and departed. Our Rio Standard Oil agent then escorted the captain and me onto his launch for a trip to his shore office.

As Hansen seated himself in the launch, he turned toward the agent, "We've got to get into dry dock. Our forepeak has to be properly sealed. Water has been forcing its way in and mixing with the fuel oil, and our smokestack has been sparking like the devil."

"Well, we've got a number of ships here waiting their turn, so it'll be at least two weeks to get you a dry dock," the agent retorted, squinting in the noonday sun. No doubt he was mentally calculating the potential profits accruing to him.

Just like in Panama and Belem, I thought.

"As you know, we're on an important mission and can't afford to be delayed," insisted the captain. It was always the same story.

At the Standard Oil office, the agent reached for the phone. Six calls later, he explained, "Sorry. Can't be done. Like I said, it will take at least two weeks to get you a dry dock."

Not to be put off, the captain, pounding his fists on the

table, exploded, "In that event, we'll take this damned wreck out as she is and run her to Cape Town, even if we have to put sails on her."

The agent took up the telephone again. He wasn't going to let the *Chamberlain* slip through his fingers. He turned to the skipper somewhat resignedly. "It wasn't easy. I've arranged to put you in ahead of the other ships, so you'll dock tomorrow at Niteroi."

After ordering fresh fruit, vegetables, milk, other mess hall supplies, and local currency for the crew, we hoisted a few slugs of whiskey in a nearby cafe.

"You see, Paul," the captain boasted after our second drink, "you've got to call their bluff; otherwise, we wouldn't get to Massawa till Christmas. Sparks says the English have been pushed all the way to El Alamein, not far from Cairo, and the Germans are attacking the naval base near there. The British sure need the Massawa harbor to repair their ships, so we've got to get there fast and clean it up."

I caught the Skipper's sense of urgency.

He continued. "Also, Flanagan told me that Johnson, Drake & Piper is building an air base for Douglas Aircraft not far from Massawa. They'll be assembling planes to be flown to the African front where Rommel is pushing the English to the wall. So the Massawa harbor has to be open to cargo ships carrying plane parts."

As we boarded the *Chamberlain*, we encountered several of our crew stumbling along in a state of inebriation and Tom Moyer sporting a black eye.

The skipper cornered the mate.

"What the hell goes on here?"

"A couple of the boys broke out a five gallon can of diesel alcohol, and they must have a corner on the pineapple juice," Jaeger complained. "We've had a few fist fights while you were gone. And the men played hell with the dishes in the mess hall."

Pointing to the launch which had brought us back to the ship and was still tied up to the gangway, Hansen snapped emphatically. "Paul, it's about time we have some discipline around here. Take that launch ashore. Phone our agents and ask them to call the police to take the troublemakers off to jail."

The captain's overreaction surprised me. He had usually been very lenient in handling any crew transgressions, and I could only guess that after his bout with the agent he had reached the breaking point.

I took the launch ashore, called our agent, advised him of the problems, and asked him to contact the police.

In the meantime, Hansen ordered Carlyle, our husky master-at-arms, to go aft, arrest the instigators, bring them midships, and lock them up. However, when G.H. brandished his pistol, the men mobbed him and took his gun away. Dejected, he returned to complain to the captain, who decided not to pursue the matter further.

It was just as well. The police launch never came. Our agent later informed us that the police hesitated to interfere with the personnel of a U.S. government vessel.

Bill McKelly, who often was in on any scuttlebutt, told me how the brawl came about. Toledo had taken a container of pure alcohol from its hiding place in the machine shop and secreted it in his locker in the galley. Wes Hewson and Tom

Moyer, who could smell alcohol through even the thickest walls, borrowed the machinist's bolt cutter to attack the locker, and Wes retrieved the can. At that moment, Bennie Godines entered the galley and pursued them, branishing his cleaver. Tom picked up a stack of plates and threw them, one at a time, at Bennie, as he and Wes rushed toward the door. In the fo'c'sle, the men fought for a share of the booze, and Moyer received his black eye in the melee that followed.

Late that afternoon, the captain ordered all men not on watch to report on deck. Standing on number three hatch, with his arms akimbo, he announced, "We'll be in dry dock tomorrow morning and you'll all get shore passes. This time I'm going to overlook today's drunken party and fights and the dishes broken in the mess hall. But let this be a warning: I won't tolerate that kind of behavior again."

On less serious occasions, the skipper invariably called any troublemakers into his cabin, shared a few of his beers, and asked for better cooperation.

The next morning the *Chamberlain* steamed to Niteroi on the shores of Guanabara Bay and entered the dry dock that had been constructed by excavating a passageway into the land mass, large and deep enough to berth a sea-going vessel. Watertight gates were then closed and the water in the basin pumped out, permitting workmen to repair the leaking forepeak tank, which stored our engine fuel oil.

Upon our arrival at the dry dock, I distributed an advance in milreis equivalent to twenty U.S. dollars to each of the men. Many of them disappeared and didn't return to our vessel until she was ready to sail five days later.

THE S.S. W.R. CHAMBERLAIN JR.
IN DRY DOCK AT RIO DE JANIERO

That evening Les Peters, Hank Rhoda, a welder and seaman, and I visited the Casino Assyrio in the heart of Rio night life. It was only 9 P.M., and we were among the first guests. An orchestra entertained with typical Brazilian music, the inevitable boomboom of the big drums, joined with the harmonics of the tambourines, kettle drums, trumpets, trombones, and saxophones.

After we ordered drinks, three Brazilian belles approached our table and offered to join us. When the waiter brought our drinks, the girls ordered cocktails. Losing no time, the waiter brought a pitcher of what appeared to be fruit juice and poured it into their glasses.

We were bug-eyed as the girls downed their drinks and motioned to the waiter, who hovered close by, for refills.

Peters complained, "They're taking us," and demanded our check.

The waiter returned with another pitcher of drinks and handed Peter a bill for 340 milreis, the equivalent of seventeen U.S. dollars.

Peters offered the waiter two hundred milreis and in a loud voice threatened, "Take it or leave it. That's all you'll get."

The waiter threw the money on the table.

I demanded to see the manager and explained to him that we didn't order the refills and were not paying any more than the two hundred milreis. He wanted to compromise on 280, but we gulped down our drinks, left the two hundred milreis on the table, and walked out, leaving the waiter arguing with the manager. We had been in the night club a scant half hour.

The next morning Hansen handed me a telegram from

Johnson, Drake & Piper demanding that we proceed posthaste to Massawa, because the clearing of the harbor was being held up.

Hansen, frustrated, pounded the ashes out of his pipe, his face flushed. "What can we do? If they had given us a ship that would do at least ten knots an hour instead of seven and was trouble-free, we would have been there by now. Write them a letter, Paul, detailing our problems. Let them know why we're delayed."

At lunch on the third day the chief complained, "The dry dock engineer told me that one of the salt water lines leading to the toilets was also connected to our condenser lines and had to be corrected. Those sons a bitches back in San Diego really messed us up. That's why we've had to feed sawdust to the condensers by the bucket. There'll still be problems since our condenser pipes are so old and have a lot of pinholes in them, but after this we'll be using less sawdust than before."

Having heard that the ship was ready to be launched, I joined the skipper in his quarters.

"Paul, let's take a tour of Rio before we leave," he suggested, a twinkle of mischief in his eyes.

As we started for the gangway, we were stopped by a U.S. army major who requested an immediate interview. So we returned to the captain's quarters.

"It's been reported to us that you have a saboteur aboard this vessel by the name of Gunnar H. Carlyle." The major went on to enumerate the same complaints that the intelligence officer in Panama had advanced, and added that Carlyle had allegedly supplied Dr. Chasen's patients with whiskey.

Apparently, the doctor had not forgotten his grudge.

"This is getting monotonous," the skipper said with a grimace. "Carlyle was fully investigated in Panama City, and I can give you my word, Major, he is not a saboteur."

"I still must make my inquiry. Do you mind if I interview some of the ship's crew?"

I knew that there were few crew members aboard.

"Go ahead!" bellowed the skipper.

While waiting for the major to investigate G.H., Hansen hauled out a bottle of whiskey and we had a couple of drinks.

Two hours later the army major reported back. "There doesn't seem to be any merit to the complaint," he concluded.

It was then too late for us to go ashore and bid farewell to Rio.

Our ship was moved from the drydock to the wharf to replenish her oil and water and take on ship supplies and food provisions. The captain's insistence for speedy repairs had paid off.

The men in the fo'c'sle, having combed the city for feminine companionship and finding it only in brothels, were astonished to learn that Bill McKelly and Carl Fromhold had met and dated two cultured Brazilian girls. We considered Bill, the youngest man aboard, to be naive and bashful, and Carl to be puritanical.

The two diesel men reported that while changing U.S. dollars for Brazilian milreis at the Niteroi Hotel, a well-dressed business man from Sao Paulo appproached them and asked if they would join him in the dining room. They agreed. To their surprise, he introduced them to his two lovely daughters who had been educated in the United States. After a sumptuous dinner, they arranged to meet the two girls again.

CARL FROMHOLD AND BILL MCKELLY
WITH BRAZILIAN GIRLS
AND SUGAR LOAF MOUNTAIN IN BACK GROUND

On the following day, Bill and Carl escorted the two girls to Sugar Loaf mountain and on a cable car ride to dine at the half-way stop on the Urca peak. They arranged for the foursome to be photographed with Sugar Loaf mountain in the background and proudly passed a copy of the picture around the fo'c'sle upon their return to the ship. Bill, totally enamored, vowed he would some day return and woo his girl.

Before departure, the dock master offered the skipper a gift. It looked to me like a mangy German shepherd, but its pedigree was a mystery.

"We've already got the beginning of a zoo aboard, so we may as well take the dog." Although Hansen never expressed particular affection for any of the animals aboard our ship, even his wife's cat, Ernie, that deserted the ship in St. Lucia, he continued to accept animals as gifts, always delegating me to care for them.

A head count of the crew disclosed three men missing. I had expected more of them would find Rio a welcome haven from the uncertainties of life aboard the *Chamberlain*, but only Chief Culpepper and two mess men were not aboard. I never could figure out how the men who had moved ashore for the duration of our stay learned about our departure time.

The captain decided to wait until morning for safer sailing and ordered our ship to be anchored in the bay to free up valuable dock space for another vessel.

He vowed, "If the missing men don't come aboard before then, we'll sail without them—Culpepper included!"

Later, a launch pulled up alongside, and to my great relief,

Culpepper climbed aboard.

"Where the hell have you been?" snapped Hansen.

"Our coffeepot in the engine room broke, and I went ashore when we were docked for supplies to get another. It cost me plenty, what with having to pay the launch to bring me back to the ship."

The next morning we sailed out of the beautiful harbor of Rio, minus the two mess men.

CHAPTER 14

A DOG"S LIFE

THE WAR: After the surrender of 25,000 men and the North African port of Tobruk in Libya to General Erwin Rommel's Panzer division on June 21, 1942, the British Army was in full retreat, falling back to El Alamein in Egypt. British headquarters in Cairo began shredding papers in preparation for abandonment of Egypt to the Axis.

The most recent addition to our menagerie, was a playful he-pup, but a veterinarian's nightmare. Now I understood why Rio's dockmaster had been so eager to unload him.

The captain dubbed the dog, Bosun. "Paul," he said, "see that he's taken care of."

The dog had diarrhea, the mange, and lice. So far as we knew, the only ailment he didn't have was a venereal disease. Open sores covered his body. I felt sorry for the pup and applied peroxide to one of the infected areas. He rewarded me with a feigned nip on my calf; then he yelped and jumped five feet into the air. No matter what other treatment I tried, nothing helped.

The doctor was unsympathetic. "I've got enough patients without adding a cur to the list," he groaned.

The land pup was miserably ill the first few days aboard, indiscriminately messing up our decks from poop to fo'c'sle. Our tied-up monkey, Flanagan, resented Bosun's playful advances and inflicted deep scratches on his face, adding to his misery. In spite of it all, he remained as frisky and good natured as if he were in dog heaven.

THE AUTHOR AND BOSUN

The first Saturday out of Rio, the captain called carpenter Frank Gray to the bridge. "We've got plenty of lumber. Make a dog house for Bosun."

So on Sunday, Gray, having loafed all week and expecting overtime pay, devoted eight hours building a deluxe abode for

Bosun. He was confident that our employer, Johnson, Drake & Piper, would compensate Sunday work upon our arrival in Massawa because it was understood that the comany was on a cost-plus basis with the U.S. Army Engineers.

Gray installed the dog mansion on deck near the fo'c'sle, but Bosun refused to go inside and never did occupy the house. Thereafter, we referred to it as "Gray's Folly."

As we departed from Rio, Doctor Chasen insisted that the men report to him for short-arm inspection. When they lowered their trousers, he discovered that two of them had contracted gonorrhea, and he promptly put the two on the sulfathiazole treatment. One of them, our baker, Feliciano Ben, was barred a second time from the galley.

Les Peters again recruited Pete Watson, our ex-navy baker, to replace Feliciano, resulting in a much appreciated improvement in our bread and pastries. The men were ambivalent in their feelings about Watson; although grateful for his contribution to their culinary appetites, they abhorred his untidy habits and found him socially unacceptable.

The doctor took the Hippocratic oath seriously and was determined to get us all to Massawa in a healthy condition. His daily health inspections of the galley and the mess hall were stricter than ever.

One morning Carlyle found a lifeless Flanagan on deck. The second engineer reported he had discovered the monkey in his room the night before chewing on a prophylactic tube. Without the benefit of an autopsy, it was presumed that death was due to his incorrigible habit of gnawing on everything in sight. The captain's order that Flanagan should remain tied up was never carried out. The loss of his pet quite depressed the usually effusive Carlyle. I sympathized with him, saddened to think that the monkey, which had become such a familiar figure on deck, was no more.

Thus our menagerie had dwindled down to the doctor's parrakeets and Bosun. The marmoset had long since disappeared. We never knew whether it had sought refuge ashore in Rio or been swept overboard during a wind storm.

As our vessel sailed southeastward from the coast of Brazil, the sea became violent, the waves crashing against the steel hull as she plowed through the South Atlantic.

Sleeping aboard was always a challenge, even on a calm sea. With just a small swell, the ship heaved and rolled without grace or rhythm, but in a heavy sea, the motions were pronounced and sudden. Sometimes the vibrations of the engines were irregular, rising in crescendo and then dropping off in a quaking motion as though in a spasm. It was impossible to have a good night's sleep during much of our journey in the South Atlantic.

I spotted our first albatross five days out of Rio. I watched it fly gracefully, its wings scarcely moving as it picked up the wind gradiant to gain energy for soaring high into the sky, then gliding effortlessly with the air currents above the wake of the ship.

Carlyle joined me at the railing, always ready to share his knowledge. "Paul, isn't it a miracle that it found our ship over a thousand miles from shore? As a matter of fact, the albatross has been known to fly as far as 3200 miles in ten days."

The bird hovered over us like a good omen. Every morning I watched it following the wake of our ship. At nightfall the albatross feasted on the ship's garbage tossed overboard from the stern by the mess men and then winged its way back into the clouds.

When I spotted one of the deck hands on the poop deck aiming a rifle at the big bird, I yelled from the deck below. "Bill, don't shoot! It's bad luck. Remember 'The Rhyme of the Ancient Mariner'!"

He scowled and put down his gun. The albatross and the ship were safe.

CHAPTER 15

THE ROARING FORTIES

THE WAR: The Japanese suffered a serious setback in the battle of Midway, the sentry post for Hawaii, which ended June 7th, 1942 with their loss of four carriers, a heavy cruiser, 322 aircraft and 5,000 men. The American casualties were one carrier, one destroyer, 150 aircraft and three hundred men. It was a critical victory for the U.S.

Gentle breezes drifted over the calm sea as the shores of the Cape of Good Hope came into view, revealing whitish-gray clouds hovering over the stately 3567-foot flat-topped Table Mountain forming the northern pillar of a chain of hills. After fifteen days at sea, the men fought for a place at the rail to gaze at the first sight of land and to admire the magestic panorama.

The captain looked over the steward's order list. He arched his bushy eyebrows. "A gallon of vanilla? Why so much?" Before waiting for an answer from Les Peters, he continued, "You know I once lost a good steward because I stopped buying vanilla for him. He could drink a pint a day."

Les, knowing the skipper's whimsical vein, replied, "Vanilla is not my idea of a drink."

Hansen turned to me. "What, no requisition from the chief?"

"I checked with him and we only need oil." In view of our past experience, we had expected another long list for the repair yards.

"The Skipper said, "Well then, we shouldn't be here more than a couple of days."

Our ship passed through the submarine nets, dropping anchor in the bay about midday. Shortly after, the shore authorities boarded us. The captain insisted, true to form, that we should have priority treatment to refuel and provision the ship in pursuit of the war effort; the officials, also true to form, promised nothing, offering only a cursory, "Stand by until you hear from us."

That evening, an icy wind blew in from the south pole, and our ship heaved and tossed at anchor until noon the next day, with no communication from the shore authorities.

At lunch, the captain remarked, "We're not going to wait here while they twiddle their thumbs. I'm going to get some action this afternoon."

Then turning to Culpepper, who was spooning his soup out of the bowl held firmly in the wooden rack while the ship tossed about, he said, "Be ready to move the ship by fourteen hundred hours, Chief."

Promptly at 2 P.M., a clanging of chains resounded throughout the ship as the windlass hauled in the anchor. We steamed toward the harbor entrance, and, in the center of the channel at the opening of the submarine nets, Hansen ordered, "Mate, drop anchor right here."

Jaeger protested, "But Captain, we'll be blocking the entrance—no ship can get in or out. We'll catch holy hell!."

The captain declared, "So be it!"

Within half an hour a tug sped out and pulled alongside. Port officials, together with a pilot, boarded us and directed the skipper to immediately move our ship alongside a dock for oil and supplies.

I had to give Hansen credit. He won again.

Right after we docked, the Standard Oil Company rep boarded our vessel, bringing a supply of South African rands for distribution among the crew. Most of the men flocked ashore to test the South African hospitality.

The ship was fully provisioned and fueled in time for departure at noon the next day. As we left the dock for anchorage in the bay, I made the rounds of the ship and reported to Captain Hansen, "Four crew members are still ashore, including our second mate."

"If it weren't for Vatne, I'd leave them behind. Grab a shore boat and see if you can locate them," he ordered.

I went to the bar near the dock where our ship had been tied up and found all four of the missing men in high spirits.

When I told the fellows that we almost sailed without them, Vatne explained, "We were down at the dock and found the ship had already left. So, naturally, we came back to the bar to celebrate."

"Well, come on," I pleaded. "The skipper is waiting to sail. I've got a taxi standing by."

"Let's have a couple more drinks," suggested Vatne.

"I'll buy you a bottle of rum if you'll come back to the ship with me now," I coaxed.

The men reluctantly agreed, left the club, and climbed into

the waiting taxi. In Cape Town, liquor by the bottle was then only available from a bootlegger. The driver was most accommodating and let me out at a nearby source. When I returned, Vatne snatched the bottle of rum out of my hands and the tippling continued in the taxi.

At the dock I arranged for transportation to the *Chamberlain* on one of the motor launches tied up there and managed to maneuver my four charges aboard. Twelve seamen from various ships boarded the launch with us, all in a festive mood. The boat zigzagged through the turbulent sea, and we had to cling to our seats as the waves threatened to overwhelm us. I sat in the bow facing the other passengers. The cold water cascaded over my back every time the boat crashed against the waves. Unfortunately, it didn't splash on my four shipmates, who could have used the sobering effect.

As the launch came alongside an anchored vessel in the harbor, weaving up and down against the steel plates of the ship, the boarding seaman had to jump to grab the Jacob's ladder. Every successful trip up the ladder was loudly cheered by the remaining passengers. After half an hour of bucking the waves, traveling from ship to ship, the launch finally arrived at our vessel. Then it was my turn to jump for the Jacob's ladder. I didn't know how the other men could make it after their alcoholic spree, but they all somehow climbed aboard. One of them even managed to hang onto the bottle. Without waiting to share in what was left of the rum, I made a beeline for my cabin to peel off my cold wet clothes.

It was too late in the day to begin steaming up the east coast of Africa. The *Chamberlain* tossed in the bay all night.

The following morning the windlass hauled up the anchor, and we proceeded south past the fortieth parallel to avoid the submarines hovering off the coast. Then we sailed east, and finally north.

The tempestuous seas between the fortieth and fiftieth parallel are known as the *roaring forties*, so named by early sailors because the strong westerly winds, blowing continuously, summer and winter, had freewheeling in the southern hemisphere, undeterred by large land masses. No sane submarine commander dared to challenge ships in those waters. It was cold and wild out there.

Upon leaving Cape Town, Hugh Anderson who had signed on as a diver's tender was ordered to watch for submarines and enemy surface vessels from the crow's nest. The skipper was not taking any chances, even in the *roaring forties*. Anderson telephoned the bridge as we entered the stormy seas, complaining that he was very seasick. When he was told to come down, he said he couldn't make it. So Jaeger sent a couple of deck hands up the rigging to help him. He spent several days in sick bay after his rescue.

There was bedlam in the fo'c'sle. The men had stocked the refrigerator with food stuffs, intending to tap this food supply when the meals served in the mess hall became intolerable or monotonous. As our ship tossed about in the *roaring forties*, the huge fridge door opened, and hams, cheeses, cans of fruit juices and miscellaneous goodies came rushing out, cascading from one side of the fo'c'sle to the other. The men bumped into each other in their attempts to corral the food.

CHAPTER 16

MASSAWA INTRIGUE

THE WAR: Rommel's panzer divisions captured Tobruk, the British African stronghold, on June 21st, 1942, and continued their steady advance toward the Suez Canal. In anticipation of observing his fifty-ninth birthday on July 29th, concurrently with a planned victory celebration upon the expected conquest of Egypt by the Axis forces, Mussolini rushed by plane to Libya. The British air force shot down one of Mussolini's escort planes in which his personal chef and barber were passengers. Since he was as a bald as a bowling ball, Mussolini never missed his barber. Rommel's panzer divisions never advanced beyond El Alamein, so the celebration never occurred.

Despite the many reports of submarine attacks in the shipping lanes off the east African coast, our smoking vessel continued to sail safely on its way without sighting any German or Japanese ships. We took on fuel and provisions at Mombasa in Kenya and, after a brief stop at Aden at the mouth of the Red Sea, proceeded toward the Eritrean port of Massawa.

On August 12th, 1942, 106 days and 15,545 nautical miles out of San Diego, the *Chamberlain* arrived safely, without escort, at its destination, much to the surprise of every man aboard.

I looked out upon the sandy countryside. I had never imagined a place as barren, inhospitable, and hot as Massawa. White houses delineated the perimeters of the city.

The harbor was a graveyard of sunken ships. Some masts, smokestacks, and flying bridges of ships barely peeked out of the water, while other vessels revealed their upper decks and superstructures or lay submerged on their sides. About forty scuttled German and Italian freighters, passenger ships, a floating dry dock, and a huge crane, rested on the bottom of the harbor and the surrounding waters.

A pilot guided our ship deftly between the wrecks to the commercial dock in the main harbor, where a shore crew began unloading the cargo of food supplies from the forward hold onto trucks for transhipment to an Asmara warehouse. Johnson, Drake & Piper (JD&P) officials had decreed that all cargo was to be hauled to Asmara and inventoried, then transported back to Massawa when requisitioned. What we didn't know then was that many items, like good coffee, never resurfaced in Massawa.

Although my research had warned me about the high temperatures at this Eritrean port, the intensity of the damp heat took me by surprise, the thermometer registering 138 degrees on the steel deck of the ship. I soon felt the contrast between the outside heat and my cool 85 degree Fahrenheit air-conditioned cabin.

Our ship's doctor, Chasen, left us as quietly as he had arrived, without fanfare—parakeets, phonograph, bagpipe music, bugle calls, and all. He had avoided Carlyle as diligently

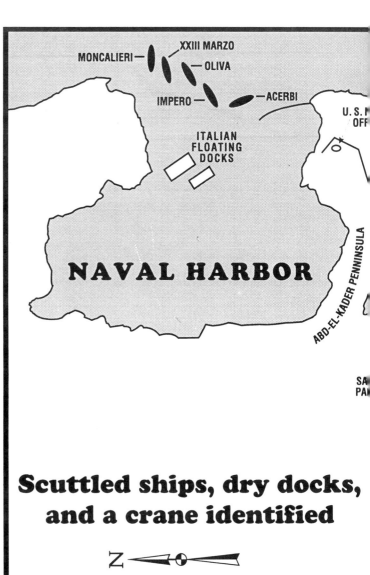

MONCALIERI
XXIII MARZO
OLIVA
IMPERO
ACERBI
U.S.
OFF

ITALIAN
FLOATING
DOCKS

NAVAL HARBOR

ABD-EL-KADER PENNINSULA

SA
PA

Scuttled ships, dry docks, and a crane identified

N

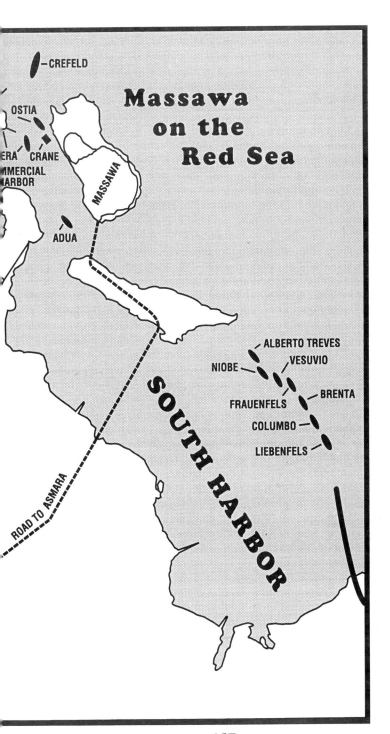

CREFELD

OSTIA

ERA   CRANE

MMERCIAL
ARBOR

MASSAWA

ADUA

Massawa
on the
Red Sea

ALBERTO TREVES

VESUVIO

NIOBE

BRENTA

FRAUENFELS

COLUMBO

LIEBENFELS

SOUTH HARBOR

ROAD TO ASMARA

as Carlyle had avoided him. I was to learn later, through an unexpected meeting with an old friend, that Chasen still nourished his grudge, even in Massawa.

The Captain and I were reviewing some reports in his cabin when a middle-aged man entered, blind in one eye, dressed in shorts and shoes, his nude, suntanned, spindly legs, and stocky upper body still oozing with perspiration. He shivered in the sudden exposure to our air-conditioning system.

Hansen got up from his desk, beaming, his eyes wide open. He grabbed the outstretched hand of the visitor. "Bill," he said in an animated voice. "Say, it's good to see you. Sit down."

"Welcome to Massawa, Tom." Bill's broad smile emphasized the wrinkles under his eyes.

"Bill, this is my purser." Then turning to me, he explained, "Paul, you're looking at one of the great deep-sea divers of our time, Bill Reed. He's Captain Ellsberg's right-hand man. Say, how are things shaping up, Bill?"

I'm ready to resign." Reed wiped his brow. "Captain Ellsberg is in Cairo to consult with General Maxwell. You know he's the American commanding general of the Middle-East area, and that includes this salvage project. Yesterday, while he was away, the Johnson, Drake & Piper gang in Asmara issued a bulletin putting Brown in charge of our salvage operation, replacing Ellsberg. This is the second time they've done this."

Captain Edison Brown had been processed in the San Diego office of JD&P, and then, together with a crew, had been flown to Port Arthur, Texas. From there they sailed the *Tug Intent*, to Massawa, arriving two and a half months before us. Brown's crew had already salvaged two German freighters. He had more than twenty-five years of salvage experience and had also played the part of a skipper in the Hollywood productions of *Mutiny on the Bounty* and *Captain Courageous.*

Hansen exploded. "But I thought the army engineers put Ellsberg in charge."

"Well he's not under JD&P control, and I don't think they can fire him. He's got no cooperation from those blockheads in Asmara, and he had to fight to get money to pay the salvage crew. That took weeks. If Brown is in charge, I'm through."

"I won't take any orders from Brown, either," Hansen threatened, knocking the ashes out of his pipe. "I had my problems with him on West Coast salvage jobs."

What a reception to Massawa! A feud between Ellsberg, a navy man, and Johnson, Drake and Piper, the civilian contractor. If Ellsberg was replaced, and Reed and Hansen resigned, what would become of me? I did have a year's contract and decided to hold JD&P to its terms, whatever decisions others might make.

This meeting was interrupted by a perspiring young man in long trousers and a white shirt open at the neck. He was obviously out of place in the ship environment.

"Captain Hansen?" he inquired, peering at the skipper. "I've got a letter for you from Mister Patterson in Asmara." He handed it to the captain and promptly left.

Upon reading it, Hansen turned to Reed. "Looks like JD&P's business manager wants me to come to Asmara tomorrow." Then he gave me an order to get all the crew's personnel records ready. As an afterthought, he added, "Better type up my resignation, too."

Bracing myself for the blast of heat, I pushed open the cabin door and stepped onto the oven-hot deck, leaving Tom Hansen and Bill Reed to reminisce about old times. Grinding sounds of winches filled the air as booms lifted cases of foodstuffs out of the bowels of our ship.

Back in my quarters, I took several salt tablets and then composed the captain's resignation, giving as the reason that he had come to Massawa with the understanding he would be working for Captain Ellsberg.

I started to cover up my typewriter when the door opened. In walked Chief Culpepper, exclaiming, "Say, Paul, I just heard that they fired Ellsberg. Well, I won't work for Brown. No way! Type up a resignation for me and get it ashore."

He stood over me as I typed his notice, then signed it and stomped out.

I was left to reflect on the latest turn of events. Ellsberg had a reputation as a top salvage man, having succeeded, while an officer in the U.S. Navy, in raising the *S-51* submarine from the bottom of the Atlantic off the shores of Rhode Island in 1926. After Pearl Harbor he had volunteered for further navy service, although now over fifty years of age. Given the rank of Commander in the U.S. Naval Reserves, he was assigned to supervise the reconstruction of the Massawa naval base and to salvage the scuttled ships in its harbor. He had arrived in Massawa on March 30th, 1942, just four and a half months before us, and had already performed miracles at the base.

Before surrendering Massawa to the English, the Italians had sledgehammered to bits most of the machinery, equipment, lathes, motors, and tools in the carpentry shop, the electric shop, the shipfitter's shop, the pipe shop, and the foundry. The British had neither the specialized talent nor the equipment available to rebuild the Massawa naval base, much less to salvage the ships that blocked its harbors.

With the help of native personnel, Italian prisoners of war, and twelve American workmen who had arrived by plane, Ellsberg rebuilt equipment and machinery by using undamaged pieces and the ingeniousness of the workmen. In spite of the oppressive heat, the naval base, although not complete by any means, was in operation by the first week in May without having received any machinery parts from the states.

In just nine days Ellsberg and his men had floated a mammoth dry dock that had been scuttled by the Italians in 1940. The navy then promoted Ellsberg to the rank of captain in the naval reserves. The dry dock was still under repair in the naval harbor when we arrived.

Ellsberg had also located a small dry dock anchored in the outer harbor of Massawa. The English had towed it from the Persian Gulf, but they had trepidations about hauling it through the narrow channel, past the sunken ships, into the naval harbor.

However, Ellsberg maneuvered it into place and notified the British naval base in Alexandria, Egypt, that the much needed Persian dry dock was prepared to repair and service ships. The air raids on the base in Alexandria precluded repairing ships there. By the time of our arrival in Massawa, the hulls of a number of ships had been scraped and painted. Further, major repairs had been performed on ships sent down from Alexandria, which had been damaged by depth charges and enemy fire in the Mediterranean.

JD&P was commissioned not only to rehabilitate the Massawa naval base under the supervision of Captain Edward Ellsberg, USNR, but also to construct air bases, rest camps, ammunition depots, warehouses, and hospitals in Eritrea, the Sudan, the Arabian peninsula, and in Jerusalem. The foreign headquarters of JD&P had been established in Asmara, Eritrea, 7500 feet above sea level and seventy miles from our naval base.

After foodstuffs and supplies were unloaded, our ship moved out of the commercial harbor, around the Abd-el-Kader peninsula, to the naval harbor.

The Italians had navigated five of their ships—the *Acerbi*, the *Impero*, the *Oliva*, the *XXIII Marzo*, and the *Moncalieri*—positioning them end to end across the entrance to the main channel of the naval base, and then detonated explosive charges planted in their holds. The *Oliva* had rolled over on its side and swung away from the bow of the *XXIII Marzo*, leaving a channel just wide enough for our ship to slip into the harbor.

Our vessel pulled up to the submarine dock, and a shore crew came aboard to unload equipment—salvage pumps and air compressors of all sizes, diving gear, other salvage material, and two motor launches, one to serve as Captain Ellsberg's official boat.

The next morning an Italian driver, perspiring in the 9 A.M. heat, awaited us dockside in his Lancia. Clad in shorts, the skipper and I climbed into the back seat. Our chauffeur took off, driving on the left side, English fashion, past bombed-out buildings and flat desert that stretched thirty miles from Massawa to the foot of the mountains. Then we climbed forty miles uphill through barren, rocky terrain, to Asmara.

The mountain road, a marvel of construction, had been cut into solid rock in the 1930's by the Italians for the invasion of Ethiopia. Mussolini's road builders, paid by the kilometer, made no effort to shorten the route, but followed ancient camel trails that wound around the mountains. We zigzagged around hairpin turns, skirting the edges of the precipices. Our driver took the curves like a true race car fanatic, almost on two wheels.

The skipper yelled, "Slow down. Not so fast."

The driver paid no attention, so we just sat back and gripped our seats. On nearby cliffs, scores of baboons scampered among the rocks and stared at us. The higher we climbed, the more moderate the climate became. By the time our car arrived on the plateau, the temperature had dropped to a point where both the captain and I shivered in our shorts. Fortunately, we had been forewarned to pack warm trousers and sweaters.

Cactus thrived on the tableland, but here and there the natives and Italians had planted small grain, vegetables, and fruit. Other than in irrigated areas, the land was barren, rocky, and arid. Our driver piloted the Lancia cautiously past natives escorting flocks of white goats and sheep, a source of meat, leather, milk, and cheese. Occasionally we passed a native accompanied by his heavily laden burro.

In Asmara, Italian officers, automatic pistols prominently jutting out from holsters strapped to their waists, and U.S. army officers strolled leisurely among civilian pedestrians up and down the crowded sidewalks of Viale Mussoini.

I couldn't help expressing my amazement. "See those Italian officers strutting around in full dress uniforms and pistols, while our American officers wear no side arms at all. That just shows—to the defeated belong the spoils!"

The captain shook his head. "It's a crazy war, Paul."

At the office of JD&P, an attractive Italian female secretary ushered us into the inner sanctum of R.G. Patterson, the business manager.

"Captain Hansen, we've been waiting for you." Patterson got up from his desk to greet us with an outstretched hand and a smile which quickly faded when Hansen, frowning, grabbed it limply.

The skipper came right to the point. "What's this I hear about Captain Ellsberg being replaced by Brown?"

"You've got that wrong." Patterson's face flushed. "We understood that Ellsberg had been transferred to Cairo by the U.S. Navy, so we appointed Brown to take over. Now that Ellsberg is back, the order appointing Brown has been rescinded. Here's a copy." He handed a mimeographed sheet to Hansen.

The Skipper scanned it and then handed it to me:

"Asmara, August 13, 1942

"To All Concerned

FROM: ASSISTANT FOREIGN MANAGER

SUBJECT: ASSIGNMENT OF PERSONNEL

"Reference is made to memorandum from this
office dated August 10, 1942, assigning Capt.
Edison Brown in complete charge of all Red
Sea Salvage operations for this Company.
Effective this date, the order is rescinded."

"You would have had my resignation and that of Chief Culpepper as well," was the captain's biting response.

"We can't afford to lose either you or the chief. So, let's get down to business." Patterson shifted some papers on his massive desk. "Now for your files, we'll need all the information on your crew."

"Mr. Behm, my purser, can give you that." Hansen got up and looked out of the second floor window. I opened my briefcase and gave Patterson copies of our crew list, data which set forth the positions for which the members were hired, their pay rates, moneys advanced to date, and their status as members of the crew.

"Mr. Behm, you will be in charge of all personnel time records in the Massawa area. That includes the hourly records for native and foreign, as well as American employees of Johnson, Drake & Piper. We're assigning several native and Italian timekeepers to your office to assist you. We'll expect you to furnish us with weekly time reports."

In charge of personnnel time records? What did I know about setting up a program for timekeepers?

Initially, during the voyage to Massawa, I planned to do as little work and minimize my accountability as much as possible, but gradually the satisfaction of being the intermediary between the captain and crew and participating in the inner council of the officers inspired me to assume more responsibility and sometimes work long hours. So the position of chief timekeeper was a challenge.

"Now to change the subject." Patterson lowered his voice and confided in a serious vein, "Let me update you on the latest war news. Montgomery is barely holding his own at El Alamein, and if Rommel breaks through, the Germans will take Alexandria and then be headed this way. We're organizing a home guard in Massawa, as well as here in Asmara. You should join the Massawa group so you'll be ready."

I didn't relish being on the firing line. I thought I had precluded that by avoiding the navy. But I agreed to get involved with any home guard.

"By the way," I asked. "What about all those Italian officers parading down the boulevard with their side arms? Shouldn't they be locked up as prisoners of war?"

"That's a strange story," responded Patterson. "After being defeated by the English, the Italians insisted on the honors of war upon surrendering. That sounded okay to the English. After the British authorities paroled the Italian officers and allowed them to live in Asmara, the Italians insisted on the right to keep their sidearms since they had surrendered with the honors of war."

"What if Montgomery is defeated by Rommel? Aren't there enough guns among the Eyties to take over Eritrea?" I asked.

Patterson shrugged. "Well, there isn't suppposed to be any ammunition in those sidearms. But who knows?"

CHAPTER 17

MY LARCENOUS NATIVE TIMEKEEPER BECOMES AN ENTREPRENEUR

*Old Jerry had us on the run, the news
was far from hot.
He had his foot in Egypt and the Sphinx
was on the spot.
The C in C with back to wall sent
signals out in sheaves
To Ali Baba Morshead and his 20,000
thieves.
So Leslie called his general staff, he
whispered in their ears.
His message went to Auchinleck.
"Drink and drown your fears.
We'll make that blanker Rommel think
he's got the desert heaves
With Ali Baba Morshead and his
20,000 thieves."*

Song shouted by Australians under the command of Major-General Leslie Morshead across the trenches to Axis troops while defending El Alamein in August of 1942.

The morning after returning from Asmara, I decided to tour the naval base. We were anchored just outside the naval harbor within easy access to the sunken *XXIII Marzo*, the first project for our divers. Its masts and superstructure hovered over the calm Massawa waters and its name appeared prominently on its flying bridge.

In its capacity as a mother salvage vessel, our ship continued to serve as an air-conditioned dormitory and to provide mess hall facilities for the salvage workers in an otherwise inhospitable climate.

One of the motor launches that we brought over from San Diego joined the *Lord Grey*, a British motorboat, in regularly transporting personnel between the naval base, our ship, and the various work projects.

The launch carried me to the floating dry dock now under repair, previously salvaged by Captain Ellsberg's men. I watched the native Eritreans scraping the barnacles from its deck and sidewalls. The salvage men, some of them members of our ship's crew, were fitting new steel plates over the bomb holes and rebuilding mechanical and electrical components.

The Italians had blasted large holes in seven of the eight compartments in the floor of the dry dock, scuttling the dock in thirty-six feet of water. When completely repaired, its compartments would be submerged, permitting a ship to maneuver onto the deck of the dry dock between the tall sidewalls. Then, after water was pumped out of its compartments, the dry dock would raise the ship above the water level for repair.

I proceeded from the dry dock to the *Liebenfels*, a six-thousand-ton German freighter which had been raised from the

depths of the harbor by Captain Brown's crew. After her gaping hole had been repaired, she was anchored in the bay for further refurbishing. Barefoot Eritreans, swinging on rope platforms fastened to the railings, half-heartedly pushed their metal scrapers along the steel hull of the ship to remove the barnacles.

The warm waters of the Red Sea encouraged the growth of these crustaceans. Living shell organisms reproduced prolifically in the marine environs of Massawa, where they fed on the plentiful plankton, the tiny organisms that drifted at or near the surface of the water. When exposed to air, barnacles soon created a stench that was almost unbearable under the hot sun.

At the Persian dry dock, the repair crew had just completed the reconditioning, scraping, and painting of a supply vessel, now ready to return to duty in the Mediterranean ferrying supplies from the naval base at Gibraltar to the English army fighting on the Egyptian front. If the the dry dock had not been available to the British naval and supply vessels, the alternative, a voyage to Durban in South Africa more than five thousand miles to the South, would have severely handicapped Montgomery's forces entrenched at El Alamein.

As the powerboat was prepared to shove off at the dry dock, Bill Reed jumped in.

"Paul, did you hear about Wood's accident?"

I had not.

"Wood is in the hospital in bad shape. While hanging up his diving gear in an empty building, he touched a power line carrying three thousand volts of current. It's a miracle he wasn't killed, but the jolt threw him clear. He'll come out of it, but he's terribly burned and will have to be shipped home. We sure needed him."

Wilford Wood, a conscientious, experienced deep-sea diver, was the first casualty of our crew. I would miss his visits to my cabin to listen to my Mendelssohn record—his favorite. Before I had a chance to see him at the Mai Habar hospital in the hills of Eritrea, he had been sent back to the States.

Over two hundred American and European workmen and about three hundred natives were employed at the Massawa naval base. The majority of the natives were skinny Eritreans with protruding foreheads and sunken eyes. Many of them wore parts of Italian uniforms that had been removed from the bodies of soldiers killed by the English in the battle of Cheren—a cap here, a pair of trousers, a shirt, or a coat there. But all were barefoot. The Eritreans, unaccustomed to hard labor in this scorching climate, made only a token effort in scraping barnacles.

In contrast, the Yemenites and the tall, dignified Sudanese were good workmen, intelligent, physically strong, dependable, and performing many diverse tasks.

The British and Americans had sought out and located qualified machinists, carpenters, welders, and other craftsmen among the Italian prisoners of war. Many had been employed on the Massawa naval base prior to the British conquest of Eritrea, and all were now eager to work for the Americans.

But as the Rommel forces harassed Montgomery's army at El Alamein, the Italian workers became defiant with threats of "Just wait until Rommel takes Alexandria and then we'll see who's boss!"

In an offensive operation beginning May 12, 1942, Rommel's

tank forces outflanked the British army and chased it from the border of Tripolitania all the way to El Alamein in Egypt, less than seventy miles from Alexandria, the site of the British Mediterranean naval base. Here, defense positions had been taken by General Auchinleck, Commander of the Middle Eastern forces. In mid-August, Churchill replaced him with General Alexander and appointed General Montgomery to the position of field commander. While waiting for reinforcements, all the English army could hope to do was hold back the German and Italian tank forces at El Alamein.

A salt marsh lying below sea level under a row of cliffs protected Montgomery's southern flank about forty miles south of the coast, in what was called the Quattara Depression. With the southern front almost impregnable, Montgomery had the advantage of concentrating his forces and attention on the western front. His army could not be outflanked, but there was great danger that Rommel's superior ground forces, with the help of his air force, could penetrate Montgomery's defenses in the west.

Although the El Alamein front was only a short plane flight to the north of us, the war was farthest from my mind as I surveyed my new office aboard the *Chamberlain*. In its conversion to a timekeepers' office, the medicines and medical equipment from the sick bay had been transferred to the shore hospital and the bunks removed to make room for my desk, table, and filing cabinets. But even after the walls and floor had been scrubbed, there remained the lingering odor of a hospital operating room.

I worked eighteen hours daily for almost a week setting up

a timekeeping routine for the native and Italian timekeepers and finally succeeded in devising a system that provided me with a maximum amount of leisure time.

A native Eritrean, Abdi by name, a gaunt lad who spoke Italian and could also communicate with the Sudanese and the Yemenites, and two English-speaking Italians were assigned to me as timekeepers.

ABDI
THE AUTHOR'S LARCENOUS ERITREAN TIMEKEEPER

One of the Italians, Renzo, became my assistant, and served as my private secretary. Before the war, he had moved from Milan, Italy, with his wife to become sales agent for Alpha Romeo automobiles in Massawa. They lived in a local apartment with their toddler. I later learned that big-hearted Bill McKelly regularly supplied Renzo with canned milk from our galley because milk was such a scarce commodity.

Whenever I wanted to communicate with a Sudanese, an Eritrean, or a Yemenite, I conveyed my message to Renzo, who in turn translated it into Italian for the benefit of my Eritrean timekeeper, who in turn translated and transmitted it to the native. This lengthy procedure also worked in reverse.

Haile Gebru, a tall Sudanese with a dark, thick, pointed beard, was one of the natives assigned to keep our deck swept and washed and to help the crew move any light equipment. G. H. Carlyle, who had not been assigned any salvage duties in Massawa, decided to appropriate Gebru's services, gave him a broom to sweep in front of his stateroom, and ordered him to stand guard. That's all he did all day long. Gebru was most appreciative and smiled broadly whenever G.H. came by. G.H. responded with a good-natured slap on the back.

I hired Abu Husain, a handsome, turbaned Arab boy, as my man Friday upon the recommendation of his former employer, a British officer. He looked somewhat like Sabu, the movie sensation of the thirties. Although he spoke only Italian and Arabic, he usually understood what tasks I wanted him to perform. If my pantomimed requests did not suffice, Renzo conveyed my message to him.

ABU HUSAIN
THE AUTHOR'S MAN FRIDAY

Abu was immaculate in his appearance, in contrast to the other natives in our employ. He wore shorts and usually a checkered shirt, but, like the other natives, he went barefoot. He kept my clothes washed and pressed, my shoes shined, and my cabin clean and orderly. Whenever he washed and ironed my clothes, he also did his own. It didn't take me long to become accustomed to the luxury of having a personal servant.

At first, the native workmen were transported from the naval dock to the various projects by motor launch on its regular schedule. They were packed so tight in the motorboat that it travelled deep in the water. The American and European workmen had difficulty crowding aboard and many never arrived at their work destination on time. After several days of turmoil, Ellsberg ordered the natives to be transported in the dhow, a seventy five foot Arab sailing vessel with no superstructure.

THE DHOW CARRYING
NATIVES TO WORK PROJECTS

Prior to our arrival, the British had compensated the native workers with an hourly wage of twenty East African cents, the equivalent of five American cents. We doubled the hourly rate, and as a result many of the workers took periodic leaves of absence to spend their extra money. They were actually overpaid, even at the British rate.

It required twenty natives to lift a heavy piece of equipment which four of our men could lift with ease. They devised numerous ways for goofing off. Whenever a heavy task came up, I often saw a Mohammedan take his neck shawl, lay it on the deck of the ship or dry dock where he was assigned, kneel facing Mecca and pray to Allah until the task was completed. Others disappeared in the interim, hiding in accessible places.

The more ambitious Sudanese and Yemenites served as capable mechanics, tending our divers and servicing the gas engines which monitored our salvage pumps. Some proved more skillful and dependable than members of our American crew. For this work, these craftsmen received the eqivalent of a dollar and twenty cents a day in local currency. In contrast, our American workers received two dollars and ten cents an hour and time and a half for overtime in excess of forty-eight hours a week.

Native workmen frequented my office with their problems, reporting lost badges, complaining about insufficient wages, or asking me to patch up their bruises. Unless a wound was promptly bandaged, it festered in the humid Massawa climate and flies attacked and infected it, resulting in an ailment known as the "Massawa rot."

Each native wore a numbered badge and was paid weekly

upon signing his name or providing a finger print. One day I made a tour of the various projects to check the natives on the payroll. I failed to find many of those reported by Abdi, my Eritrean timekeeper, on his daily runs. I located some workmen sleeping between decks on ships and some in compartments on the dry dock. All those I did not find working were removed from the payroll.

Abdi had expanded the payroll by daily reporting thirty natives who never appeared for work. With the help of a few cohorts, he collected the wages for all thirty, himself. Although ingenuity was to be admired, I discharged him. His not-so-clever replacement was difficult to work with, and I regretted losing my intelligent, albeit larcenous, timekeeper.

He returned after a few days and requested a contribution from me for a trip into the hinterland of Eritrea and Ethiopia in search of souvenirs—native weapons and other handicraft. I gave him the equivalent of twenty American dollars, scarcely expecting to ever again see him, much less the promised souvenirs.

But three weeks later he returned laden with a large collection of native spears, hand-forged swords, castrating knives, and rhinoceros hide shields. I selected a few of the treasures and our crew members enthusiastically bought the remainder, giving him more than enough local currency to engage in a second foraging. Abdi had become a successful entrepeneur.

CHAPTER 18

MASSAWA ADVENTURES AND MISADVENTURES

THE WAR: Rommel's German panzer divisions advanced on the Alam Halfa Ridge within striking distance of Alexandria, Egypt. Montgomery's forces repulsed the attack, and Rommel, in need of reinforcements and supplies, took defense positions on the El Alamein battle lines early in September of 1942.

First Assistant Engineer Gibson was full of resentment. He couldn't forget Horace Armstrong's insubordination and his contemptuous remarks dished out en route from San Diego. In the past, while in the merchant marine service, he was accustomed to respectful treatment from his oilers, firemen, and water tenders, no matter how much he vilified and abused them. But the men in our engine room had agreed to work aboard ship only as a means to get to Massawa. They also were used to being treated with respect and consideration in their jobs before joining the _Chamberlain_.

Upon our arrival in Massawa, Armstrong, in his capacity as boilermaker, was assigned to work on the large dry dock.

Gibson approached Lloyd Williams, foreman of our salvage operation, to inform him that Armstrong was a troublemaker and could not be trusted.

"I'll judge the fellow myself," was the foreman's cool response. When Armstrong came on the job, Williams relayed Gibson's warning. Armstrong was enraged and vowed to his friends that as soon as he met up with the first assistant, he was going to teach him a lesson.

That evening Armstrong joined his shipmates for a few beers at the JD&P canteen. Word had gotten around to all of its patrons that he was laying for the first assistant.

When Gibson stepped into the canteen, there was sudden silence. The men watched him make his way to the beer counter without recognizing anyone. Armstrong got up, took long strides toward Gibson, who was facing the bartender, and tapped him on the shoulder. In a loud voice he exclaimed, "I've been waiting for you!"

Gibson's face reddened as he faced the former pugilist. There was not even the sound of one clanking glass. All eyes were on the two antagonists.

"What the hell d'ya want?" he demanded.

"You tried to queer me with Williams, you dirty rat!" Armstrong couldn't contain himself any longer. Anger had built up in him during the 106 days of being cursed at and forced to do the filthiest jobs in the engine room, and Gibson's comments to Williams provided the final trigger. Armstrong pummeled him with both fists.

Gibson hit the floor, his face bloodied and several front teeth missing. He picked himself up and headed for the JD&P first aid station, mumbling something about setting the authorities on Armstrong. Armstrong's friends let out a loud cheer.

In the weeks that followed, Gibson tried to claim payment

from JD&P for the loss of his teeth, but we never learned whether he succeeded.

Massawa provided entertainment centers, including a night club, the Torino, where the bartenders served unsavory beer, wine, and liquors. Over seventy sex-starved males competed for the attention of six bar girls, some Italian, some half Caucasian and half Arab. They bought the girls high-priced non-alcoholic drinks for the privilege of taking them in their arms and waltzing them around the dance floor. But the girls refused to associate with the men away from the Torino, undoubtedly because a few days' visit to the local filthy jail awaited them if caught by the British authorities.

Perhaps the integrity of the Massawa brothel had to be protected against competition from the bar girls, since it was operated by the British army. An army sergeant was delegated to collect the going rate of fees from its patrons and to distribute prophylactics to them. The British army also provided the services of a doctor for bi-weekly physical examinations of the brothel girls in an effort to minimize sexually-transmittable diseases among the girls and their patrons.

Some of the men from our ship rented houses in Asmara or Massawa for appoximately twenty-five dollars a month and then hired Italian or native housekeepers to keep and play house. Permission had to be obtained from the British army office for a rental house, and, in addition, a housekeeper had to undergo a physical examination before approval. Some of the men boasted that they had a real home away from home, oblivious to the promises made to wives and sweethearts upon takeoff from San

Diego.

JD&P arranged for water, bottled at a local plant, to be delivered daily to all salvage projects, including the *Chamberlain*, together with a large supply of ice to make the water drinkable. Because of the intense heat, perspiration oozed from our bodies, even without exertion. In a climate with normal humidity, the evaporation of the sweat provides some relief from the intense heat; but in Massawa, the degree of humidity being one of the highest in the world, it clung to our bodies, increasing the discomfort. The perspiration also leeched out the body mineral salts, so vital to maintain protection against fatigue and the sun's heat. Besides gulping lots of liquids, we frequently swallowed salt tablets.

During the early part of our stay in Massawa, there was an adequate supply of coke, root beer, and grape and pineapple juice. Every few weeks a truckload of American beer was shipped from Asmara to our canteen. It was rationed, one can at a time, so five of us made trips between our table and the beer counter until twenty-five cans or more had been accumulated. We then returned to the ship for an evening of tippling.

As time passed the beer trucks arrived less often, and the supply of root beer, coke, and grape and pineapple juice was not replenished.

On rare occasions the British officers' bar sold me a bottle of Haig and Haig Scotch whiskey, but word traveled fast and friends emptied my bottle in short order.

After sampling the beer, wines, and liquors produced by the Mellotti brothers in Massawa and served at the Turino night club, I diligently avoided imbibing further, because all the local alcoholic beverages tasted foul and were harsh to the throat.

During the first week of our arrival, prickly heat eruptions that itched unbearably covered my body. After the initial attack, I spent more time in my air-conditioned office and the rash subsided.

But the workmen who labored under the Massawa sun suffered interminably. After a week or two, working twelve to sixteen hours a day, some at strenuous labor, most of them developed extensive heat rashes and convalesced for a few days in Asmara or Ghinda, enjoying the cool breezes of the plateau. Frequently the open sores became infected by contact with rusty metal, barnacles, and sometimes by the African flies that clung to the skin like honey and abounded ashore in great numbers; but fortunately they seldom frequented the dry docks or the ships at anchor.

Enormous cockroaches invaded our deck, and my assistant and I often interrupted the preparation of time sheets to go on a swatting spree to keep them in check.

After only a few weeks on the job some of the American workers made an exodus to the JD&P office in Asmara to hand in their resignations. At first the administrative officers gave a number of them a raise in pay and talked them into returning to Massawa and continue working. To others they offered construction jobs in the cool hill areas. Men who faithfully stayed on the job, without complaining, were ignored and continued working at their original pay scale.

After awhile JD&P authorities no longer pampered the complainers but accepted their resignations. The work contract required that the resigning employee be returned to the place where he had been hired, but transportation out of Massawa or Asmara was unavailable for weeks at a time. Meanwhile, his pay having been terminated, he had to provide his own food and lodging at great expense. Furthermore, upon returning to the United States, a young ex-employee faced the possibility of a call from his draft board.

Through it all, we never lacked for news or scuttlebutt about what was going on in our little part of the world.

One evening an American worker was found injured and unconscious on the road into Massawa. Tire marks on the dusty road indicated that he had been hit by a jeep. None had been released from the JP&D car pool for that evening, but the authorities suspected Wes Hewson of having hot-wired a jeep and gone out on the town. At the Massawa base, he was assigned to service the launches that transported the men from job to job.

Although Wes vehemently denied the charge, and there was no proof of his guilt, the Provost Marshal locked him up because of his combined reputation as a skilled electrician, a mischief maker, and an auto craftsman. Even though the American worker recovered, Wes remained in custody. He was fed well enough, and his faithful friends supplied him with an ample quantity of liquor. Although kept locked up, he had little surveillance.

During Wes's confinement Captain Ellsberg's private launch was taken out for a joy ride. When it was returned and backed up to the dock, the propellor was badly bent, thus depriving Ellsberg of his sea transportation. Bending the propellor back to its original shape was a delicate task, since a little variance would put the boat in jeopardy. Ellsberg knew that Wes was capable of fixing it, but since Wes was locked up, he had not suspected Wes of causing the damage. In actual fact, Wes had managed to pick the door lock of his confined quarters and travel about whenever he was so inclined.

When Ellsberg sent for him, Wes insisted that the Captain come to see him in his locked room. Ellsberg finally consented. When he asked Wes to repair the propellor, Wes demanded a complete pardon for the jeep affair. Reluctantly, Captain Ellsberg signed the pardon, which Wes had already conveniently prepared. He then bent the propellor back to its original shape, regained his freedom, and the launch was returned to service.

After his release, Wes accumulated lumber together with tools and other supplies from the carpentry shop and set about building a boat for himself so that he could get around the harbor without depending upon the infrequent launches. From time to time I watched it take shape. It evolved into a six-footer that resembled a craft frequently seen at lake resorts. He managed to acquire and equip it with an outboard motor and thereafter often went ashore. It was a long ride to the dock. Watching him take off, I sometimes wondered if he would make it safely back to the ship.

He bought a motorcyle from an Italian workman. One evening, having imbibed freely from his private stock, he mounted the motorcycle, sped down the naval dock and catapulted into the water. He only sustained a few bruises, but the vehicle sank to the bottom. The next day he dove into the warm water, tied a rope on the cycle and with the help of a few friends, pulled it out.

On another occasion, he barged into my office and handed me a wine bottle. "Thought you'd like a souvenir of the deep."

Taken in by his offering, I thanked him profusely and asked, "Where did you get this bottle?"

"Oh, Ellsberg, Huck, Buckey and I decided to get a peek at the cargo of that passenger liner lying deep in the channel. Huck went down into the hold and discovered a cargo of wine. He brought up a few bottles and when we took a closer look we found that worms had eaten through the corks." Pointing to the bottle, he said, "So this is only good as a souvenir."

He could afford to give it up.

CHAPTER 19

WORK ON THE XXIII MARZO

THE WAR: After landing on Guadalcanal on August 7th, 1942, U.S. Marines constructed the Henderson Air Field which was opened to U.S. combat aircraft on August 20th, 1942. This airfield proved invaluable as a base to aid the U.S. forces to defeat the Japanese in the South Pacific.

In the Massawa naval harbor, the *Chamberlain* was secured by two of the ship's anchors that had been dropped to the sea bottom and by eight lines, three fastened to the deck of the sunken *XXIII Marzo* just a stone's throw away, three connected to floating buoys, and two anchored to underwater cement blocks.

Locating the underwater cement blocks, positioned by the British before our arrival, had proven elusive in the murky Massawa waters.

The British naval establishment ignored our request for information on their emplacement, adding to the prejudice of some of our crew against the British navy. One of our divers finally succeeded in locating the blocks and fastening the lines.

Our ship's boilers had been shut down, and it would have taken hours to reactivate them before our ship could navigate on its own power.

Twenty days after our arrival, gale winds swept across the Massawa harbor. While preparing time sheets for the Asmara office, I was unexpectedly thrown backwards in my chair as our ship swung wildly. Dashing out on deck, I found that we were floating perilously toward the Persian dry dock, which supported a freighter undergoing repair. Our lines to the *Marzo* had snapped!

THE CHAMBERLAIN ANCHORED BY
THE SCUTTLED S.S. XXIII MARZO

I hastened around to starboard to check the lines attached to the anchor blocks and the buoys. Fortunately they held, and those lines, together with the anchors, prevented a great catastrophe—the sinking of the dry dock, the freighter it was carrying, and not least, the *Chamberlain.*

With the winds came the desert sands. Visibility was almost zero. There was no protection from the grit. It filtered into my hair, ears, nose, and mouth, and even under my fingernails. My sunglasses didn't protect my eyes from the irritating particles. I covered my face as best I could to keep from breathing in and swallowing the gritty stuff. It piled up on deck. Even after the winds subsided, a thick haze hung over the harbor. I took refuge in the cozy comfort of my cabin.

Third Mate Olsson entered. The captain had placed him in charge of supervising the salvage work on the *Marzo.* He was a slender man of forty-seven years, soft spoken, courteous and friendly. Having spent many years in isolation from the world, captaining small fishing boats, he preferred the seclusion of his cabin when not on duty reading adventure stories in preference to consorting with the crew.

"That was a helluva storm!" he exclaimed. "Lucky we weren't out there working on that wreck. Say, could I borrow one of your books?"

I scanned my shelf and took down *Pearls, Arms and Hashish* by Henri de Monfreid and Ida Treat. "I think you'll enjoy this, Mate. It's a saga of a Frenchman searching for pearls in the Red Sea area. Has a lot of local color."

"Thanks, Purse. Sounds interesting."

"Say, by the way, Mate, when do you start working on the

Marzo?"

"Tomorrow morning," he replied. "What about joining us to get a close look at her? We'll be shoving off around eight bells."

Early the following day Olsson led the way down the gangway. Two divers, Huck Daughtery and Patty Geitner, and two diver's tenders, Arthur Dalton, and Hugh Anderson, were already in the launch. They were surprised to see me.

PATTY GETINER, IN DIVER'S SUIT,
HUCK DAUGHERTY AND ART DALTON ON
BARGE TO WORK ON SALVAGING XXIII MARZO

"You diving, too, Purser?" Huck asked.

I laughed. "No way. Just wanted to watch you fellows at

work."

Dalton steered our boat to the diving platform. Because it was impossible for divers to work from the deck of the *Chamberlain* high above the water level, the carpenters had constructed a large raft to be used as a platform from which the divers could jump to inspect and repair the damage to the *Marzo*. A canopy, supported by pipes fastened to the floor of the raft, had also been constructed to provide shade from the hot Massawa sun.

The raft was tied to the *Marzo's* superstructure on the starboard side, thus protecting it from the fury of the storm. Patty brushed the accumulated sand off the raft and the diving suits. It was then hauled to the bow of the *Marzo*.

I noticed that the divers were wearing heavy woolen underwear. "In this heat, Huck, how come you're wearing longies?" I inquired.

He grinned. "If I didn't wear 'em, I'd be drowned in sweat down under. The underwear absorbs it. You know the water temperature is ninety-eight degrees."

With the help of the divers' tenders, Huck and Patty crawled into their one-piece rubberized canvas suits. Dalton and Anderson put the brass breastplates over their heads, then fastened them to the suits with thumb screws. The breastplates provided protection to the chest and neck from the heavy pressure of the water. Next, the divers put on their helmets equipped with an exhaust valve that could be adjusted by hand on the outside and also by leaning the face against it on the inside.

After hooking the telephone connections into the earphones in the helmet, they fitted the twenty-seven pound shoes. A heavy belt was buckled around each diver's waist and suspended with straps from the shoulders. The tenders connected air hoses to the helmets and fastened the divers' lifelines with straps under their right arms. They then forced air into the suits by an air compressor that had just been activated. The suits were now air and watertight. Huck and Patty were ready to take the plunge.

"What's the day's diving schedule?" I asked Olsson.

"They'll examine the hull from the outside to check on the damage, and in this murky water they've got a problem. They must do a lot of work by feel. After they look over the outside of the *Marzo*, they're going inside to map the layout of the ship and look for bombs."

As we talked, the divers let themselves down from the platform and disappeared into the sea, leaving a trail of bubbles. The tenders watched the air pressure and listened intently to the divers' reports as the lifelines and the communication cables lengthened. Huck examined the hull on the port side, and Patty inspected the starboard side.

Even with the canopy to protect us from the hot rays of the sun, the heat was stifling and I longed for the comfort of my air-conditioned office. I now understood why a number of our crew reported sick from time to time and took off for the rest camps in the cool highlands.

After examining the hull for three hours, Patty reported that the starboard side was intact, but Huck found two large holes in the port hull of the *Marzo*. I was relieved when the divers returned to the raft and our shore boat ferried us back to the

Chamberlain for lunch.

In the next few days the divers located an undetonated bomb in number one hold and lifted it out carefully. The British navy personnel exploded it on the beach.

The jagged metal protruding from the holes in the hull was cut away with underwater acetylene torches. To cover the holes, cofferdams consisting of large wooden patches were constructed. These wooden patches, one on the outside of the ship and another on the inside, were then bolted in place, and sacks of cement inserted between the patches were forced to the bottom. More cement was then poured in to make the patch watertight.

When all the *Marzo's* valves and decks were closed or otherwise covered and the holds made watertight, the plan was to pump out the water, permitting the air to rush into the holds from the vents protruding above the water level, thus making the ship buoyant.

However, the work on the *XXIII Marzo* never progressed beyond the cofferdam stage. With a severe shortage of salvage men, Captain Ellsberg assigned the *Chamberlain* crew to work on other projects that were more critical. After observing all of the effort put into preparation to salvage the *Marzo*, I was disappointed to learn that she was destined to remain in her Red Sea grave—at least during our Massawa stay.

CHAPTER 20

WE LOSE ARMSTRONG

THE WAR: On August 19, 1942, Allied troops, under cover of naval and airforce bombardment, invaded France at Dieppe, but the German defense forces had been alerted by reports from their patrolling E-boats which had encountered the invading flotilla in the English Channel. It was a disaster for the Allies, with a heavy loss of life.

About the last of August, Ellsberg started work on the small dry dock completely submerged in the naval harbor, the top surface of its sidewall chambers more than nine feet under water. Explosives planted by the Italians had blasted large holes in seven of the eight floor compartments. It had been scuttled near the large dry dock, which had been salvaged months before and was still undergoing repairs.

Usually, after breakfast and before the heat of the sun made life outside of my air-conditioned room uncomfortable, I traveled in the scheduled motor boat between the various projects in the naval harbor to observe the progress of our salvage activities.

Carpenters had constructed a wooden walkway eleven feet above each of the submerged decks of the dry dock's two sidewalls. The first time I saw Ellsberg, he was directing operations from the newly constructed walkway, his shirt in tatters but the gold braid epaulets signifying his captain's naval rank still in place on his shoulders.

THE SCUTTLED DRYDOCK ON THE
BOTTOM OF THE MASSAWA HARBOR

I learned from the salvage crew that Ellsberg was dedicated in his determination to get the Massawa naval base ready to repair and service allied fighting and supply ships. Not a man to sit in his office directing the salvage, he was on the site whenever any critical job was in progress. Sometimes he worked continuously on a twenty-four hour stretch, helping where needed, assigning jobs to supervisors and solving any technical problems that might occur. He never asked any workman to perform a task which he, himself, would not undertake.

CAPTAIN EDWARD ELLSBERG, USNR AND
DIVER DOCK KIMBLE ON SUNKEN DRYDOCK WALKWAY

The huge Sutorbilt low-pressure salvage air compressor and assembly, unloaded from the *Chamberlain*, was secured on a barge moored to the outside of the starboard wall of the sunken dry dock. It had the combined capacity of four of the compressors used in raising the first dry dock prior to our arrival. A second Sutorbilt air compressor ordered by Ellsberg had been shipped to Massawa on a cargo vessel, unloaded, and placed on a train bound for the Asmara warehouse of JD&P to be inventoried, never to resurface.

Ellsberg repeatedly questioned JD&P personnel as to the whereabouts of the compressor, but they informed him that it had disappeared en route and could not be traced. They also reported that an entire loaded railroad train had disappeared between Massawa and Asmara. How a compressor and its assembly, as big as a room, and an entire train could vanish in seventy mile stretch of railroad through the sparsely populated arid land of Eritrea, remained a mystery.

Starting September 10th, an Ingersoll Rand compressor, one fourth the capacity of the missing Sutorbilt, pumped air into the port sidewalls, and the original Sutorbilt pumped air into the starboard sidewalls, pushing water out through holes at the bottom.

Air bubbles rose to the surface of the water from holes in the roofs and sidewalls of the compartments. Alerted to the location of leaks, Al Watson, wearing a face mask, and Don Kimble, in his diving suit, submerged to caulk them. Three days later the starboard wall rose to the surface. As soon as any part of the submerged sidewall appeared above water, natives set to work scraping the barnacles.

As the starboard sidewall, made buoyant by the injection of compressed air, emerged above water level, welders, shipfitters, and mechanics entered the compartments to plug leaks that appeared in its roofs and walls. The air compressors kept running day and night, and because few experienced personnel were available, the men worked twelve to sixteen hours a day. Even the night did not provide relief from the intense heat. The air compressors had to be serviced around the clock.

THE DRYDOCK PARTIALLY SALVAGED

But the port sidewall would not budge from the bottom of

the harbor.

The day after the starboard wall rose out of the water, the air compressors became overheated and had to be shut down. Ellsberg ordered them to be restarted as the starboard wall began to sink. Suddenly the port wall, so firmly stuck in the mud, rose three to four feet, while the starboard wall sank slowly down below the water level, flooding the compartments in which many workmen were caulking leaks in the side walls.

As the water entered the sidewall compartments, workers emerged and swam to the wooden walkway, the only part of the starboard wall structure still above water. Foreman Lloyd Williams attempted to identify and account for all his men.

But Armstrong, Larson, and Jones were missing. They had entered the aft compartment to close a particularly large hole in the wall. Since no diver was immediately available to go after the men, Captain Ellsberg dove into the water, pushed open the submerged compartment door and dragged them out, one at a time. All three men were unconscious. Larsen and Jones were revived, but in spite of intense resuscitation efforts, Armstrong could not be brought back to life. His death was a great blow to the morale of the base.

The air compressors had cooled off and were finally restarted. Five hours later, the starboard sidewall floated up again and additional compressors pumped air into the port sidewall. By sunrise on September 15th, the port and starboard walls were well out of the water. The dry dock had been raised in sixteen days, a feat the English salvage men on the base had deemed an impossibility.

One of the first tasks of the divers was to enter the eighth

*THE DRYDOCK NOW FLOATING
BARNACLES AND ALL*

*BAREFOOT NATIVES AT WORK ON
THE SALVAGED DRYDOCK*

compartment, which had not been blasted. They found a bomb loaded with two hundred pounds of TNT. A manila bridle was attached to it and a dozen men carefully lifted it out of the hold. It was detonated on the beach.

That evening, Bill Reed, the Skipper, and I discussed the events of the day. Bill's voice was strained and subdued. "That guy Armstrong, he's sure going to be missed. Just a couple of weeks ago, the British cruiser, the Dido, was being repaired on the Persian dry dock by the English workmen sent down from the shipyard at Alexandria. The Eyties in the foundry ashore cut a steel plate to patch a leak in the ship's stern, but they didn't knuckle it like the plate that had been removed. The English workmen, some of them husky, said they couldn't knuckle the plate and that no one could do it without special machines. Ellsberg sent for Armstrong and Cunningham. In an hour and a half, with a couple of heavy sledge hammers, they had knuckled the plate so that it fit perfectly. We just can't replace Armstrong."

Horace Armstrong was the second of our crew to die. "Hoot" Ralph, had succumed to pneumonia a few weeks before. Wood, the diver who had been seriously injured when he touched live electric wires, arrived safely at his home in California, and the prognosis for his recovery was good.

CHAPTER 21

THE WINTHROP ERA

THE WAR: Although Hitler had signed a non-aggression pact with Russia in August of 1939, the German army invaded Russia on June 22, 1941, on a nine hundred mile front in an operation designated BARBAROSSA, besieging Leningrad and coming within nineteen miles of Moscow by December 5, 1941. In spite of the rigors of the Russian winter, the Germans retained their advanced positions and by November of 1942 had occupied Sevastopol on the Black Sea and threatened to overrun Stalingrad.

Bill Reed strode into my office in early September, his bushy eyebrows underlining deep furrows on his forehead. "Paul," he said. "Prepare a complaint 'To Whom It May Concern' about JD&P's policy on supplies and equipment ordered by Ellsberg from the States. It just doesn't make sense. After the stuff is unloaded from ships here in Massawa, it is shipped all the way to Asmara to be inventoried, instead of being delivered directly to us here.

"Lots of times the trucks carrying supplies, equipment, and foodstuffs from the Asmara warehouses to us in Massawa, will pass trucks loaded with similar items on the way from the

Massawa docks to the Asmara warehouses. It's a sheer waste of time and effort, gasoline, and wear and tear on trucks. And more often than not, the items we order from the States that are hauled to Asmara, never get back to us.

"And also emphasize that we need those salvage men JD&P are stealing from us. I'll make an appointment with the local army intelligence officer. He can pass the complaint on to the army big shots in Cairo."

I was only too familiar with all of these problems, having heard Reed, Hansen, and Williams discuss the failure of JD&P's personnel to cooperate with the salvage staff. I prepared the detailed complaint.

Reed lost no time getting in touch with the U.S. army intelligence officer. About nine o'clock the next morning I was shocked to see a broad-shouldered, heavy-set U.S. army lieutenant with a prominent nose and a debonaire mustache enter the officer's mess.

"Bob Winthrop!" I sputtered. "You—the intelligence officer?"

I knew Winthrop back in Los Angeles. Travel was our common interest. He lectured about his China experiences, and I gave a few talks about my European and Central American adventures. We had big plans to travel by kayak from Point Barrow, Alaska, to San Francisco, expecting to arrive there for the opening of the Golden Gate International World's Fair on February 18, 1939. But the plan was scrubbed for lack of funds. I always admired how clever it was of him to arrange to reside in a building called the Winthrop Apartments. Initially, I had thought he was its owner, instead of just a tenant.

"Paul!" His eyes opened wide as he held out his hand. "What

the devil are you doing here?"

We were bringing each other up to date when Bill Reed, who was pacing the floor, interrupted us.

"Let's get our business over with first, Lieutenant. We're not getting any cooperation from Johnson, Drake & Piper." Reed handed the complaint to Winthrop somewhat impatiently. "See that the army authorities in Cairo receive this. If we don't get the salvage materials and equipment we need and keep our men on the job, we'll have to shut down the naval harbor and give up." He stomped off.

Winthrop looked at me quizzically. "Say Paul, I've got a complaint in my files about somebody on your ship by the name of Carlyle. I was going to contact your captain. Is he a spy? What do you know about him?"

So Chasen was still on the warpath..

"Carlyle's okay, Bob. I bet you heard from Dr. Chasen. He complained to army intelligence in Panama and in Rio. Carlyle was thoroughly investigated. Chasen just wanted to give him a hard time. Carlyle's a friend of mine."

That was the end of the Chasen-Carlyle affair.

During our stay in Massawa, the army designated Winthrop to serve in various capacities at different times: as intelligence officer, provost marshal, quartermaster procurement officer, and finance officer, in that order. To whatever post he was assigned, he assumed a supercilious, pompous manner, accentuated by a swagger stick which he waved flamboyantly at every opportunity. He could have been taken for a British officer masquerading in a U.S. army officer's uniform.

The men piloting the shore boats complained that when he

stepped aboard he pointed his swagger stick to his destination. If it was our ship, he barked in an authoritative voice, "Take me to the *Chamberlain*," even though the next scheduled stop was the small dry dock. They were intimidated by his commanding presence and initially followed his orders. It delayed the arrival of workmen at their projects and upset the carefully arranged schedule of the boatmen. They complained to Lloyd Williams, who told them in no uncertain terms that no one, except himself, Bill Reed, and Captain Ellsberg, was to change the schedule of the boats.

I later inquired of Bill Reed whether he had any response to the complaint we had given to Winthrop.

"Looks like it's been buried up there in Cairo, unless it never got there."

I asked Winthrop about our petition.

"Oh, I passed it on to Cairo," was his only comment. Nothing further was heard about our "To Whom It May Concern" letter.

Having found an old friend, and with time on his hands, Winthrop persistently demanded my attention, requesting that I accompany him on numerous junkets. I didn't object, since life was getting somewhat humdrum aboard the Chamberlain.

He had an Italian driver for his Lancia, who on numerous occasions drove us to the local open air theater to view such films as *The Boys from Syracuse*, *The Hunchback of Notre Dame*, Hardy comedies and a multitude of lesser known flickers projected from a sixteen millimeter machine, which often broke down at the most exciting parts. The air was filled with nasty invectives when the operator put the film in upside down or failed to focus properly, and intermission was punctuated by catcalls and shouting.

One day Winthrop barged into my office.

"Paul, I've got a couple of Italian rifles from the armory. Let's go hunting."

Although hunting was not my sport, I decided to go along for the ride. I put Renzo in charge, grabbed my sun hat, and we were off. It was early November, and the thermometer was a cool ninety degrees Fahrenheit.

Winthrop's Italian driver awaited us on the dock in the Lancia. He took us fifty miles westward over ungraded desert roads into the hinterland. Occasionally we passed a caravan of camels carrying twigs, water, and unidentifiable cargo. Our driver spied half a dozen gazelles grazing in the distance. Leaving the beaten trail, he sped over the parched Eritrean wasteland at an accelerated pace. To my relief, as soon as the gazelles detected us they were off and away. Had they competed on a race track with War Admiral, the latter would have been left far behind.

We followed the fleeing gazelles over hills and through riverbeds. Sometimes it seemed as though our driver intended to take us right through the bushes, but he always swerved just in time. Finally, we got within rifle range. Bob took careful aim. As he fired, the driver took a sharp turn to the right to avoid a large rock. By the time Bob had inserted another bullet in his single-shot rifle, the gazelles, fortunately, were out of sight. It was impossible to hit anything from the bouncy Lancia. Every time our driver stopped so we could take aim, the gazelles had fled, to Bob's disgust and to my relief. I had no desire for such a trophy.

As we headed for home, our gear shift broke and the Lancia could only travel in high gear. Fortunately, we encountered no steep hills.

Winthrop was a devoted souvenir hunter and fiercely possessive of his acquisitions. I spent many an hour waiting for him while he visited Asmara shops in search of jewelry and precious stones, cut and uncut. He had the facility to bargain and, before purchasing a stone, insisted that it be tested for authenticity. I was impressed by the collection he displayed in his quarters.

On one of our outings en route from Asmara to Massawa, we detoured to Gura, the American air base operated by the Douglas Aircraft Corporation on the site of a former Italian air depot constructed for Mussolini's conquest of Ethiopia.

Winding our way to the Gura complex, we passed tremendous boulders towering high over the barren lands of the plateau. Hangars, hospital facilities, housing, and a 7500 foot runway came into view. Winthrop and I got out of the car and approached a Douglas employee at the entrance to one of the warehouses.

Winthrop opened the conversation. "You've got quite a city here."

"Yes, we've got over a thousand workmen in this complex."

"I'm Bob Winthrop, army finance officer, and this is Paul Behm. He's from the salvage group in Massawa."

"Al Zampolino, Superintendent of the Accessories Division," the Douglas employee replied. "Are you looking for anyone?"

"No, we're just poking around."

Zambolimo took us on a walking tour of the air base, pointing out the various facilities where planes were being repaired and aircraft assembled.

"Every day, damaged RAF planes arrive from the Egyptian front," he explained. "Some are flown in, many have been disassembled and arrive on trucks, others are unloaded from boats at Massawa and trucked here. We've repaired hundreds. Some of our personnel have even been flown to the North African war front to repair the planes on site.

"And we've also received a number of shiploads of airplane components from the States to be assembled and flown to the war front."

After leaving the Douglas complex, we returned to Massawa. Our driver took us to the famous salt beds where the hot African sun evaporated almost two million gallons of water daily in the extensive flat basins connected by canals to the Red Sea, leaving vast quantities of salt.

Natives scooped up the deposits in buckets and hauled it to a dumping ground beyond a high dam surrounding the basins. After it was all removed from the basins, they were again filled with water from the Red Sea. Before the war, Eritrea exported boatloads of salt to Japan.

For a time Winthrop acted as the officer in charge of the American Volunteer Guard that had been organized to stop any invasion of Massawa by the German army. He ordered several of its members to act as sentinels aboard the *Tripolitania*, a passenger vessel that Brown's men had raised from the bottom of the Massawa harbor. Bob had decided that guards were needed to prevent the removal and theft of parts of the vessel. He promised they would receive overtime compensation for their efforts. Actually, Winthrop had no authority to make such a commitment.

The men acting as guards were also employed in the salvage operation, and only Lloyd Williams was authorized to promise any kind of remuneration. Upon learning of this affair, Williams refused to sanction the overtime pay, and the persons who had spent time guarding the *Tripolitania* didn't hesitate to vent their anger on Winthrop whenever they met up with him.

While discussing Winthrop at a shore gathering of JD&P salvage and other personnel, Edward Mahoney, the assistant business manager resident in Massawa, remarked, "If you see anyone running around shaking his head and muttering, 'He shouldn't have done it,' you'll know he's talking about Winthrop."

Winthrop diligently appeared at meetings of our American Volunteer Guard, but the training sessions were a farce. We had access to the rifles taken from the Italians when Eritrea was invaded by the British army in 1941. I was assigned the rank of lieutenant but had purposely obliterated all memory of training rules and procedures taught in a summer session with the National Guard in Wisconsin more than twelve years before. No one in our local guard was qualified to initiate a training schedule for the thirty men who had volunteered, but, fortified with the Italian rifles, we managed to go through the basic motions of shouldering arms and marching in formation. At the second meeting, only a few of us attended.

But when it came time for target practice, all thirty men participated, traveling in a number of jeeps to a beach away from Massawa proper. Using the captured Italian rifles, we fired at target boards and bottles, most of the shots going astray. We blamed the Italian rifles. My ears rang for days after the shooting spree.

Our ship's radio kept us informed daily of the skirmishes by Rommel's panzer divisions on the El Alamein front and the bombing missions of his air force over the Alexandria naval base and British troop positions. There was the ominous possibility that Massawa would be overrun by the Germans and Italians.

On August 30th, Rommel began his major assault. Montgomery's lines held. While the British were consolidating their lines, little news of any British reinforcements leaked out. On October 23rd Montgomery's planes, tanks, and infantry took the offensive. The battle ensued for twelve days, resulting in great casualties for both the British and the Axis forces. By November 3rd, Rommel was in full retreat.

But even before the news of Montomgery's success reached us, enthusiasm for the Home Guard had waned and meetings were canceled for lack of participants.

Winthrop was transferred to yet another post in the hills of Eritrea, and I lost touch with him.

CHAPTER 22

ORDERS TO SAIL

THE WAR: *On November 8th, 1942, Allied forces commanded by General Dwight D. Eisenhower invaded North Africa in an operation code-named "Torch," against stiff resistance by Vichy French forces. After three days of fighting around Casablanca, Oran, and Algiers, the Vichy French capitulated.*

Before arriving in Massawa, Captain Hansen had imbibed in alcohol only moderately. Although he drank regularly, he was always in complete control aboard ship. Life in Massawa changed all that. In his capacity as salvage master, he had been assigned the project of raising the *XXIII MARZO* from the depths of the Massawa harbor. In the initial stages, it only required the involvement of Third Mate Olsson and the divers and their tenders to seek out and put temporary underwater patches on any holes in the ship's plates. As a result, our captain had a lot of free and boring time on his hands.

He managed to get plenty of beer and whiskey from the British naval base canteen and occasionally traveled to Asmara where spirits were easily obtainable. Frustrated by inactivity and lack of involvement in salvage activities, he began drinking excessively. The JD&P authorities in Asmara saw Hansen in an inebriated condition on several occasions and thereafter treated him as a sot. That bothered me a lot because I had come to respect his many good qualities and was very fond of him.

Don McAllister came by one evening as I stood at the railing viewing the wrecks of the vessels in the calm waters off our starboard bow, highlighted by a half moon, the silence disturbed only by the swishing of the water against the steel plates of our vessel and the continuous splashing of jumping fish.

Upon our arrival in Massawa, Don had taken over the position as steward on the *Chamberlain*, having served in that capacity aboard the *Tug Intent* on its voyage from the States. In spite of his many years at sea in the galley, he had retained his lanky figure, in contrast to many a chef and steward whose corpulent body attested to a ravenous appetite and a weakened will in a culinary atmosphere. His debonaire manners and solicitous concern for others captivated not only the officers, but the crew as well.

We had excellent food ever since he came aboard to relieve Peters as steward. However, in spite of his likable personality and his talent to procure the best provisions from Asmara and from suppliers ashore in Massawa, he never did manage to serve us the good coffee that we knew had been transhipped to Asmara.

Some of our men contributed a supply of fresh fish almost daily. The local waters proved to be well-stocked and the fish very cooperative. In fact, they leaped into our launch on a number of occasions as we returned from an evening ashore.

"Out for some fresh air?" I asked.

"No. I've got a message for the captain."

Being curious, I followed him to Hansen's quarters, where Lloyd Williams and Hansen were drinking beer. I joined Williams on the settee while McAllister took a chair.

The salvage men were fiercely loyal to Williams, a six foot-three, brawny-shouldered construction worker from New York, who was always sympathetic to the needs and problems of his men.

McAllister faced Hansen. "Captain, I got a written order from Asmara to stock up the *Tug Intent* with food from our galley. You want me to do that?"

Ordinarily the steward would have complied with the request, but he knew that Hansen was not on speaking terms with Brown, the tug's captain, and he didn't want to antagonize our skipper.

Williams chimed in, "Say, I heard rumors that Captain Brown plans to take the big shots from Asmara on a fishing expedition."

Hansen's naturally red face took on a darker hue. He got up from his chair and paced the room. His blue eyes peeked out below his furrowed brow. He rolled his lower lip over his upper lip, and you could see his jaw firming.

"Steward," he began in a low voice, enunciating each syllable. "Not one ounce of food is going aboard the *Intent* from this ship. I'll teach those bigwigs in Asmara that they can't expect any help from me after the way they're treating me. And Brown doesn't get any favors from me, either." He lit his pipe and puffed furiously.

Williams complained, "Those JD&P big shots know nothing about salvage operations, and yet they're trying to run us. Ellsberg doesn't get any cooperation from the Asmara gang.

They're waiting to put Brown in charge because Brown caters to them."

The next morning, the skipper came into my office to borrow scissors to cut holes in his hat for ventilation.

"It's just too damned hot." He wiped his brow. "I'm getting fed up with this life here. Nobody consults me, and I'm supposed to be one of the bosses. With overtime, the men are getting paid twice as much as I. The men were even paid overtime for Sundays on the trip over. Jaeger got fed up and quit." The captain paced the floor.

"You're not thinking of quitting, too?" I asked.

"Yeah! this isn't the life for me. Type up my resignation, effective immediately." Thinking, no doubt, that he had some responsibility as captain, he added, "Better make it to take effect as soon as they can replace me."

Jaeger and Carlyle had taken the same plane out of Asmara. Jaeger, plagued by severe heat rash, used that as an excuse to get a medical discharge from his contract.

Carlyle, not having been assigned any duties in the salvage operation, merely sat around blowing off steam. He failed to follow the medical rules that permitted us to survive the Massawa heat and to ward off malaria. I tried to get him to take tablets to replace the body salt lost by perspiration and quinine to protect him against an attack of malaria; but as a Christian Science adherent he refused.

As master-at-arms during the voyage he had custody of the rifles and ammunition acquired in Panama in exchange for the six pistols and misfit ammunition supplied by Flanagan in San Diego. After our arrival in Massawa, he had loaned out the guns to members of the crew for hunting grouse and gazelles in the hinterland of Eritrea. When the Guard was formed in Massawa, Major Albert, the then Provost Marshal, having been informed of the rifles aboard the *Chamberlain*, issued a requisition to Captain Hansen that they be produced within ten days. Carlyle was able to reacquire five of them. The sixth he had given to one of the seamen, who refused to return it.

Carlyle had an attack of malaria the day before he was to turn in the rifles, and, in a weakened state caused in part by his deficiency of salt, he was taken to Mai Habar hospital, halfway up the hill, where he remained in critical condition for thirty days.

Back in my cabin, I typed up the captain's resignation addressed to C.A. Nelson, the assistant foreign manager. After Hansen signed the letter, I delivered it to the Massawa office of JD&P. Since the resignation was to become effective upon the replacement of Captain Hansen, and there was no captain in Massawa who was eager to take over, nothing further was heard about it.

News came over the radio that on November 18, 1942, U.S. forces under General Eisenhower had landed in North Africa, encountering strong resistance from the Vichy French forces at Casablanca, Oran, and Algiers. About the same time, following the defeat of Rommel's army at El Alamein, the German and Italian desert armies were in full retreat. Now the more accessible and superior navy yard at Alexandria was again available to the ships of the Allied navies, and our naval facilities at Massawa would serve only as a secondary repair base for Allied war ships.

Meanwhile, rumors circulated that Captain Ellsberg had been transferred and that Brown would soon take over the Massawa salvage supervision.

But Ellsberg remained committed in Massawa. He made preparations to salvage a heavy floating crane which the Italians had scuttled off the shores of Massawa Island in the commercial harbor.

Members of an English salvage crew had worked many months attempting to raise the crane. In the process, they had seriously damaged the main deck, making it impossible to salvage by the traditional method of sealing the bomb holes and forcing air into the platform compartments to make them buoyant. They had failed to budge the crane, which was deeply mired in Massawa mud, and reported that it could not be salvaged. They requested permission to use explosives to remove the crane since it was a navigational hazard. But that would have deprived the naval base of a valuable addition to its facilities.

Captain Ellsberg had divers insert slings, attached to steel cables, under the platform of the sunken crane, a tedious job for the divers, sawing the cables back and forth under the crane in the muddy waters. Then using four huge empty gasoline tanks as pontoons, each forty-five feet long, he had two of them placed on each side of the crane. After water was pumped into them, they sank into position. The divers fastened the cables that were attached to the cradles underneath the crane, to the pontoons.

The unsuccesful English crew watched the efforts of Ellsberg's men, betting long odds with our salvage men that the crane was there to stay on the bottom of the Massawa harbor.

Meanwhile, air was forced into the pontoons from the pumps, and valves were opened so that the water was forced out, thus providing buoyancy to the pontoons. On the first attempt, one of the pontoons upended. On the second, the pontoons came up evenly, successfully floating the crane thirty-five days after Ellsberg began work on it.

Two of our men climbed up the derrick and hoisted the American flag. There was a loud cheer from the docks by our workmen who had been watching the operation. The Englishmen who had wagered paid their bets grudgingly.

Hansen sought me out at breakfast. "Paul, stop in my office after chow."

Rumors persisted that Ellsberg was leaving that day. Was it possible that Asmara officials would finally get their way and prevail in their determination to appoint Brown as superintendent of salvage?

The captain's exuberance was evident both in his voice and his demeanor as he greeted me.

"Paul, looks like we'll be leaving Massawa soon."

I waited impatiently while he puffed on his pipe.

Then he explained, "Ellsberg called the salvage officers together yesterday and told us that General Maxwell has ordered him to report to General Eisenhower in Oran to salvage ships there. He said that the Oran harbor was littered with twenty-seven sunken ships, many of them scuttled by the French. Several of them are blocking the entrance to the harbor. He wants us to load all the salvage gear on the *Chamberlain* and be ready to join him there as soon as he sends for us."

The captain was very unhappy about his Massawa experience and would be glad to leave. But I had mixed emotions, having found a lot of satisfaction in my work supervising salvage timekeepers. I considered deserting the ship and asking for a position ashore with JD&P, possibly in the cool hills of Asmara. But my loyalty to Hansen prevailed.

He dictated a list of what had to be done in preparation for our departure pending the arrival of Ellsberg's sailing orders. It included recruiting a full complement of men, obtaining a doctor or nurse, getting the ship into dry dock, and assembling and loading all the salvage equipment and supplies for the long voyage.

I proceeded ashore to Mahoney's office with the typed list and informed him that our ship was getting ready to leave for North Africa.

Mahoney looked up at me and frowned. "You know, Paul, Johnson, Drake and Piper gives the orders. Not Ellsberg. The *Chamberlain* and its crew will continue doing salvage work here in Massawa as long as there is a ship to raise. After all, your contract hasn't expired."

He immediately called Murphy, in charge of construction, and Nelson, assistant foreign manager, at their JD&P Asmara offices and was reassured that Ellsberg was no longer in charge of salvage operations and that the *Chamberlain* and its crew were to remain in Massawa.

Perplexed by these reactions, I then approached Major George V. Guisleman, the U.S. army's executive officer at the Massawa base and reported Mahoney's comments.

The major pounded his desk. "When the order comes from Captain Ellsberg to pull out, the *Chamberlain* and its crew will go, even if the men have to be sworn in as members of the U.S. armed forces. And Johnson, Drake & Piper won't have any say in it." The major left no doubt in my mind. It was a relief to have that issue settled.

On Thursday, November 26th, 1942, McAllister arranged a Thanksgiving feast of turkey from our frozen food supply, salad, nuts, canned sweet potatoes, and ice cream. I had a pang of nostalgia wondering how and where my California buddies were observing this holiday.

Our ship moved into dry dock to have her barnacles scraped, the first step in its preparations to sail to North Africa. Barnacles clinging to the hull of a ship retard her movement, and they proliferated on the *Chamberlain's* hull during the five months of exposure to the warm waters of the Massawa harbor.

JD&P officials R.P. Bayard, general manager, and H.R. Burroughs, chief of personnel, descended upon Massawa on December 2nd, and appointed Edison Brown to the position of superintendent of salvage for the third time. Now there was no Captain Ellsberg to rescind the order.

Word had not yet arrived from Ellsberg for us to join him in North Africa.

Early in December, I mailed the following Christmas greetings to my stateside friends, without revealing our location to the censors, whose inevitable scissors mutilated our letters:

A MERRY CHRISTMAS AND
A HAPPY NEW YEAR
I've come to the land where the camels run free,
And white man's as scarce as a mulberry tree;

Where prophets have never predicted snow
As far back as Adam and history books go.
'Tis a land of sun and a land of sand;
But I hope the censor will understand,
I'm merely trying to convey
A CHRISTMAS GREETING FOR THIS DAY.

A week passed and Mahoney was certain that we would continue salvage work in Massawa. "Ellsberg is gone. You won't hear from him again. So you may as well settle down and expect to finish your contract here under Brown."

Then he told me that the New York office of JD&P had intervened in Washington with the Navy Department to recall Ellsberg. "Chances are he's on his way back to the States right now," he added.

But three days later, the Skipper handed me an order reading:

SUBJECT: Orders

TO: Captain E.D. Brown, *Tug Intent*
      Captain T.H. Hansen, *S.S. W.R. Chamberlain, Jr*
      Captain Byglin, *Tug Resolute*

1. In accordance with oral instructions previously
    given, you will prepare your ship for sailing from
    this port for salvage duty elsewhere in Africa, on
    short notice. Each ship is to be fully loaded with
    oil and provisions, as may be required. The salvage
    outfit which each vessel was to carry, as previously
    outlined to you, is to be taken aboard and the vessel
    in all respects prepared to sail within twenty-four

hours after receiving word to proceed. Your sailing orders, together with destination and route to be followed will be communicated to you later. Upon receipt of these orders you will proceed with all possible dispatch either separately or in convoy as may be indicated to you by the Naval Authorities along the routes you are to follow.

2. Before proceeding, you will ensure that a full supply of ammunition for your guns is on board and that your crew will be properly drilled in the use of the guns and ready for action if necessary. You will further see that your degausing equipment is in order and is used in such waters as require it.

3. You will keep me advised at each port you make, as to your anticipated date of sailing and your next port.

(s) Edward Ellsberg

EDWARD ELLSBERG

Captain, U.S.N.R.

Officer-in-Charge

After perusing it, I chuckled, "Mahoney will blow his fuse!"

Hansen couldn't suppress his glee. "It'll be good to be out of this hellhole. Better get started assembling a full crew."

Mahoney's sour comment was, "Looks like Ellsberg's ghost is still around!"

One of the first men I approached was Jim Cook, the one-time delegate for the crew, who declared, "I wouldn't sail on that pisspot again for all the gold in Fort Knox."

But I did manage to locate thirty-two men from our original

- 220 -

crew who agreed to accompany us to Oran. We had carried seventy-nine salvage personnel and crew members out of San Diego, but now our ship required a complement of only forty-six men.

We located a Norwegian, John Silseth, to replace John Pearson, who had resigned as second assistant engineer. Our third mate, Hjalmar Olsson, who held captain's papers, was boosted to the position of chief mate to replace Otto Jaeger. Ray "Huck" Daugherty was designated third mate. As owner of a fishing boat in Redondo Beach, he held captain's papers.

Don McAllister, our steward in Massawa, stayed on. With the help of the British Admiralty, we recruited a Polish cook, a Russian mess man, engine room wipers, firemen and water tenders from Norway and Malta, and deckhands from Denmark. Our international crew was complete by the middle of December.

The salvage men who had sailed with us from San Diego and had not signed on for the trip to Oran remained in Massawa as JD&P employees and were assigned to construction jobs.

The air-conditioning system had broken down and was never reactivated because it required too much fresh water. The diesel engineers had devised a system of cooling the motors with big rotating fans and draping water-soaked towels over the motors. The water evaporation cooled the refrigeration motors. But early in December, even these devices failed to keep the motors running.

No doctor was available in Eritrea for the trip to North Africa, but John Vargas, who had sailed with us from San Diego in the capacity of male nurse, agreed to accompany us.

Since Ellsberg had ordered us to sail from Massawa directly upon receiving further instructions from him, every day the skipper dictated a list of items to be attended to and supplies that had to be loaded, and every day I took the list to Major Guisleman.

"I'll have my men on these items right away," was his usual comment. Only after repeated requests were the various demands fulfilled.

The skipper and I had often complained about the lack of cooperation of the British naval and military authorities, but after this annoying experience with a U.S. Army official, it occurred to me that we should bite our tongue before again complaining about the British.

In the middle of December, the captain received orders from Ellsberg for us to sail from Massawa posthaste and join him in Oran.

The same day, the U.S. army command in Cairo ordered both Chief Engineer Culpepper, and First Assistant Engineer Gibson to fly to Cairo to testify at the trial of an American civilian JD&P employee caught with five hundred dollars worth of jewelry that had been stolen from Gibson.

They were gone two weeks, and, since both of them were needed to prepare our ship for sailing, our departure was delayed yet another week after their return.

CHAPTER 23

FAREWELL MASSAWA

THE WAR: After the armistice between Vichy France and the Allies was negotiated on November 11, 1942, terminating hostilities in Morocco and Algeria, Hitler abrogated the terms of the treaty entered into between France and Germany in 1940 and ordered German forces to take over unoccupied France. At that time, the greater part of the French fleet was anchored at the Mediterranean port of Toulon. As the German troops occupied Toulon, and, before they were able to seize the French ships, Admiral Jean de La Borde ordered 62 of them scuttled, including three battleships, four heavy cruisers, three light cruisers, one aircraft tender, twenty-five destroyers, and twenty-six submarines.

Strong alcoholic fumes pervaded the captain's quarters as I entered on the eve of our departure. I found Second Assistant Engineer John Silseth's body draped over the settee and Second Mate Art Vatne sprawled awkwardly on the floor, both in a deep drunken sleep. The skipper listlessly waved a bottle of Scotch to the rhythm of, "She's only a girl in a gilded cage ..." off key, as usual. Several empties lay scattered on the floor.

There was no point in inviting the skipper to my farewell

party, scheduled to start an hour later. Eight of my onshore friends assembled in my quarters to say goodbye, among them Mahoney, Hudson, an English engineer, and Jones, an English shipfitter. My bottle of White Horse lasted one sparse round.

Gordon Kerr, who had shared some of my timekeeping duties, slapped me on the back. "Congratulations on leaving this miserable place."

As the fellows gathered around me, singing, "For he's a jolly good fellow," Hansen came staggering in moaning the same old song and demanding a drink.

I held up the empty Scotch bottle. "It's all gone, Captain."

He stood in the doorway, eyeballing my British friends, and to my great embarassment, exclaimed, "Those damned English. They can't do anything right, and they always think they're better than us."

In his inebriated condition, he began mumbling one of his long tirades. One after the other of my guests bade me farewel, ignoring the captain as they made their way past him into the Massawa night.

"Since you don't have anything to drink, I may as well turn in," the skipper complained. I accompanied him to his cabin and saw him disappear into his bunk room. Art and John were still out cold.

I paused at the railing, taking in the cool night air. The five sunken ships blocking the entrance to the naval harbor were just shadows in the dark quiet waters.

In the inner sanctum of my quarters, I put on a Victor Herbert record and sat a long time reflecting with satisfaction on my ten months with JD&P.

In spite of all the personnel problems, substantial benefits had been achieved for the war effort by Ellsberg, Brown, and our salvage crew. Besides opening the harbor of Massawa to Allied shipping and rebuilding the Massawa naval repair base, the salvage men had raised five ships from the muddy waters of the Massawa harbor—the *Liebenfels, Gera, Brent, Frauenfels* and *Tripolitania*—together with two dry docks and a floating crane.

The large dry dock was now in service, the bomb holes in its compartments covered with steel plates, the barnacles scraped, and the machinery repaired. The equipment in the machine shop had been rebuilt and replaced. The Persian dry dock, which had floated unattended and unused in the outer harbor when Ellsberg arrived, had since serviced eighty ships, including a number of British war vessels.

The *Liebenfels*, completely reconditioned and renamed the *General Russell Maxwell* in honor of the U.S. commanding general in Cairo, lay at anchor, ready for active service as a supply vessel in the Allied cause. Other salvaged ships, when renovated, would become a welcome addition to the Allied war effort.

At 6 A.M. after a restless night anticipating the morning departure, I decided to check on the captain. His door was open and I heard his gruff remonstrance: "What do ya wake me up for? Get outta here!"

The third mate's voice cajoled, "Remember, Captain, we're sailing this morning. The pilot is aboard already."

A few minutes later, the bleary-eyed skipper and Huck came out of the cabin.

"Are we leaving on schedule?" was my first concern, in view

of the captain's condition.

"Looks like it," Huck answered.

The mate shouted to the deck crew to haul in the lines, and we steamed between the wrecks of the *XXIII Marzo* and the *Oliva* into the Red Sea,

Twenty minutes after leaving the mooring, we paused to permit the pilot to board his shore boat, and we were on our own, plowing through the mine-infested waters of the Red Sea.

After seeking but failing to obtain more alcohol, Hansen returned to his cabin to sleep it off.

The British naval authorities had warned us that the Red Sea was extensively mined. Although a path had been swept for passage through the hazardous waters, any deviation by a vessel would spell certain disaster. I walked the deck, fearing that any minute we would hit a submerged mine and be blasted into the sky.

I was worried, knowing that Huck was in sole charge of the vessel. As a fishing boat captain, he had never before navigated a ship this large, much less charted such a dangerous course. None of the other deck officers, including the captain, appeared on the bridge.

The naval authorities had debated about sending our vessel through the Suez Canal into the Mediterranean en route to Oran. But they ignored her reputation as a charmed ship and, after evaluating the U-boat menace, plotted her course over the long route around the Cape of Good Hope.

Early that afternoon the usual deck vibrations stopped, indicating that the engines had been shutdown. I made my way to the chart room and found the third mate studying his sea charts.

"What's up, Huck?" I asked.

"Oh, nuts! The chief's got the usual condenser troubles."

For three long hours our engines paused. At least the cool invigorating breezes floating in from the south were a welcome contrast to the hot air of Massawa.

At evening mess Culpepper, in his usual loud staccato style, asked no one in particular, "Where the hell are the deck officers? I haven't seen any of them all day. Helluva way to run a ship!"

"Huck's on the bridge," McAllister related. "I sent some chow up to him this noon and tonight. He seems to be holding up so far."

The sobered-up skipper finally resurfaced in the messhall for the evening meal on the following day, his blue eyes still bloodshot. He acted in an officious manner, as though the last day and a half had not occurred.

After Hansen left, I asked Huck, "How long were you on duty on the bridge?"

"I got stuck for nine watches, without relief, until Art sobered up and took over this afternoon." With good reason, after thirty-six hours on the bridge, he looked pooped.

McAllister asked, "The pilot wasn't aboard very long. How did we manage to get through the mine fields?"

"Well, the pilot did give me a map to take us through." Then Huck shook his head. "But if those damned mines had shifted, we'd have been blown to bits."

We were still on our lucky streak, but I was afraid to say it.

After anchoring in the Aden harbor overnight, we sailed on

to the Kenyan port of Mombasa, where the ship's crew loaded salvage gear that originally had been destined for Massawa.

Although the captain now had complete control of himself and of the ship, he no longer had the enthusiasm to insist at each port of call that departure of our vessel should be expedited for the sake of the war effort. He allowed the port officials and the U.S. authorities ashore to determine the timetable for necessary repairs, refueling, and loading supplies and cargo.

During the eight days that our ship rested in the Mombasa harbor, some of the men embarked on excursions to Lake Victoria on their motor bikes acquired in Massawa from the Italians, while I made a fast trek to Nairobi by train and took a taxi into the veldt to view the giraffes and zebras in their native habitat.

An amazing transformation took place in Huck when he assumed the duties of third mate. His demeanor changed from that of a carefree adventurer to a serious minded, responsible officer. Houghton Ralph had been his mentor. Since Hoot's death from pneumonia, Huck took his place as father confessor to the men, settling disputes and knocking heads together when the occasion demanded. Although as an officer he no longer bunked in the fo'c'sle, a lot of his waking hours away from his watch were spent with his friends there.

While our ship was anchored in the Mombasa harbor, Wes Hewson, having imbibed heavily from his private supply of alcohol, took offence when Toledo, a slight fellow in his early thirties, who had formerly served in the officer's mess, did not give him prompt service at the noonday meal.

"Get the lead out of your butt," Wes shouted at Toledo. "Bring me some soup, and be quick about it."

"Aw, go fly a kite!" the mess man responded.

Getting up from the table, Wes punched Toledo in the chest with his right fist and began to swing with his left toward Toledo's face when Huck, who was dining in crew's mess that day, jumped up from his seat at a nearby table, yelling, "Cut it out, Wes."

He grabbed Hewson's left arm and swung him around, unbalancing him. Wes fell to the deck. Getting up, dazed, he stared at Huck in disbelief and slunk out of the mess hall.

WES HEWSON, CARL FROMHOLD AND
RAYMOND (HUCK) DAUGHERTY

I thought that would be the end of their amicable relation-sip, but they remained close friends. After that, Wes tried to control his temper, even when under the influence.

Since the *Chamberlain* was no longer air-conditioned, the hot and humid nights in Mombasa forced the crew to desert their sleeping quarters in the fo'c'sle and find deck space for their mattresses under the open sky.

I found little relief in my cabin, even with the porthole and door open. My bedsheets were soaked with perspiration.

The navy routed many ships around Madagascar but decided that our vessel should take the shortest and fastest route through the Mozambique Channel and brave the submarines lurking there.

Axel Fredricksen, who had survived a severe beating in San Diego prior to departure and who was hearty enough to withstand the Massawa heat, was hospitalized in Mombasa. Neither the ship's log nor its correspondence record revealed the exact nature of his illness or disabiity. The skipper had a close affinity to Axel as a fellow Norwegian. Had his illness been adjudged to be due to alcoholism or a social disease, the work contract provided for termination of pay and release from the vessel. In the case of Axel, his pay continued, and he was provided transportation back to the port of San Diego.

Axel, like a number of crew members, was an alcoholic and imbibed excessively. The fo'c'sle typewritten newspaper, the *Hawse Pipe Herald*, reported: "Axel Fredricksen gave a pint of blood to a man who died almost immediately of acute alcoholism. Axel says, 'I was framed. It must have been something he et.'"

CHAPTER 24

CAPERS AT THE CAPE

THE WAR: After the Japanese lost nearly 24,000 men, including 600 airmen, in their attempt to dislodge the U.S. Marines from Guadacanal, they abandoned their positions on the island and evacuated 11,000 men by February 9, 1943. The U.S. marines suffered losses of 1600 killed and 4100 wounded. Both sides lost many ships. The occupation of Guadacanal provided an important base to the U.S. forces in the battle to dislodge the Japanese from their Pacific conquests.

One morning after we had safely passed through the Mozambique Channel, Hansen, having finished his breakfast, pushed the dishes to one side, and, with his elbows resting on the table, lit his pipe. He looked around the mess hall focusing on Daugherty and Olsson, who sat at the adjoining table.

"At Mombasa the navy again warned that we'd have a better chance of avoiding the subs by sailing south into the *roaring forties* before turning into Cape Town. You know what that means. Only this time we'll be bucking the winds, so make sure all the deck cargo is secure."

Turning to Culpepper, he added, "Chief, better get your

repair list ready for the Cape Town shipyards. It'll be the last chance we have before Oran.

"By God, my list will keep the shipyards busy for a month," the chief rasped. His prophesy almost proved correct.

As we approached the fortieth parallel, the westerly winds pounded our vessel with relentless fury, blowing ruthlessly and without respite. Our ship plowed tenaciously southward, braving the foaming waves that noisily sloshed over her decks. She tossed, pitched, and rolled, floundering in the South Indian Ocean, and as we sailed into the trough of a wave, the sea often threatened to engulf us. Life aboard was a battle of balance and survival.

The light of day slowly vanished, and the dark sky unveiled the flickering stars. We pushed on southward in spite of the pounding wind.

Between mouthfuls of food the next morning, I asked the captain when we would reach Cape Town.

"I don't know. We've tried to steer the ship to the West, but the winds are so strong, we can't change course. So it's anyone's guess. We might end up in the antartic or at Prince Edward Island."

With my little knowledge of navigation, I almost believed him.

Fierce winds continued to harass us. One of our lifeboats broke loose and was swept overboard. Our ship still had five lifeboats and four life rafts available, which, in case of emergency, were adequate for our crew of forty-five men. Several hydrogen tanks strapped down on deck came loose and started to roll. The deck crew managed to corral and secure them.

Sometimes a swell built up to forty feet, hovering over us like a mountain. The sound of waves hitting the steel plates intermingled with the pounding of the engines.

Then again, the winds almost pushed the ship over on her side. Walking on deck became a hazard. On starboard I collided with cabin walls, and on port I fought to keep from sliding overboard.

Finally, after we sailed more than two hundred and fifty nautical miles south of Cape Town, pounded constantly by the westerlies, the winds subsided for a short time, long enough for the helmsman to change course and steer westward.

That night in the mess hall the skipper and the mates were relaxed.

"I'm sure glad we didn't end up in the antarctic," I said gleefully.

"It was touch and go for awhile," Hansen remarked. "We should be in Cape Town tomorrow."

Although there were many items on Culpepper's long repair list, the principal complaint was the leaking throttle valve. A replacement had been requested before leaving San Diego, again in Panama and Massawa. But each time the part was unavailable without considerable delay, and Culpepper didn't press the matter in Massawa. While traveling unescorted, the leaky main throttle valve wasn't a hazard, but in a convoy, the vessel would have to respond immediately to an order from the bridge, and exactly to any change of speed.

It was summer in South Africa. The temperate climate and the sandy beaches of Cape Town were a welcome relief after the heat and humidity of Massawa and its desolate shoreline.

Hansen patronized the local bistros daily, but I was not so fortunate. Each morning, he sketched out work that kept me occupied most of the day, but I did manage to get away evenings.

As I came aboard one night after a round of night clubbing, I heard screams from the fo'c'sle and found Tom, an oiler, tearing a wide adhesive tape from seaman Hugh's ankle. Obviously, both had been drinking.

"What happened?" I asked.

"Well we got lost finding our way back to the ship," Hugh explained. "It was damn dark, and when a watchman comes by, we tells him we was lost. He asks us to wait there 'cause an ambulance would soon come along. When it finally comes, we climbs in and tells the driver we wants ta get back to our ship. I guess he didn't understand 'cause when we stopped, here we was in front of a hospital.

"We stumbles in, an' a sour nurse wants ta know what's da problem. I tells her I turned my ankle. She steers me to the dressin' room, and 'fore you could sneeze, a coupla nurses push me on a operatin' table. Well, I was gettin' scared, so I tries to get off, but Tom, here, holds me down an' insists I hurt my ankle bad. The nurses tape it up. Then we plays peek-a-boo with 'em 'till a couple of men grabs us and pushes us into a ambulance. And here we are."

Our Cape Town agent, Attwell & Co., in gratitude to Hansen for using that company to provision and repair the *Chamberlain*, invited our officers to dinner and an evening of tippling. But after a gourmet meal and drinking the best Scotch, the agent's staff set up a crap table and hauled out a pair of dice.

All of the officers, except Hansen, participated. The agent more than recouped the cost of providing the evening's entertainment from those of us who played craps. We paid dearly for the food and libation, except for Huck, who left with a bundle.

The shipyard foreman had estimated that the repairs would be completed in ten days, but when the ship left the dock on a trial run, the main throttle valve failed the test and we had to return to the repair dock. Then, as the ship was moved to anchorage ready for departure, the anchor chain separated, and both it and the anchor dropped to the bottom of the bay. A buoy was lowered to mark the spot and our ship returned to the quay.

Winds and heavy rain made it impossible to recover the anchor. When the weather cleared, Huck, together with two of our seaman, took one of our shore boats to the buoy. They reported back that another ship had been moored directly over our anchor, making it impossible for us to retrieve it until that vessel moved. After several more days, they returned to the buoy, and Huck, in his diving suit, located the anchor in three feet of sand, sixty feet below the water surface. He was unable to secure a rope around it. On the third try, with the aid of a tool from our ship, he succeeded in digging it out of the sand and attaching a line to it. The *Chamberlain* steamed over and heaved up the anchor.

One day Chief Culpepper spied a copy of a letter on my desk, addressed to the captain, from Major Milton J. Landvoigt, in charge of the U.S. Army Engineer office in Cape Town. It described the cargo of acetate and rubber cement that had been loaded on our vessel. He threw up his arms, commenting,

"Aw, shit! What chance have we got if we ever get hit by a torpedo. We'd be blazing in no time."

"Look at it this way, Chief. This is a charmed ship. No matter what we take aboard, she'll get there." Those were brave words, but I by no means felt that confident.

Twelve U.S. navy men joined our ship to man our guns. They had been beached in Cape Town when their cargo vessel was torpedoed off the South African coast.

Our Cape Town holiday ended after twenty-seven days. We lost four of our crew. An oiler suffered a concussion when he collapsed on the street after a drinking spree, a deck hand drowned off the dock while exploring on his own, and two disenchanted seamen deserted.

The morning after our departure, the captain knocked on my door at 6 A.M. as he had done frequently since leaving Mombasa, and, as usual, I offered him a drink of Scotch.

To my surprise, he answered, "No, Paul, thanks anyway."

As the days wore on, it became obvious that the skipper had taken the pledge. That was amazing, because up to that time, I would have wagered there never was a day when he didn't have a drink. I was further mystified to learn that he had given the chief mate his entire supply of a case of Scotch acquired in Cape Town.

Then, by sheer chance, I spied a supply of sulphathiozole tablets in his medicine cabinet, and the thought hit me like thunder that he must have contracted a venereal disease at the last port of call. Perhaps his wife's advice to pay for female companionship, when the need arose, was not so good after all.

I never thought I'd miss hearing his old ditty "She's only a

girl in a gilded cage, , ,"

HJALMAR OLSSON, CHIEF MATE ENROUTE TO ORAN
CAPTAIN THOMAS HANSEN AND AUTHOR

CHAPTER 25

OUR RESTLESS CREW

<u>THE WAR:</u> *The Germans experienced a severe set-back on February 3rd, 1943, when General Frederick Paulus surrendered an army of 90,000 men at Stalingrad, having suffered 110,000 casualties; and the Russians, taking advantage of the severe winter weather, advanced all along the 900 mile front. In spite of the reversal, the German army took the offensive, taking Kharkov by March 15th and driving the Russians into defensive positions.*

A pilot directed our vessel past a tiny fishing hamlet into the Lagos harbor, the principal port of Nigeria. Imposing villas nestled amidst bright green grass and picturesque gardens. Occasional palm trees graced the shoreline. Located in a lagoon, the harbor was one of the most beautiful on the African continent, and to me, after another twelve days at sea, it looked like paradise.

We anchored for just a day to hospitalize Bill McKelly, who had contracted pneumonia, and two men who were infected with a venereal disease—a member of the Navy Reserve gun crew and one of our carpenters.

No fuel was available in Lagos. Upon leaving, a pilot boarded to guide our vessel through the ship-crowded lagoon and out into the Atlantic, en route to Takoradi.

The pilot telegraphed "full speed ahead" to the engine room, and our ship shot forward. "Hard right," he shouted to Buckey at the helm. But the *Chamberlain* kept going straight ahead. We were on a collision course with a freighter. Hansen, Huck, and the pilot almost collided in grabbing the telegraph lever to signal the engine room to go into reverse.

"What the hell's wrong down there?" the captain yelled into the communication tube.

The ship came to an abrupt stop and reversed. After the pilot had signaled for the ship to stop, the chief yelled up from the engine room through the tube, "Nobody turned on the steam for the steering gear! Its okay now."

The thought crossed my mind that some of our past engine room problems might have been generated by our engineers or members of our black gang.

Two days later we arrived at Takoradi, on the Gold Coast. For six days, while temperatures prevailed in the upper eighties along with high humidity, our ship lay anchored in the bay, awaiting fuel. The restless crew was not allowed shore leave. After finally taking on oil, we sailed to Freetown in Sierra Leone.

From the time of our arrival in Lagos, Takoradi and Freetown, mosquitoes plagued us day and night, and I religiously swallowed quinine to avoid contracting malaria.

In most ports, launches regularly made the rounds in the harbor between ships at anchor and the dock, but Freetown had no such service. Our crew was jubilant when the mate launched one of our boats powered by an outboard motor to provide shore-going tansportation.

After an exploratory trip ashore, most of the men swore off further visits. They found Freetown dusty, its shops run-down, and the city completely lacking interesting entertainment. In the hot and humid tropical atmosphere, and without any duties to perform, they became restless aboard ship, picking fights with each other, arguing about everything from who had the right to the available liquor to who on board ship was a virgin.

Frank Gray and Lawrence Kealey, both seamen, Tom Cahill, an oiler and Terry Engal, a carpenter, were in a high stakes poker game in the fo'c'sle. All had been imbibing in great abandon.

After Cahill shuffled the cards and the deck was cut by Gray, a fight started between John Sattler and Clarence Smith, two firemen, at their bunks, drawing the attention of the card players. Huck, who had been watching the poker game, left the table to separate the two.

Cahill dealt himself a ten-high flush, while Engal ended up with three kings. Wild betting ensued between the two players, Gray and Kealey having thrown in their hands after Cahill raised the opening bid.

When the cards were shown and Cahill was raking in the pot, Engal jumped up and shouted, "You cheating bastard! You switched decks!"

Cahill, too, jumped up. "Nobody calls me a cheat and gets away with it."

He lunged forward, swinging his clenched right fist at Engal who towered over him by five inches. Engal staggered drunkenly, and Cahill's blow missed him by a foot. Enraged, Engal regained his balance and lunged toward Cahill.

Huck strode over and grabbed Engal's arm, stopping his charge, demanding, "What's the problem?"

"Cahill must have switched decks," Engal complained.

"Before you kill each other, why don't we check the cards and see what the score is," Huck advised.

Gray picked the cards off the table and examined them. "This is the same deck we've been playing with. See that coffee stain on the deuce of clubs?"

Kealey chimed in, "Yeah, an' I watched Tom shuffle the cards, an' I cut 'em, so his deal was on the level."

Engal bowed his head, shamefaced.

Thanks to Huck, another confrontation was avoided.

Although the skipper had issued an order for all of our men to take quinine in this tropical area, apparently he, himself, did not deem it expedient to mix it with his sulpha drug treatment. When we arrived in Freetown, he complained of nausea, headaches, and fever, and nurse John Vargas diagnosed it as an attack of malaria.

Hansen called me to his quarters. "Paul, we're supposed to join a convoy leaving here tomorrow, and there's a meeting of captains ashore this afternoon. I'm just too sick to take the ship out. I want you to attend that meeting and advise the commodore that our ship has to stay behind because of my damned fever."

That afternoon, I reported to the British lieutenant commander in charge of the escort vessels and gave him the skipper's message. At his request I joined the captains and other officers at the briefing. We all listened intently as the lieutenant commander spoke in a clipped British accent.

"Good afternon, gentlemen. I am Lieutenant Commander Williams and I will be the senior officer in command of your escort. There will be two corvettes and one frigate guarding your convoy. Captain York will be your commodore.

"Each of you has received your sealed orders which include your position in the convoy. Thirty-five ships will be sailing in the usual seven-column formation. An oceangoing tug will accompany us, and only the tug is to stop and pick up any survivors of torpedoed ships. Let's hope there will be no torpedoes. No other ship in our convoy is to stop if we are attacked. It would be a prime target for any sub still lingering in the area."

Williams then turned the meeting over to the commodore. Captain York spoke with authority. "You know how important it is to maintain your position in the convoy and to change course immediately when I give the signal. Keep your eyes open for our flag hoist or signal lamps. You have a copy of the code.

"Keep your ship blacked out at night. And no smoking on deck! Enforce this rule on your ship! A light at night can easily betray the convoy. That's it, gentlemen. Let's hope we all arrive safely at our destinations."

I reported the details of the meeting to Hansen.

CHAPTER 26

IN CONVOY

THE WAR: After the capitulation by the Vichy French High Command in Morocco and Algeria, the U.S. and British forces converged on Tunisia, a most important objective, since its airfields and ports could provide a jumping off place for planes and ships to attack Axis convoys in the Mediterranean and also serve as staging areas for the invasion of France, Sicily, and Italy. A combined Anglo-U.S. force advanced within 12 miles of Tunis by late November of 1942, but it was not until February 2, 1943, that Montgomery's 8th Army entered Tunisia from Libya on the heels of Rommel's panzer divisions. Because of the fortified positions held by the Axis forces in mountain strongholds overlooking key roads and valleys, the Allies, bogged down as they were by winter rains, did not dislodge the Germans and Italians in North Africa until May 11th, 1943, although they were superior numerically in troops and planes.

Although we had traveled 24,000 dangerous miles from San Diego on our own, the navy now insisted that we must be escorted to Oran. The seas on the West Coast of Africa were honeycombed with enemy subs. The port of Freetown harbored over five hundred lucky seamen who had managed to reach shore after their ships had been torpedoed.

By our sixth day in Freetown, Hansen recovered sufficiently to go ashore and request U.S. Navy Commander McFall to expedite our departure. No convoy was expected to depart from Freetown in the foreseeable future. McFall convinced the British Admiralty to assign two British corvettes to escort our ship to Dakar, where we would be in position to join a convoy scheduled to pass nearby en route to the Mediterranean. The corvette, designed during World War II for antisubmarine duty, ranked below the destroyer in size and was lightly armed and highly maneuverable,

A day out of port, while breathing in the fresh tropical air on deck and spying on one of our escorting corvettes with my binoculars, I saw what looked like a periscope rising out of the sea, about midpoint between our ship and the escort vessel. I froze. Was this to be doomsday for the *Chamberlain*? Visions of being trapped on a burning ship flashed through my mind.

I managed to yell, "Submarine!" But nobody heard me. While rushing up to the bridge to inform the mate on duty, I heard several dulled detonations. I saw the corvette circle the spot where the periscope had appeared, and the sea suddenly erupted into a column of foaming churned-up water where the corvette must have dropped depth charges. There was no evidence of debris on the surface of the sea. The submarine apparently escaped, and so did we.

A pilot boat welcomed us to Dakar at 2300 hours. During normal times and in seas that are not at risk from submarine attacks, the usual procedure requires a vessel arriving after nightfall to wait until the following morning before being admitted into port.

Dakar had one of the best harbors on the West Coast of Africa and also served as the African anchor for intercontinental plane travel. A French possession before World War II, it had been dominated by the Vichy French who cooperated with the Germans after the Franco-German Armistice of June 22, 1940.

So long as the Vichy French were in control, the Allies were deprived of the use of Dakar. After the successful invasion of North Africa by the U.S. forces, the friendly Free French took possession of the port.

Dakar had sidewalk cafes,, restaurants, shops and a European environment. Petroleum being unavailable, taxicabs were equipped with charcoal burners called gasogenes, which produced a gas to run the motors. After a bumpy ride over streets abounding in chuckholes and ruts, and after inhaling the smell of the burning charcoal, a glass of French wine at the local bistro served as a balm to my jangled nerves and nauseated stomach.

The U.S. army loaded hospital equipment destined for Casablanca into our number four hold, but someone in the engine room flooded the fuel tank, soaking all of that cargo with oil.

When the skipper heard about it, he rebuked Culpepper, "What kind of engine room are you running, Chief?"

"What can you expect from a bunch of damned amateurs?" replied Culpepper.

The Skipper often went out of his way to pursue his concept

of justice. Just before departing from Dakar, he handed me a letter from Captain R.A. Erickson, the U.S. Army Transport Officer, reporting that a native had been apprehended with a bedsheet from our ship in his possession, and that it was his duty to see him punished.

"Paul," he said. "Write a letter to Captain Erickson. Just say that we've had trouble with our men stealing things from the ship and each other. We're ready to sail, so there's no time to line up the crew and find the man who sold the sheet to the native. I don't think he should be punished, only reprimanded."

Three corvettes escorted us out of Dakar to join a convoy of ships in mid-ocean, many of Norwegian nationality. Their ships in the past had invariably been assigned to the outside position in a British convoy, thus making them more vulnerable to sub attack. A number of Norwegian skippers had pulled their ships out of previous convoys, deciding to go it alone instead of being a buffer for English ships. After this mutiny, the English Commodores required their own vessels to share the hazards of sailing on the outer rim.

The *Chamberlain* was destined to be a buffer ship assigned to sail fifth in line on the outside right column.

Periodically, our convoy passed through pools of oil, floating lumber, life jackets and other debris from sunken vessels. Once we observed a seaman's body, attired in a rubber suit and life preserver, tossing about in the turbulent sea. Our convoy instructions were not to stop for any reason. Later we watched as one of our escort vessels rescued eight men aboard a life raft.

It was a spectacle to see our parade of ships gliding effortlessly through phosphorescent waters at sundown, masts flying gay signal flags under a sky tinted with superabundant shades of pink, yellow and red.

At irregular intervals, the commodore's ship signaled with flags and lamps a change of course and sometimes of speed to the five columns of vessels. The leading ships in the convoy then changed course or speed, followed by the second in each column, and the others in turn until all were synchronized.

It was slow going, about one hundred and thirty knots a day. At night, we towed a light to warn the ships following us of our location, and yet not bright enough to aid the prowling subs.

Every night, at least one neutral ship sailed through our convoy, its lights ablaze, a beacon for subs on the prowl and revealing the dark outlines of the ships in our convoy. My luck, tied so intimately with that of the *Chamberlain*, still held.

CHAPTER 27

NORTH AFRICAN INVASION TALES

THE WAR: *The details of the April 8, 1942, bombing raid on Japan by Colonel James H.Doolittle's force of sixteen B-25 bombers from the U.S. aircraft carrier, the Hornet, were not released until April of 1943. At the time of the attack, the news gave Americans a great psychological boost, but the scattered bombing did no great damage to Japanese industry. Shortly thereafter, the Japanese improved their home defenses and captured the Chinese bases where the American pilots had landed, bases that the U.S. had planned to use for future bombing attacks on Japan. The Japanese captured eight of Doolittle's men, fifty-five returned to the U.S. to fight again, five flew their planes to Russia and were interned there, one was killed, two were missing, and eight joined Major Lee Chenault and his Flying Tigers in China to defend the Burma Road.*

The *Chamberlain* left the convoy in mid-ocean and was escorted by a corvette to the entrance of the Casablanca harbor, where a pilot boarded and directed our vessel to the wharf for the unloading of the well-oiled hospital supplies and equipment that had been stowed in number four hold.

Two U.S. Army officers boarded shortly after our ship docked. In the captain's cabin, they introduced themselves as Colonel Clarkson and Lieutenant Gibbs.

The skipper's first question was, "Is Captain Ellsberg still in charge in Oran?"

"I've no way of knowing, Captain," answered the colonel, a middle-aged man with a military bearing. "We want to welcome you to Casablanca and do everything we can to speed you on your way. Incidently, Captain, you'll be loading a thousand tons of gas bombs and ammunition for the trip to Oran."

"With the combustible liquid we already have aboard, and now the ammunition cargo, we'll really be a munition dump," Hansen complained, squinting in displeasure.

As the officers got up to leave, he asked, "Would you gentlemen join us for lunch?"

"Sorry, I have another commitment," responded the colonel. Then turning to the lieutenant, he suggested, "Why don't you accept?"

Gibbs, a young fellow in his early twenties, agreed.

Culpepper and Gibson were already eating when we entered the mess hall. The captain introduced the lieutenant and then commented, "We're loading a cargo of ammunition here to take to Oran."

"That does it," the chief exploded. "I'm getting off here."

Gibson scowled and snapped, "That goes for me, too. To hell with this floating disaster!"

The lieutenant listened to these outbursts, and then whispered to me, "I'll lay odds they'll sail on to Oran."

To change the subject, I asked, "Were you in the invasion of

Casablanca?"

"Yes, in the first wave."

The captain queried, "Did you have any opposition?"

"Opposition wasn't our problem. I'm lucky to be alive." The lieutenant paused for a minute. "The invasion was so badly planned that it's a miracle we captured Casablanca. We were packed in an assault boat in the dark and headed for shore, expecting the French to defend every inch of the coastline. We were supposed to land on a sandy beach; instead, we hit rocky reefs, and our boat sank, taking down with it most of our radios, machine guns, bazookas, mortars and shells.

"We piled out into the cold Atlantic, making our way to shore over sharp rocks. My hands, arms and legs were badly cut up. It was miserable, soaked as we were. Luckily most of the men from our boat made it to shore. But then we didn't have anything to fight with. We ended up a couple miles from where we were supposed to land."

"Any enemy fire?" I asked.

"No, if there had been, we probably wouldn't be here now. After a couple of hours of hiking along the coast, we finally ran into our outfit and got some dry clothes and guns. None of the boats landed where they should have. And none of the radios that we were to use to contact the ship, worked. They had been ruined by salt spray and were useless."

All conversation in the mess hall halted when the lieutenant started talking, and when he paused, the only sounds were the footsteps of the mess man.

"Have you been here since the invasion?" asked Olsson.

"No. After Casablanca was secured, the army sent my unit off to fight in Tunis. I've been detached from my outfit for only a few weeks and now I'm assigned here."

That afternoon, Culpepper and Gibson visited the colonel's office to deliver their resignations. Both engineers were back at mess that evening, looking glum.

"Give us the news, Chief. Are you getting off here?" I asked.

"No such luck. The colonel said he was sending us back to the States on the *Chamberlain* via Oran. So we're stuck with this son of a bitchen ship—at least until Oran."

The Casablanca harbor was crowded, not only with supply ships waiting to be unloaded, but also with sunken vessels blocking off valuable dock space. A damaged French battleship, the *Jean Bart*, destroyers, and cargo vessels lying mast deep in the water, attested to the ferocity of the fighting between the Allies and the Vichy French forces.

On the streets of Casablanca, U.S. soldiers and sailors and merchant seamen mingled with natives dressed in their colorful robes. The city was under martial law and an eight-thirty evening curfew. Although there were no air raids during our six-day stop, some of our men, fearing aerial attacks on our munition-laden ship, took shore leave in the safety of the Old Medina, the original Arab commercial and residential quarter. It was an uneventful stay.

Two hundred nautical miles and thirty-one hours after leaving Casablanca, the *Chamberlain* crept under escort into the harbor of Gibraltar, crowded with Allied invasion craft, cruisers, destroyers, corvettes and supply vessels. We could only surmise where this invasion force would strike next.

The noise from the detonation of depth charges released by

the British Navy in the Gibraltar harbor reverberated each night of our six-day stay. These depth charges were designed to discourage saboteur swimmers from attaching timed explosives to the hulls of ships. In spite of such precautionary measures, the bows of three vessels were blown off during our visit.

Spain, under General Franco, was known to be sympathetic to the Nazi cause and it harbored German spies and saboteurs who took advantage of the safety of the Spanish mainland to prey upon the Allies in Gibraltar.

CHAPTER 28

WHAT A RECEPTION!

*THE WAR: All Axis resistance on the African conti-
nent ceased on May 11th, 1943. The German and
Italian soldiers and officers fled from the battlefields
near Tunis in their own trucks on traffic-clogged roads
to surrender to the Allies at the compound where prisoners of war were collected. For them the war was over,
and many were to be shipped to America, while U.S.
troops faced more combat and death on the battle
fields of continental Europe. Over 175,000 Axis soldiers, including sixteen German and ten Italian gen-
erals, became prisoners of war. This Allied victory was
as significant as the Russian success at Stalingrad. The
tide had turned.*

After a thirty-four hour voyage from Gibraltar, chaperoned by
British corvettes and U.S. fighter planes, we anchored in the
Oran harbor within view of scuttled and bombed freighters and
navy auxiliary vessels revealing only their masts and some
superstructures. The entrance to the harbor had been cleared of
sunken ships by Ellsberg and his men.

No sooner were we anchored in the bay than Major T.A.
Olson of the U.S. Army Corps of Engineers climbed aboard from

a navy launch. I escorted him to Hansen's cabin. After introducing himself, he got right to the point. "Captain Ellsberg was shipped back to the States on sick leave in February. You'll be turning the *Chamberlain* over to the navy, and your crew will be discharged. We'll try to get you transportation out of here to New York as soon as possible."

I stepped back in shock and disbelief. Was the saga of the *Chamberlain* and its crew to end so abruptly after we had come 11,431 nautical miles from Massawa?

Captain Hansen puffed his pipe and shuffled papers. Then a smile lit up his face. "Well, Major," he said. "This comes as quite a surprise, but I'm not a bit sorry to get off this ship. As you know, we're carrying explosives, so my men are anxious to get as far away from this ship as possible, as soon as possible."

"I'll get your vessel alongside a dock when there's room, but you've got to be patient. It may take a few days." As an afterthought, the major asked, "By the way, what kind of vessel do you call this anyway?"

Hansen grinned. "It's one of a kind. Would you believe it was an old lumber steamer before the shipyard in San Diego got a hold of it?"

The major just shook his head.

Then he demanded crisply, "Get your payroll and personnel records ready. I'll be back to pick them up."

That meant full-time work for me.

Cheers overwhelmed the accoustics when the skipper announced at evening officer's mess that we would be shipped back to the States; but the men's enthusiasm was drowned out in the chatter of their discontent when he added that we'd be stuck aboard for a few more days.

Darkness engulfed Oran under an enforced blackout edict. As I stumbled back to my cabin, the moonlight from the starry, cloudless sky revealed the eerie dark outlines of freighters, tankers, and navy vessels anchored in the harbor, easy targets for enemy planes.

I stared at the payroll worksheets spread out on my desk, realizing the finality of my purser's duties and contemplating my future plans. From the day I set foot in Flanagan's office to the present, many of the experiences, both on shipboard and ashore, had exceeded my fondest expectations for adventure and travel. Now my only regret was that the journey was ending; I never before had it so good.

Having gone through the depression of the thirties, when a job and the next meal often were elusive, I relished the comfort of my cabin aboard the *Chamberlain* and the three squares a day.

I thought of the antics of our men whose daily lives had been so intimately interwoven during our fifteen months together, and the camaraderie, rivalries, and feuds among us. Once back in the States, would my path ever again cross those of good old Hewson, McKelly, and Daugherty, not to mention Hansen, Carlyle and Winthrop? And would we safely make it back there at all?

Some of the highlights of our salvage mission flashed through my mind, such as our exhilaration when the small dry dock slowly rose above the water level in the Massawa harbor, and the cheers when our men attached the American flag to the top of the floating crane after it emerged from the muddy

waters. Also, I thought of the barefoot natives working apathet-
ically in the hot Massawa sun, scraping away the endless masses of barnacles on the drydocks and ships.

My meditation was interrupted when the skipper entered,
sat down, and quietly puffed his pipe. I had gotten used to his
brooding, so I waited for him to break the spell.

"Paul, after leaving this ship, I'm going to the West Coast
and sail out of there. I'll probably be looking for a purser. If
you're out that way, look me up."

I had to reflect on that. Although pleased that he thought of
my future, I didn't know what my immediate plans would be
upon landing in New York. Not ready to commit myself, I said,
"I would certainly like to sail with you again, Captain."

"I'll give you my San Francisco address. You can contact me
there. Meantime, we've got to get the men ashore into hotels
and arrange for their pay until we sail out of Oran. Paul, you take
care of . . ."

The sudden loud rata-tat-tat of antiaircraft fire drowned out
the captain's orders. He rushed out, heading for the stairway to
the bridge. I followed him on deck and joined Huck at the railing. Neither of us spoke. It was as though time stood still.

The skies were illuminated with streaks of light from anti-
aircraft. The scream of sirens from shore pierced the air.

As the men from our navy gun crew uncovered the machine
guns on the flying bridge, weapons of other ships anchored in
the harbor fired away at the wave of enemy planes coming in
from the north, their bomb bays open. The roar of their engines
drowned out the shouts of our men rushing out of the fo'c'sle
and the officers quarters. When flak from the antiaircraft bat-

teries hit our deck, they dove for cover, and the only persons visible to Huck and me at the railing were the navy gunners at their stations behind our machine guns, firing away blindly. The gun on the starboard bridge remained unmanned and silent.

Huck gave me a quick look, squared his jaw, dashed to the companionway, and headed for the deck above. I rushed to my cabin, switched off the lights and propped the door open so that I could view the progress of the approaching planes.

My stomach muscles tightened and my heart pounded as I visualized the terrible consequences of a direct hit on our munition-laden vessel. Our rapid-firing fifty-caliber machine guns resounded over the roar of the approaching planes. The thunderous boom of the bombers increased in intensity.

The first wave of German aircraft swept over us, heading for the city of Oran. The next wave dropped bombs over the ships in the harbor.

One of them hit its mark on a ship five hundred yards from our starboard bow. It must have been carrying explosives. The entire harbor became aglow with the first blast. Three more explosions followed. The blazing vessel lit up the sky and highlighted the anchored ships.

"Poor devils," I thought. "That could have been us."

Then I saw Huck's bulky body squatting behind the machine gun on the starboard bridge deck, firing away at the approaching planes.

Directly overhead, a plane released a bomb that splashed into the water a mere forty feet from our bow, causing a geyser reminiscent of Yellowstone's Old Faithful.

A group of Allied fighter planes appeared from the south,

attacking the German planes that were bombing the city. The Axis bombers changed course, heading for the coast of France with the Allied planes in pursuit. One die-hard pilot dove his roaring plane toward us.

I held my breath.

It looked like the tracer bullets from Huck's machine gun might find their target as the plane came closer. But I was greatly relieved to spot two Allied fighter planes pursuing the German bomber. Their machine guns and cannons blazed away. The bomber burst into flames and fell into the water off our starboard bow.

The ordeal over, bedlam broke loose. The men poured out of the doorways, shouting wildly as they lined the railing, shaking their fists at the fleeing planes.

I made my way to the mess hall where the officers were gathering.

In our exhilaration, we took turns pounding Huck on the back. He just smiled in his usual unpretentious manner. Even though allied fighter pilots were directly responsible for the downed plane, all of us admired Huck for his heroic efforts to save our ship.

"How come you manned the fifty-caliber, Huck?" asked Olsson.

"Well, There was no one on the starboard machine gun, so I just took over," Huck said nonchalantly.

Culpepper was fidgety, pacing up and down the messhall. "I'm going to be damn happy to turn this bucket over to the navy," he thundered. "If they're smart, they'll take it out to sea and sink it. The condensers are still leaking like hell; the steering engine crank shaft could go any minute; and the boilers are ready for the junk heap."

On the following day no one was permitted to go ashore. Some of the navy officers who were scheduled to take over our ship came aboard to preview their quarters and examine the vessel.

I couldn't help but resent the lieutenant who fell heir to my cabin. He spied my phonograph and record collection and the Ethiopian spears acquired from my Massawa timekeeper. With a lump in my throat, I accepted his offer to buy the lot since I did not want to be unnecessarily encumbered returning to the States.

On the third day, the pilot directed our vessel to a berth alongside the dock, and the men lowered their motorcycles, tools, souvenirs, and gear onto the pier. I had my hands full with my large rhinoceros skin shield, the long Ethiopian hand-forged sword, my trusty portable typewriter, clothing, and numerous other personal possessions.

Stepping off the gangplank for the last time, I deeply felt the drama of the moment. The *Chamberlain* had been home to me for over a year. Although it was a dilapidated vessel with endless problems, it had carried me 29,976 nautical miles out of San Diego safely through some of the most dangerous waters. It had indeed been a charmed ship.

THE FATE OF THE CHAMBERLAIN

In May of 1943 when we bade the *Chamberlain* goodbye in Oran, we were certain that the old bucket had seen her last days. In view of all the problems we encountered in our twelve and a half months' adventuresome voyage, we fully expected her to be bombed to oblivion by the German air force or abandoned to a graveyard after a thorough inspection by the U.S. Navy. We should have realized that the ship had a life all her own.

It gave me great satisfaction and made me proud to read later in the *Dictionary of American Naval Fighting Ships* (Volume VII) and other official navy records that she valiantly served in the U.S. Navy, having been renamed the *TACKLE(ARS-37)*, and participated in a number of invasions in her salvage ship capacity. The navy should have re-named her the *Intrepid.* In spite of the fact that on a number of occasions her boilers, deck machinery and steering gear required repairs, and that she was the target of German bombers in air attacks in Naples, Italy, and sustained considerable damage from a mine explosion during the invasion of southern France, she survived the war and received two battle stars. On July 24th, 1946 she was transferred to the Maritime Commission, then converted to merchant service. She was finally scrapped in 1949.

U.S. MERCHANT SHIPS LOST TO GERMAN SUBMARINE ATTACKS IN WORLD WAR II PRIOR TO APRIL 28, 1942

NAME OF VESSEL	DATE	LOCATION	LIVES LOST
S/V ALBERT F. PAUL	3/13/42	26.00N/72.00W	8
S.S. ALCOA GUIDE	4/16/42	35.34N/70.08W	6
S.S. ALCOA PARTNER	4/26/42	13.32N/65.57W	10
S.S. ALLAN JACKSON	1/18/42	35.57N/74.20W	22
BARGE ALLEGHENY	3/31/42	37.34N/75.25W	2
S.S. ARIO	3/15/42	34.37N/76.20W	8
S.S. ASTRAL	12.2/41	Mid-ocean	37
S.S. ATLAS	4/9/42	34.27N/76.16W	2
M.S. AUSTRALIA	3/16/42	35.07N/75.22W	4
S.S. AZALEA CITY	2/20/42	38.00N/73.00W	38
S.S. BARBARA	3/7/42	20.10N/73.05W	19
BARGE BARNEGAT	3/31/42	37.34N/75.25W	-
S.S. BYRON D. BENSON	4/4/42	36.08N/73.32W	10
S.S. CARDONIA	3/7/42	19.53N/73.27W	1
S.S. CARIBSEA	3/11/42	34.35N/76.18W	21
S.S. CATAHOULA	4/5/42	19.16N/68.12W	9
S.S. CHINA ARROW	2/5/42	37.44N/73.18W	-
S.S. CITIES SERVICE EMPIRE	2/22/42	28.00N/80.22W	14
M.S. CITY OF NEW YORK	3/29/42	35.16N/74.25W	26
S.S. COLLAMER	3/5/42	44.18N/63.10W	7
S.S. COMOL RICO	4/4/42	20.46N/66.46W	3
S.S. CONNECTICUT	4/23/42	23.00S/15.00W	27
S.S. DAVID H ATWATER	4/2/42	36.46N/75.05W	23
S.S. DELPLATA	2/20/42	14.45N/62.10W	-
S.S. DELVALLE	4/12/42	16.51N/75.25W	2
S.S. DIXIE ARROW	3/26/42	35.00N/75.33W	11
S.S. E.M. CLARK	3/18/42	35.50N/75.35W	1
S.S. EFFINGHAM	3/30/42	70.28N/35.44E	12
S.S. ESPARTA	4/19/42	31.00N/81.10W	1

NAME OF VESSEL	DATE	LOCATION	LIVES LOST
S.S. ESSO BOSTON	4/12/42	21.42N/60.00W	-
S.S. EUGENE V R THAYER	4/9/42	2.35S/3955W	11
S.S. FEDERAL	4/30/42	Near Cuba	5
S.S. FRANCES SALMAN	1/18/42	Near Newfoundland	28
S.S. FRANCES E. POWELL	1/27/42	35.45N/74.53W	4
S.S. GULFAMERICA	4/10/42	30.00N/81.15W	19
S.S. GULFTRADE	3/10/42	Near New Jersey	18
S.S. INDIAN ARROW	2/4/42	38.48N/73.40W	26
S.S. J.N. PEW	2/21/42	12.40N/74.00W	33
S.S. JOHN D. GILL	3/14/42	33.55N/70.39W	23
M.S. LAKE OSWEGA	2/20/42	43.14N/64.45W	30
S.S. LAMMOT DUPONT	4/23/42	27.10N/57.10W	19
S.S. LEHIGH	10/19/41	8.26N/14.37W	-
S.S. LEMUEL BURROWS	3/14/42	Near Atlantic City	20
S.S. LESLIE	4/12/42	28.35N/80.19W	4
S.S. LIBERATOR	3/19/42	35.05N/75.30W	5
S.S. LIHUE	2/23/42	14.30N/64.45W	-
S.S. MAJOR WHEELER	2/6/42	East Coast U.S.	35
S.S. MALCHACE	4/9/42	34.289N/75.56W	1
S.S. MARGARET	4/14/42	East Coast U.S.	29
S.S. MARIANA	3/5/42	27.45N/67.00W	35
S.S. MARORE	2/26/42	35.33N/74.58W	-
S.S. MARY	3/3/42	8.25N/52.50W	1
S.S. MENOMINEE	3/31/42	37.34N/75.25W	16
S.S. MOBILOIL	4/29/42	23.35N/66.18W	-
S.S. MUSKOGEE	3/22/42	28.00N/58.00W	34
S.S. NAECO	3/23/42	34.00N/75.40W	24
S.S. NORLAVORE	2/24/42	35.02N/75.20W	28
S.S. NORVANA	1/22/42	Near North Carolina	29
S.S. OAKMAR	3/20/42	36.22N/68.50W	6
S.S. OKLAHOMA	4/8/42	31.18N/80.59W	19
S.S. OLGA	3/12/42	21.32N/76.24W	1
S.S. OREGON	2/28/42	20.44N/67.52W	6
S.S. OTHO	4/3/42	36.25N/72.22W	31

NAME OF VESSEL	DATE	LOCATION	LIVES LOST
S.S. PAN MASSACHUSETTES	2/19/42	28.27N/80.08W	20
S.S. PAPOOSE	3/18/42	34.17N/76.39W	2
S.S. PIPESTONE COUNTY	4/21/42	37.43N/66.16W	-
S.S. R.P. RESOR	2/28/42	39.47N/73.26W	48
S.S. REPUBLIC	2/21/42	27.05N/80.15W	5
S.S. ROBINHOOD	4/15/42	38.39N/64.38W	14
S.S. ROBIN MOOR	5/21/41	6.10N/25.40W	-
S.S. ROCHESTER	1/30/42	37.10N/73.58W	4
S.S. SAN JACINTO	4/21/42	31.10N/70.45W	14
S.S. SELMA CITY	4/6/42	17.11N/83.20W	-
S.S. STEEL AGE	3/6/42	6.45N/53.15W	33
S.S. STEEL MAKER	4/19/42	33.48N/70.36W	2
S.S. T.C. McCOBB	3/31/42	Near British Guiana	4
S.S. TAMAULIPAS	4/10/42	34.25N/7600W	2
S.S. TEXAN	3/11/42	21.34N/76.28W	10
S.S. TIGER	4/1/42	Off Virginia	1
S.S. VENORE	1/23/42	34.50N/75.20W	17
S.S. W.D. ANDERSON	2/22/42	27.09N/79.56W	35
S.S. W.E. HUTTON	3/18/42	34.25N/76.40,	13
S.S. W.L. STEED	2/2/42	33.25N/72.43W	34
S.S. IMBODEN	4/20/42	41.14N/66.00W	-
S.S. WEST IRMO	4/3/42	2.10N/5.50W	10
S.S. WEST IVIS	1/26/42	East Coast U.S.	35
S.S. WEST ZEDA	2/22/42	9.13N/69.04W	-

LOCATION: North Latitude/West Longitude

87 SHIPS LOST   1167 MEN LOST

INFORMATION FROM: *A Careless Word . . .*

. . . A Needless Sinking

By Captain Arthur R. Moore

U.S. MERCHANT SHIPS LOST TO JAPANESE
SUBMARINE AND SURFACE VESSEL ATTACKS
IN WORLD WAR II PRIOR TO APRIL 28, 1942

NAME OF VESSEL	DATE	LOCATION	LIVES LOST
S.S. BIENVILLE	4/6/42	17.48N/84.09E	24
S.S. CYNTHIA OLSON	12/7/41	34.42N/145.29W	35
S.S. EMIDIO	12/20/41	40.33N/125.00W	5
S.S. EXMOOR	4/6/42	19.52N/86.25E	-
S.S. FLORENCE LUCKENBACH	1/29/42	12.55N/80.33E	-
S.S. LIBERTY	1/11/42	8.5S/115.28E	-
S.S. K MALAMA	1/1/42	26.21S/153.24W	2
S.S. MANINE	12/17/41	South of Hawaii	2
S.S. MONTEBELLO	12/23/41	35.30N/121.51W	-
S.S. PRUSA	12/19/41	16.45N/156.00W	10
S.S. ROYAL T. FRANK	1/28/42	20.34N/155.43W	21
S.S. VINCENT	12/21/41	22.41S/118.19E	2
S.S. WASHINGTONIAN	4/7/42	7.25N/73.05E	-

LOCATION: North Latitude/West Longitude

13 SHIPS LOST   101 MEN LOST
INFORMATION FROM: *A Careless Word ...*
                  ...A Needless Sinking
        By Captain Arthur R. Moore

U.S. MERCHANT SHIPS LOST TO GERMAN SUBMARINES
IN THE PATH OF THE *S.S. W.R. CHAMBERLAIN, JR*
DURING IT'S VOYAGE THROUGH THE CARIBBEAN

NAME OF VESSEL	DATE	LOCATION	LIVES LOST
S.S. ALCOA CARRIER	5/25/42	18.45N/79.50W	0
S.S. ALCOA PILGRIM	5/28/42	16.28N/67.37W	31
S.S. BEATRICE	5/24/42	17.23N/77.00W	1
M.S. CHALLENGER	5/17/42	12.11N/61.18W	8
S.S. EDITH	6/7/42	14.33N/74.35W	2
S.S. GEORGE CLYMER	6/7/42	14.48N/18.37W	1
S.S. JACK	5/27/42	17.36N/74.42W	10
S,S, L.J. DRAKE	6/5/42	In Caribbean	41

LOCATION: North Latitude/West Longitude

8 SHIPS LOST   94 MEN LOST

INFORMATION FROM: *A Careless Word . . .*
. . . A Needless Sinking
By Captain Arthur R. Moore